Rosicrucian Manual

Rosicrucian Manual

Prepared under the supervision of

H. SPENCER LEWIS, Ph.D., F.R.C.

Imperator of the Rosicrucian Order for North America

KALPAZ

ISBN: 978-93-5128-589-2

First Published in1918
Indian Reprint in 2017

Published by

Kalpaz Publications
C-30, Satyawati Nagar,
Delhi – 110052
E-mail: kalpaz@hotmail.com
Website: kalpazpublications.com
Ph.: +91-9212142040

Cataloging in Publication Data—DK
Courtesy: D.K. Agencies (P) Ltd. <docinfo@dkagencies.com>

Lewis, H. Spencer (Harvey Spencer), 1883-1939, **author.**
Rosicrucian manual / prepared under the supervision of H. Spencer Lewis (Ph.D., F.R.C.).
pages cm
"First published in 1918"—Title page verso.
ISBN 9789351285892

1. Society of Rosicrucians. 2. Rosicrucians. I. Title.

BF1623.R7L49 2017 DDC 135.43 23

The Rosicrucian Library

▽ ▽ ▽

VOLUME

I. Rosicrucian Questions and Answers with Complete History of the Order.

II. Rosicrucian Principles for the Home and Business.

III. The Mystical Life of Jesus.

IV. The Secret Doctrines of Jesus.
(In Preparation.)

V. "Unto Thee I Grant . . . "
(Secret Teachings of Tibet.)

VI. A Thousand Years of Yesterdays.
(A Story of Reincarnation.)

VII. Self Mastery and Fate with the Cycles of Life.

VIII. Rosicrucian Manual.

IX. Mystics at Prayer.

X. Rosicrucian Healing.
(In Preparation.)

XI. Mansions of the Soul; The Cosmic Conception.
(A complete outline of the Doctrines of Reincarnation.)

XII. Lemuria—The Lost Continent of the Pacific.

XIII. The Technique of the Master; The Way of Cosmic Preparation.

(*Other volumes will be added from time to time. Write for complete catalogue.*)

TABLE OF CONTENTS

▽ ▽ ▽

TABLE OF CONTENTS—*Continued*

The
IMPERATOR'S GREETINGS

▽ ▽ ▽

I am delighted that the Rosicrucian Press, Printing and Publishing Department of the Supreme Grand Lodge of the A. M. O. R. C., has again decided to publish another edition of the official Manual. I know that it is greatly needed and will be sincerely appreciated. Years ago we issued a small, private Manual for our Lodges but the issue soon became exhausted. The new Manual will take the place of the older ones and will contain so much additional matter that it will be truly a Guide to the Work and Studies of the Order.

Naturally such a book as this must be limited in its contents and carefully worded.

I know that many benefits will come through this book to our members as well as to general readers. It should be a weekly guide to the lectures and lessons for every member, and a help to every officer of our hundreds of branches throughout the North American Jurisdiction. The many diagrams and plates have been carefully prepared so as to make plain many points in the lectures of the various grades.

Members and Officers will do well to recommend the use of this Manual to all members, for it will help in many ways to promote a better understanding of the Order and its teachings, and bring about a better agreement in regard to the terms, rules, regulations, and practices of all our work.

Therefore, through the pages of this Manual, I again greet our members and the student reader and wish them every success and joy in the Glorious Search for Light, Life, and Love.

In Peace Profound,

H. SPENCER LEWIS, F. R. C.

IMPERATOR.

October 1, 1932.

WHAT THIS MANUAL CONTAINS

This Manual contains many helps for the members as outlined herewith:

1st. A Manual of the Order generally, its purposes, formation, arrangement of Lodges, description of Officers, their duties, etc., and the various regulations of membership. This is of unusual value to every member and officer.

2nd. The plates and diagrams used in the various lectures of all grades. Some of these diagrams are intended for the members in the grades of the National studies (as described previously) and others for members in the higher grades of the Temple lectures or the Postulant studies. Explanations of the diagrams are given in the proper places, in the weekly lectures, and cannot be given to members in advance of the particular lectures to which they refer.

3rd. Diagrams and illustrations of many of the symbols used in our Order and in the ancient teachings of the Rosicrucians and other mystics. These illustrations are for all members.

4th. A Glossary of the principal terms and words used in the Teachings throughout all the grades. It is not a complete dictionary of all the terms used, for this would require a very large volume and would be unnecessary. Such words as "Alchemy" are not included, for the definition given in any standard dictionary is identical with the sense in which we use the term. Only where terms have special meanings have we included them in the Glossary.

5th. General instructions which should be carefully read by our members from time to time until they are very familiar with them. This will help all of us to give you greater service in the work.

6th. Other matter of help to all members.

HOW TO USE THE MANUAL

National Lodge Members should have this Manual early in their studies, preferably with the first or second lesson of the First Grade. They should read it through and note what matter is indicated for "National Lodge Members." This will aid them in their lectures. And matter marked for "All Members" will be of help to them. But matter marked for "Temple Lodge Members" or "Postulants" will be of little help until they reach the proper grades of study.

Temple Lodge Members will find many plates and diagrams indicated for them in addition to the general matter. For them this Manual will serve in place of the many diagrams they have had to make in their note books in the past. (National Lodge Members will receive identically the same lectures as those given in the temple or lodge, after they have completed the three National Grades and met certain requirements.)

PRELIMINARY INSTRUCTIONS

This Manual is divided into several sections and a proper understanding of its plan will greatly help in deriving the utmost benefit from it.

THE FORMS OF MEMBERSHIP

There are two distinct forms of membership in the AMORC of North America, as there are in some foreign Jurisdictions of the Order.

NATIONAL LODGE MEMBERSHIP: This form of membership is for those who live in small towns or sections of the country where we have no TEMPLE LODGES, or for those who, because of certain forms of employment or other conditions, cannot attend a TEMPLE LODGE in their locality.

National Lodge membership means *correspondence membership*. By a vote at the National Convention of Rosicrucian Delegates in Pittsburgh, Penna., in the summer of 1917, the National Lodge was established to provide correspondence instruction to those who could not attend the Temple Lodges. Such instruction, sent in weekly lectures and lessons, was especially prepared and contains a summary of the Rosicrucian principles with a wealth of personal experiments, exercises, and tests as will make each member highly proficient in the attainment of certain degrees of mastership. These correspondence lessons and exercises compose three GRADES and cover a period of practically ten months. Each grade has its own initiation ritual, to be performed by the member at home in his own Sanctum and before his own altar. Such rituals are not like the elaborate rituals used in the Temple Lodges and conducted by the staff of fifteen Officers in Egyptian form.

National Lodge members pay their dues directly to the National Lodge, located at the Supreme Lodge Headquarters. They constitute a very large body of members with their own signs, grips, pass-words, and benefits. However, they have the privilege of visiting any Temple Lodge on special occasions or whenever there is a Feast or General Ceremony. Members of the National Lodge and the Temple Lodges alike hold official membership cards, have many signs and symbols in common, and in every possible way are related in membership.

Furthermore, National Lodge members who complete the preliminary three grades, covering ten months, *may be permitted* to receive the lessons of the higher teachings of the Temple Lodges throughout the nine grades in the same manner that they received the preliminary instructions, with the provision that they have passed all of the requirements, satisfactorily.

TEMPLE LODGE MEMBERS are those who attend the regular Lodges in the many cities of the North American Continent (and Dependencies) and receive the higher teachings from the Masters thereof, after having been initiated in such Lodges. They pay their dues directly to such Lodges and receive no instructions by correspondence unless they also join the National Lodge. The benefits of Temple Lodge Membership, and association with other members in the study and discussion of the lessons, are many and important. The monthly magazine contains a list of the important Temple Lodges, and others can be located by addressing the Grand Secretary.

CHAPTER MEMBERSHIP consists of membership in the small study groups which are established conveniently in all parts of the country. New Chapters are occasionally organized, and if you do not find one listed in our monthly magazine which is convenient to you, write to the Grand Secretary. Members in these Chapters are usually National Lodge Members paying their monthly dues direct to the National Lodge and have no additional dues to pay to the Chapter. Chapters carry on special discussions and have special lectures and other benefits truly worth while to the Correspondence Members of the National Lodge. The Chapters throughout the United States, Canada, and Mexico, constitute a chain of active centers covering almost every large county of every State or Province.

Part One

THE AMORC AND ITS ORGANIZATION

Every member of the AMORC should be familiar with the facts of the establishment of the organization, its Constitution, and its secret or private system of operation.

The widespread confusion in the United States because of the popular use of the word *Rosicrucian* by so many movements, publishers, and small research societies—a condition not permitted in foreign lands—makes necessary the understanding of the following facts; and we trust that every member will refer to these pages in any discussion of the authority and rights of AMORC:

*The history of the Rosicrucian ORDER in foreign lands has been well covered in many books of recent years, though all are warned against giving any credence to the statements made in most of the *encyclopedias* wherein it is said that the Order started in Germany in the eighteenth century and ended there. Such a story has been copied and recopied without investigation and is without foundation. But the real facts, as we have said, have been published in many books and we need not take space here to repeat the European and Oriental origin and history of this very old Order.

We are more concerned with its introduction into the New World. We find here, too, many books and records which give reliable and precise details of the coming to America of the first Rosicrucian colony from Europe, under Sir Francis Bacon's original plan, in the year 1694, and its establishment for many years, first at Philadelphia, then at Ephrata, Pennsylvania, where many of the original buildings still stand.

The first foundation here in America in 1694 (which left Europe in 1693) grew into a large and potent power of considerable importance in the affairs of the birth of the American nation, as can be seen by records in Philadelphia and Washington. But the ancient law that each 108 years was a cycle of rebirth, activity, rest, and waiting, made the great work in America come to a close, so far as public activities were concerned, in 1801 (108 years after the founders left Europe). Then for another 108 years the Order in this country was

*See: "Rosicrucian Questions and Answers with History of the Order," published by the Rosicrucian Publishing Department (AMORC) San Jose, Calif., U. S. A.

in its rest period with only certain *descendants of the last initiates* passing to one another the rare records and official documents.

Then came 1909—108 years after the year 1801—and the time for rebirth and reorganization in a public form was at hand. The story of how our present Imperator, H. Spencer Lewis, was chosen to bear the burden of reorganization, has often been told, investigated, verified, and acknowledged by the highest Rosicrucian authorities of Europe and other lands.

Having had passed to him in the proper way certain knowledge preserved by the descendants of the first foundation in America, he prepared himself, through various courses of study and association with scientific and metaphysical bodies, for the work he was to undertake in 1909. Then in the month of July of that year he went to France, where he was introduced to the right authorities and inducted into the mysteries and the methods of carrying out his life mission.

Returning to America, he held many secret sessions with men and women who had been initiated into the Order in France and India and other lands, who formed with him the first foundation committee. Together they labored for six years so that in the seventh year of preparation they could announce to the American public the reestablishment of the Rosicrucian Order. The first official *Manifesto* was warmly greeted by a gathering of over three hundred prominent students of the ancient Rosicrucian teachings who examined the official papers, seals, and warrants possessed by Imperator Lewis, and formed the first American Council of the Order. A report of that session was sent to France, to the body of men who undertook the burden of supporting the foundation work in America, and a few months later the Grand Council of the *Ordre Rose Croix* of France recognized the Imperator for the Order in America.

Thereafter further organization meetings were held until a point was reached when two officials of the International Council of the Order visited America, approved of the organization as established here, and, upon their report to the International Convention in Europe, the American Order was made an independent Jurisdiction coming directly under the guidance of the International Council of the Order instead of under the sponsorship of the French Jurisdiction.

And this gave the Ancient and Mystical Order Rosae Crucis (AMORC) of North America a representation in the International Council, in its National and International Conventions and Congresses, and made the American AMORC a part of the AMORC of the world. Therefore, the AMORC is today the ONLY Rosicrucian movement in America having such authority and connections.

But, there are other Rosicrucian movements here. They use the term or word *Rosicrucian*. But none of these Rosicrucian movements or publishing companies or societies uses the term ROSICRUCIAN ORDER, nor do they use the title Ancient and Mystical ORDER Rosae Crucis.

Ever since the AMORC was organized in America it has made its *definite and unequivocal* claim of genuineness. Its Supreme Lodge was duly incorporated, not as a society or fellowship of Rosicrucians, but as "The Ancient and Mystical Order Rosae Crucis of the Great White Brotherhood." Please note the word Order and the Latin term *Rosae Crucis* in the title. Its Colleges and Universities were also incorporated, and a Patent was secured from the United States Government protecting the name and symbols of the Order in the United States and Dependencies. AMORC is the only Rosicrucian movement in North America having a patent on the symbol of the Cross with ONE rose in its center, which is the true ancient symbol of the Order in all lands.

Therefore, AMORC repeats again its statement: It is a part of the international Rosicrucian Order, most Jurisdictions of which use the same name except for slight variations due to translation in foreign languages. It is a part of the ONE and ONLY Rosicrucian ORDER that is truly international. It is the only Rosicrucian movement, society, or body in North America having membership and representation in the "Conseil Internationale, Antiqum Arcanum Ordinis Rubeae Rosae et Aureae Crucis" with its international "siege social and secretariat general" in Europe and its sacred Sanctums and monasteries in India and other lands in the Orient, with the Holy Assembly of Masters in Tibet. The AMORC of America, therefore, is duly represented in the International Congresses and Conventions held at stated periods in Europe and adheres to the ancient traditions and customs in all of its standards and practices. This means that it does NOT publish books claiming to contain the private Rosicrucian fundamentals, rituals, secrets, rites, or TEACHINGS; does not deal with sex problems, sex practices, or indulgences under the guise of higher occult teachings; is strictly non-religious, non-commercial, and not *affiliated* with any secret society, fraternity, fellowship, or movement *except* the international Rosicrucian ORDER.

If our members will read the foregoing statements again they will see that AMORC has never claimed and could not claim to be connected with the honorable fraternity of Freemasons, even though that body has in one of its higher degrees one grade named in honor of the Ancient Rosicrucians; and AMORC is not connected in any way with any publishing firm, group, or movement using the word Rosicrucian unless it is also using the word AMORC and the true patented symbols of the Order.

Nothing said herein is intended to cast any aspersions on the work being done by any group of students using the word Rosicrucian to indicate the sincerity of their search for Truth. The AMORC always maintains the attitude of broadmindedness and tolerance toward every person or group of persons seeking to contribute to the uplift of man. And this attitude we desire to have expressed by every member of the Order.

AN ANCIENT KNIGHT ROSAE CRUCIS

SIR FRANCIS BACON, K. R. C.
IMPERATOR OF THE ROSICRUCIANS IN THE SEVENTEENTH CENTURY
(Modern Symbolical Drawing)

FRA. MICHAEL MAIER

GRAND MASTER OF ROSICRUCIANS IN GERMANY IN THE SEVENTEENTH CENTURY, AND SIR FRANCIS BACON'S DEPUTY ON THE CONTINENT

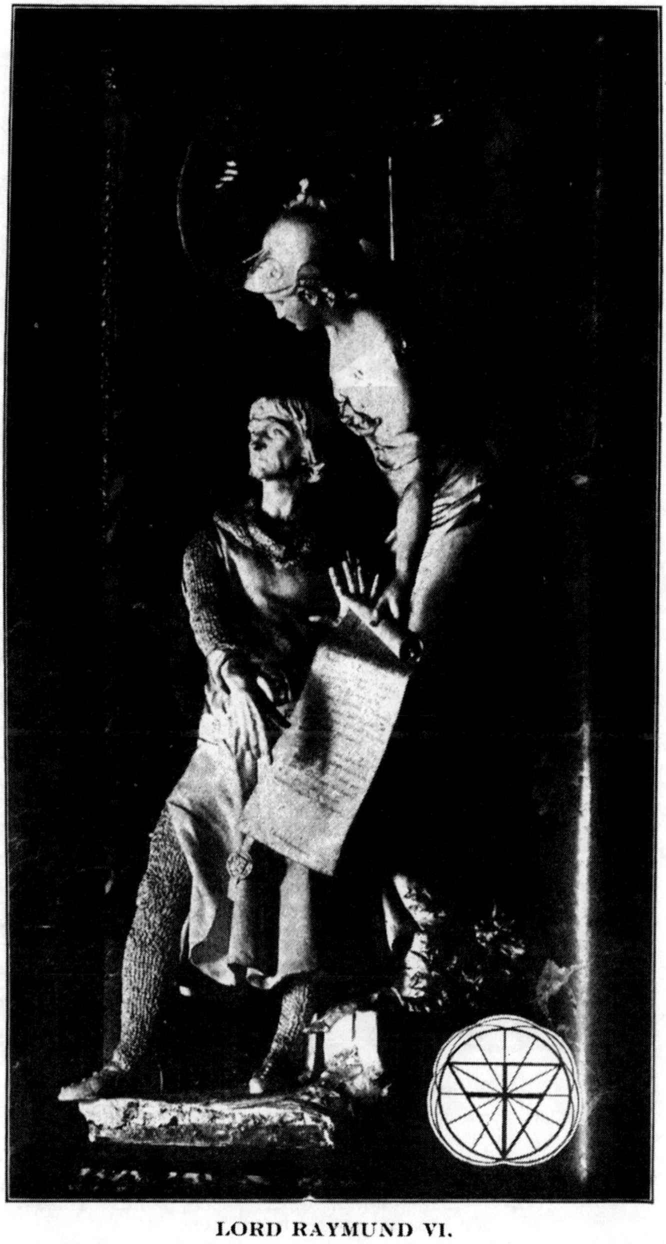

LORD RAYMUND VI.

WHO, AS COUNT OF TOULOUSE, REFUSED TO PROSECUTE THE MYSTICS WHO LAID THE FOUNDATION FOR ROSICRUCIANISM IN SOUTHERN FRANCE IN THE THIRTEENTH CENTURY. AS A MYSTIC MARTYR, HIS BODY WAS REFUSED BURIAL IN "HOLY GROUND," BUT WAS PRESERVED FOR 600 YEARS IN THE KNIGHTS TEMPLAR BUILDING, BUILT BY HIS FOREFATHERS.

H. SPENCER LEWIS, PH. D., F. R. C.

IMPERATOR, A. M. O. R. C. OF NORTH AMERICA — MEMBER OF THE SUPREME COUNCIL R. C. OF THE WORLD — LEGATE OF THE ORDER IN FRANCE — MINISTER OF THE FOREIGN LEGATION — ORDAINED PRIEST OF THE ASHRAMA IN INDIA — HONORARY COUNSULAR OF THE "CORDA FRATRES," ITALY — SRI SOBHITA, GREAT WHITE LODGE, TIBET — REX, UNIVERSITATIS ILLUMINATI.

MRS. MAY BANKS-STACEY

CO-FOUNDER AND FIRST GRAND MATRE IN U. S. A.

(See Biographical Reference on Page 129)

MASTER KUT-HU-MI, THE ILLUSTRIOUS
D... G... M... OF TIBET (BOD-YUL)
BELOVED HIEROPHANT OF THE R. C.
(See Brief Biographical Reference on Page 137)

A MODERN ALCHEMIST IN HIS LABORATORY

MONSIEUR F. JOLLIVET CASTELOT, PRESIDENT, FRENCH ALCHEMICAL SOCIETY AND HIGH OFFICER OF LA ROSE-CROIX OF FRANCE, WHO HAS DEMONSTRATED THE ROSICRUCIAN DOCTRINES AND HAS PRODUCED GOLD BY TRANSMUTATION.

PHOTOGRAPH OF THE ORIGINAL DOCUMENT OF FRENCH SPONSORSHIP OF THE AMORC IN AMERICA. "PRONUNZIAMENTO NUMBER R.. F.. R.. C.. 987-432" WAS MAILED IN A SPECIAL METAL CONTAINER. IT WAS SEALED AND SIGNED BY THE PRINCIPAL OFFICERS OF THE ROSE CROIX OF FRANCE. STOLEN TWICE, COPIED AND FORGED ONCE, THE ORIGINAL HAS BEEN AN AMERICAN "PRIZE" EVER SINCE THE FIRST AMERICAN SUPREME R. C. COUNCIL EXAMINED AND VERIFIED IT. IT IS ADDRESSED TO OUR IMPERATOR, FRATRE H. SPENCER LEWIS, F. R. C.

Great American Manifesto

Issued by the Charter Members of the Supreme Grand Lodge as Founders of the Order in America

The Ancient and Mystical Order Rosae Crucis in the United States of America, its Territories and Dependencies, shall be an independent organization operating under its Constitution.

Its purpose shall be the same as that of the "Order Rosae Crucis" throughout the world, and its Constitution shall be identical in spirit with that which guides and directs this Order in other lands. The Order in America shall, however, retain its fraternal and spiritual relation with this Order in other countries, regardless of its independent jurisdiction, and shall maintain its adherence to the traditional principles and laws of the ancient Rosicrucians.

Since both the ancient and modern form of government of the Order are autocratic in nature, the government of the Order in America shall adopt strictly autocratic principles of government, but because of the necessary division of America into many jurisdictions operating under one American Constitution, the said Constitution shall embody such changes or modifications as will properly meet the requirements of this jurisdiction.

Therefore it is declared that the attached Constitution, of which this Pronunziamento is a part, was prepared after consultation with all possible authorities and with proper discussion by all the Founders of the Order in America, and was finally approved and adopted by the Charter Members of the Supreme Grand Lodge in America and shall be adopted and ratified by all Lodges now organized or hereafter to be organized and Chartered by the Supreme Grand Lodge or the Imperator of the Order in America.

Decreed and Issued June, 1915, at a meeting of the First American Supreme Council held in the City of New York, N. Y.

Part Two

EXTRACTS FROM THE CONSTITUTION OF THE GRAND LODGE OF THE *ANCIENT, MYSTIC ORDER ROSAE CRUCIS* NORTH AMERICAN JURISDICTION

Obedient to the edict of the Imperator and in pursuance of the will of the members, as was expressed by their vote during the Convention of 1930 A. D., duly assembled July 23-30, the special committee, which was appointed for the purpose, submitted for the approval of the Trustees of the Grand Lodge the New Constitution and Statutes of the Grand Lodge of AMORC, jurisdiction of North America, on the date of January 15, 1931. The Trustees, in turn, on February 9, 1931, submitted for the Imperator's approval and promulgation the New Constitution and Statutes.

On the date of March 18, 1931, in a communication addressed to the members of AMORC and duly published, the Imperator expressed his approval and put it into effect as of March 21, 1931, for the governance of the Grand Lodge and all members of the North American Jurisdiction until altered or amended by duly constituted authority.

Members of the Rosicrucian organization can procure a copy of the complete Constitution and Statutes of the Grand Lodge by writing the Grand Lodge at San Jose, California, and enclosing ten cents to cover cost of same. It is advised that every member procure a complete copy.

ARTICLE I.

Section 1

This Lodge shall be known as THE GRAND LODGE OF THE ANCIENT AND MYSTIC ORDER ROSAE CRUCIS, or, in its abbreviated form, as THE GRAND LODGE OF A. M. O. R. C.

Section 2

This Grand Lodge is subordinate to and derives its existence and powers from the Imperator and the Supreme Grand Lodge of A. M. O. R. C.

Section 3

This Grand Lodge shall be located at the Adytum of the Imperator unless otherwise directed by the Supreme Grand Lodge.

Section 4

The members are known as ROSICRUCIANS and the Order may also be known as THE ROSICRUCIAN BROTHERHOOD.

Section 5

All members within the jurisdiction of this Supreme Grand Lodge are members of this Grand Lodge, and membership in this Grand Lodge is prerequisite to membership or participation in any Subordinate Body.

ARTICLE II.

Section 6

All matters within the Official cognizance and concern of this Order are divided into two classes, namely: Doctrinal-Ritualistic and Administrative. The administrative work is classified as: Legislative, Executive, and Judicial.

ARTICLE III.

Section 7

The Imperator is the Supreme Doctrinal-Ritualistic Officer of this Order. This work of the Order shall be directed by him through such officers as he may designate from time to time, together with their respective duties, functions, obligations, privileges, and tenure of office. He has sole, complete, and exclusive jurisdiction over the Doctrinal and Ritualistic work of the Order and all Ritualistic Officers. He may function through the Supreme Grand Lodge or other Subordinate Bodies or Officers. All communications, directions, and acts of the Imperator or of the Supreme Grand Lodge under the hand and seal of the Supreme Secretary shall be binding, conclusive, and final on this Grand Lodge, its Subordinate Bodies and all Ritualistic Officers and Members.

Section 8

In the direction of the Doctrinal and Ritualistic work of this Order the Imperator exercises Supreme Autocratic Power, limited only by adherence to the Ancient Landmarks and the Unwritten Laws of this Order as recognized by the International Council of this Brotherhood. All provisions of this Constitution and all laws and regulations are subject and subordinate to the Doctrinal and Ritualistic Power and jurisdiction of the Imperator.

ARTICLE IV.

Section 9

Subject to the Supreme Authority and Power of the Imperator and of the Supreme Grand Lodge as herein defined and limited by it, this Grand Lodge is the Authority and Power of this Order—Legislative, Executive, and Judicial.

ARTICLE V.

Section 10

Its Legislative Powers extend to every case of legislation not expressly delegated by itself to the Subordinate Bodies or withheld from it by the Imperator or the Supreme Grand Lodge; and this Constitution, the Statutes, and General Regulations for the Subordinate Bodies which it may promulgate from time to time under the limitations herein imposed, shall be final and binding upon all Subordinate Bodies within its jurisdiction until modified, amended, or repealed.

ARTICLE VI.

Section 11

Its Executive Powers include the granting of Charters to establish and perpetuate Subordinate Bodies within this jurisdiction and in other territories where no Supreme Grand Lodge exists; the revocation or suspension thereof; and the exercise, generally, of all such administrative authority on all members and Subordinate Bodies necessary to carry all orders and commands of the Imperator and of the Supreme Grand Lodge and its own legislation into complete effect.

ARTICLE VII.

Section 12

Its Judicial Powers are of two kinds:

A. Original, including the decision of all controversy between:
   - (a) Any of the Subordinate Bodies.
   - (b) One or more of the Subordinate Bodies and a member or members of another.
   - (c) One or more Subordinate Bodies and one or more National members.
   - (d) Between members of two or more Subordinate Bodies.
   - (e) National Members.

B. Appellate, embracing the revision of all matters of controversy or discipline proper for investigation by the laws of the Order, which may have arisen in any of its Subordinate Bodies and over which it has not retained original jurisdiction.

Section 13

All disciplinary matters, together with the establishment of necessary judicial forums and the procedure thereof, shall be prescribed by the Supreme Grand Lodge, and it shall be put into effect by this Grand Lodge.

Section 14

Any controversy to which the Grand Lodge or any of its officers, and any controversy to which the Grand Council or any of its members in their official capacity, are a party, shall be referred to the Supreme Grand Lodge.

ARTICLE VIII.

Section 15

The officers of this Grand Lodge are:

1. The Grand Master.
2. Deputy Grand Masters.
3. The Grand Counsellors.
4. The Grand Secretary.
5. The Grand Treasurer.
6. The Doctrinal and Ritualistic Officers.

Section 16

The Grand Master, Grand Secretary, and Grand Treasurer shall be appointed by the Supreme Grand Lodge, with the advice of the Grand Council, and shall serve during the pleasure of the Supreme Grand Lodge and until their successors are appointed.

Section 17

Deputy Grand Masters shall be appointed by the Grand Master by and with the consent of the Imperator. The number of the Deputy Grand Masters shall be such as the interests of the Order may require as determined by the Grand Master from time to time. They shall serve and hold office during the pleasure of the Grand Master and until their successors are appointed.

Section 18

The Doctrinal and Ritualistic Officers of this Order, their appointments, tenure of office, and their duties, are prescribed under Sections 7 and 8 of this Constitution.

ANNUAL CELEBRATION DAYS

There may be held two special assemblies each year in North America. One shall be the New Year Feast and the other the Outdoor Fete.

A

The New Year Feast will occur about the 21st of each March, the exact date being proclaimed by a Pronunziamento issued by the Imperator every February. It is to celebrate the New Rosicrucian Year which begins on the minute when the sign "Aries" rises on the horizon on that day in March when the "Sun" just enters the sign of "Aries." (The year 1916 A. D. corresponds to the Rosicrucian year of 3269, which began on March 21, 1916, at 1:06 A. M. Eastern Time.) Such New Year Celebrations shall be held in the Temple of all lodges and attended by the Council, Officers, and members of the Lodge and such especially invited guests or visiting members of the Order and whose presence the Master desires for reasons good and sufficient unto himself. There shall be a symbolical feast consisting principally of *corn*, or its products; *salt*, or that which tastes most strongly of it, and *wine*, in the form of unfermented grape juice, and any other delicacies or refreshments suitable to the occasion. All Officers shall wear their full regalia and all others their aprons or other insignia. There shall be only sacred music, symbolical addresses, and sincere rejoicing for the New Year.

B

At this New Year Feast it has been customary for the Master to bestow such honorary titles on his members as he may contemplate, to make new appointments to fill vacancies, etc., and to turn his control over to any newly elected Master and Officers.

C

All other regular or special Convocations or meetings of each Lodge are to be postponed in order that the New Year Feast may be held on the day decreed by the Imperator.

D

The Annual Outdoor Fete may be held at the discretion of the Master of each Lodge, on or about the 23rd day of September of each year. It shall be that day when the Sun enters the sign of Libra.

This Annual Outdoor Fete should be held by each Lodge independently, to celebrate the laying of the foundation stones of the Great Pyramid in America. Each Lodge shall arrange to go on this day (or the following one, should it rain or be stormy) to an open space in the suburbs near such Lodge, and with prayer and addresses, have each member of the Lodge deposit in one small pile a simple little stone or pebble, symbolical of "placing a stone for the foundation of the Great Pyramid in America." Full regalia and insignia must be worn by all Officers and members. Secrecy of the Fete need not be maintained, but the public or the uninitiated must not be given, in the prayers or addresses, any of the secret "work," signs, or symbols of the Order. Such a Fete may be held at sundown, if desired.

CHAPTER VIII.

PUBLICITY AND PUBLICATIONS

Section 146

The general propaganda work of the Order shall be officially conducted by the Supreme Grand Lodge exclusively, assisted by such other subordinate bodies or committees as the Supreme Grand Lodge may indicate from time to time.

Section 147

Local propaganda work may be conducted by a subordinate Lodge or by the Grand Lodge, provided that no propaganda work or publicity of any nature whatsoever shall be undertaken or attempted by any body subordinate to the Supreme Grand Lodge, except by its express approval and consent given in writing, and, in that event, only in accordance with the instructions given by the Supreme Grand Lodge, and at all times under its supervision and not otherwise.

Section 148

No body subordinate to the Supreme Grand Lodge shall issue or cause to be issued or tolerate the issuance or utterance of any book, pamphlet, treatise, lecture, exposition, or interpretation concerning this Order or its ideals, principles, laws, rituals, teachings, symbols, statutes, or any other phase of the work of this Order, unless same shall have been first submitted to the Supreme Grand Lodge for approval. All authorized publicity, publication, or propaganda matter shall state on its face that it is issued under the authority of the Supreme Grand Lodge of A. M. O. R. C.

Part Three

OPERATING MANUAL

We present to our members a complete Manual regarding the Work, Symbols, and other matters pertaining to our Order. This Manual will answer many questions continually asked, and will be a guide for officers and members in promptly and more efficiently advancing in the principles of the Order.

The matter has been prepared under the direction of the Imperator and must conform with the National Constitution of the Order as well as the unwritten laws used by the American Supreme Council in its procedures. *Wherever the following may differ from the Constitution, the Constitution is binding.*

This Manual should have a careful reading and study, and should be consulted often.

PURPOSES AND WORK OF THE ORDER

All Applicants for Admission—and, in fact, all serious inquirers regarding the Order—should be correctly informed as to the Purposes and Work of our Order.

The only correct way of so informing the inquirer is to adhere to the following statements:

The Order is primarily a Humanitarian Movement, making for greater Health, Happiness, and Peace in the *earthly lives* of all mankind. Note particularly that we say in the *earthly lives* of men, for we have naught to do with any doctrine devoted to the interests of individuals living in an unknown, future state. The Work of Rosicrucians is to be done *here* and *now*; not that we have neither hope nor expectation of *another* life after this but we *know* that the happiness of the future depends upon *what we do today for others* as well as for ourselves.

Also, our purposes are to enable men and women to live clean, normal, natural lives, as Nature intended, enjoying *all* the privileges of Nature, and all benefits and gifts equally with all of Mankind; and to be *free* from the shackles of superstition, the limits of ignorance, and the sufferings of avoidable *karma*.

The Work of the Order—using the word "Work" in an official sense—consists of teaching, studying, and testing such laws of God and Nature as make our members Masters in the Holy Temple (the physical body), and Workers in the Divine Laboratory (Nature's domains). This is to enable the Brothers and Sisters to render *more efficient help* to those who do not know, and who need or require help and assistance.

Therefore, the Order is a School, a College, a Fraternity, with a laboratory. The members are students and workers. The graduates are unselfish servants of God to Mankind, efficiently educated, trained, and experienced, attuned with the mighty forces of the Cosmic or Divine Mind, and Masters of matter, space, and time. This makes them essentially Mystics, Adepts, and Magi—creators of their own Destiny.

There are no other benefits or rights. All members are pledged to give unselfish Service, without other hope or expectation or remuneration than to Evolve the Self and prepare it for a *greater* work.

JURISDICTION

Masters of Subordinate Lodges, in all Jurisdictions, have autocratic power within their individual Lodges, limited by the Constitution of the Order, the Grand Master of the Jurisdiction, and the By-Laws of the individual Lodges.

Members, belonging to one Jurisdiction, but visiting Lodges in another Jurisdiction, must be subject to the rulings and laws of the Jurisdiction in which they are visiting.

Masters, visiting any Jurisdiction, will likewise submit to the rules and laws of the Jurisdiction visited, except when *honorary* exceptions are made by the Grand Master of such Jurisdiction.

Men and women may become members of our Order through being *invited* to make *Application for Admission,* and then having such application passed upon.

The Applicants must, therefore, bear the burden of Supplication. They may be invited to make application, but having been invited, and having accepted the invitation to make application, each applicant makes plea for admission, and must *humbly* seek and pray for admission, as though he or she had not been invited to do so. In other words, the invitation to make application does not indicate that the Applicant is desired to such an extent that supplication for admission is not necessary.

When an application blank is given to a man or woman, with the invitation to make plea for admission, the Member thus inviting another must advise the prospective Applicant that admission to the Order depends upon the Applicant's *plea* and his or her *qualifications*; and the members must also make it plain that a Membership Committee will pass upon the application in a formal and *regular way*.

Applications which pass the Membership Committee and seem worthy of further consideration will be handed to the Secretary and the Master shall appoint some Member or Members to call upon such Applicants (or have them call upon the Members), and *interview* them.

The said Application blanks are then voted upon by the Lodge or the Lodge Council (see Constitution of the Order), and if there are not *two or more* reasonable objections against the admission of the Applicant (*two* black balls cast upon reasonable and sufficient grounds) the said Applicant is elected to Membership and must be so notified; he shall then call upon the Secretary and advance the proper Initiation Fee and be informed of the date of Initiation.

ENTERING THE LODGE—(*Guardian's Examination*)

In order to enter one of our regular Lodges, each Applicant for Admission, claiming to be a Member, must submit to an Examination by the Guardian, at the door of the Lodge. This is an ancient custom, and should be rigidly adhered to by all Guardians, as a matter of form. In fact, it will be proper for the Guardian not only to demand the proper Password from each applicant for admission, as well as a *Membership Card,* but to *test* the Members occasionally, as regards the rightful possession of the Password.

The possession of either a Membership Card or the Password of any Degree, or both, does not constitute a benefit or right by which the possessor can *demand* admittance into one of our Lodge Temples. Both, or either of these possessions, may be unlawfully known or owned by a man or woman. It is the duty of the Guardian to *learn* whether this is so or not.

A legitimate Member, properly possessing a Membership Card, may present a Password of some higher degree than that in which he or she may be properly registered. Therefore, the mere possession or knowledge of a Password is not *sufficient* evidence of a Member's standing in the Order. This point must be determined by each Guardian, to his or her own *thorough satisfaction.*

Naturally, the question arises—and perhaps will never be thoroughly settled—as to what constitutes *thorough satisfaction,* in some cases. All that each Guardian can do, and MUST DO, is to make himself or herself feel that every fair test has been applied, *when there is any doubt,* and, if still doubtful, leave the matter to the Master of the Lodge, who will make the final test and decide.

The Guardian and Master cannot be too exact in the questions asked, and the answers returned. In other words, the Member should PROVE his or her Initiation into the Degree where admission is now sought, regardless of the possession of the Password or Membership Card or even Demit.

All such tests should be given in private, where the Member cannot be coached by any other person. Likewise, the Guardian should be sure, in testing or asking a Member for the Password at the Temple door, that no one else hears such Password given. The Password should always be whispered to the Guardian at the door.

Vouching for Visitors. A visiting Member may be vouched for by another Member of a Lodge, *if* the Member so vouching can assure the Guardian that he or she has *actually seen* the visiting Member in one of our Lodges, at some time when a regular convocation or lecture was in session; or if the Member so vouching can assure the Guardian that the visiting Member has passed every test as to the rightful possession of a Password, and the vouching Member *further* knows, by lawful or satisfactory evidence, that the visitor is a duly and properly Initiated Member of some Degree of our Order. In such a case, the Guardian can demand the Password in the usual way, ask for the Membership Card, and then admit the visitor to the Lodge.

Membership Cards must be shown, upon demand, by all Members, and the Card must show that all dues of the Lodge to which the Member belongs have been paid up to *within three months.* No one shall be admitted to any Lodge (their own or another), unless dues are paid up to within three months. In some Lodges or Jurisdictions, if dues are in arrears three months (more or less), the Member cannot enjoy the privileges of *Active* Membership. The only guide for Guardians, in the case of visiting Members, is to set *four months* as the limit for arrears. Naturally, Members presenting *Demits* should have a Membership Card, showing all dues paid up to the time of Demit. New dues in the Lodge to which transferred, must begin at the time of admission to such Lodge.

Responsibility for Admission to Lodges. The Guardians as well as the Masters are responsible to the Order and the Supreme Grand Lodge for the admission into any Lodge of any one who is not a properly Initiated Member in good standing.

If a visitor wishes to attend one full Degree, or take an Initiation, he should secure a Demit from his own Lodge for the time of his visit.

VISITORS

Visitors to a Lodge must submit to the rules and laws of such Lodge and the Constitution of the Order. Visits to a Lodge cannot extend over a period of more than *three months,* after which time a visitor must be transferred to such Lodge. During the time of visiting a Lodge, whether in the same city or another city than that in which the Member's own Lodge is located, a visitor must pay his or her regular dues to the Lodge to which he or she belongs. By showing a Membership Card to the Secretary of a Lodge, indicating that the dues have been paid to one's parent Lodge, one may visit any Lodge without paying dues to such Lodge. Arrears in dues to any parent Lodge of more than three months (including the present month), will *prohibit* a Member from visiting a Lodge.

Visitors to a Lodge are to be considered as guests of the Lodge, and, if officers of another Lodge, are to occupy seats in the East with the Master of the Lodge visited.

Visitors may attend only those sessions of such Degree as they were in during their regular attendance at the parent Lodge. If a visit is made to a Lodge during any other Degree session, the Master may, if deemed advisable, suspend all Degree Work for a half hour, open the

Lodge in the First Degree, and permit the visitor to be introduced to his Lodge.

National Lodge Members, or those in the Postulant Grades (Correspondence Grades) of the Supreme Lodge, may visit or attend only general sessions or Feast Ceremonies of a regular Temple.

TRANSFERS

Members may be transferred from one Lodge to another only when the Member intends or expects to be a Member of the Lodge to which he is transferred, for *three months* or more. If a Member wishes to attend another Lodge for less than three months, he or she must be classed as a visitor to that Lodge, and be subject to the hospitality of such Lodge.

Continued visits to any Lodge should be made only when a Member is in another city than that in which his own Lodge is located.

When a Member is transferred to a Lodge, and presents to that Lodge a properly signed demit, the Secretary of such Lodge should give *precedence* to such transferred Member over all other Applicants for admission to that Lodge, should there be a waiting list for admission.

Upon transfer, the Member must assume all the obligations and dues of the Lodge to which he is transferred, regardless of what they may have been in a former Lodge.

DEMITS

Section 136

A member in good standing in a subordinate Lodge may affiliate with another subordinate Lodge. He shall apply to the Secretary of his Lodge in writing stating the name of the Lodge with which he seeks affiliation. The Secretary shall forward the letter to the Grand Secretary who shall send a certificate to the Secretary of the Lodge wherein membership is desired, showing that the applicant is a member in good standing, and the subordinate Lodge shall admit him to membership without further proceedings or initiation.

Section 137

No certificate of good standing issued by the Grand Lodge shall be valid or recognized by any subordinate Lodge after thirty days of its issuance. If the member cannot or does not complete his transfer within thirty days, he must, in the interim, maintain good standing in the Grand Lodge or his former subordinate Lodge, as the case may be.

Section 138

A member who has paid or offers to pay all his dues in a subordinate Lodge may apply to the Secretary for a demit from such subordinate Lodge. The Secretary shall issue the demit and inform the Grand Secretary of that fact. Such demit shall not affect Grand

Lodge standing of the member who shall thereafter have the status of Grand Lodge National Member.

Section 139

A member who has paid or offers to pay all his dues in the Grand Lodge may apply to the Grand Secretary for a demit and the Grand Secretary shall issue same. The member receiving such demit shall have the status of inactive membership in the Grand Lodge. He may resume active membership at any time if, during inactive status, his life and conduct has been such as required of active members in good standing.

THE ANTE-CHAMBER OF A TEMPLE

This is the room in which the Initiates are first prepared for Initiation in the various Degrees. On such occasions it shall be guarded by the Guardian of the Temple, assisted by the Deputy Master. In the First Degree Initiation, this room is in charge of the Conductor of the Lodge, and no one may enter it without the permission of the Conductor, unless so decreed by the Master.

THE CHAMBER OF A TEMPLE

This is a Secret Room, wherein the first part of the First Initiation is conducted. It is the Chamber of the Cross, the Abiding Place of Life and "Death," the Tomb of Silence, and the Place of Terror. All these names have been applied to it in the past, and each expresses to the mind of the Initiate its function in the First Degree Initiation.

This Chamber is guarded, at First Degree Initiations, first by the Conductor in the Ante-Chamber, then by the Herald, and then by the Torch Bearer.

When not used for Ceremonies, it should be reverenced and kept undefiled by the uninitiated. Nothing should ever occur in it to profane it (such as levity, unbecoming conduct, or profane labor).

THE THRESHOLD OF THE TEMPLE

This is the Most Beloved place in each Lodge to the Initiated, for it represents the Doorway to Light and Knowledge.

It is the Entrance from the Chamber to the Lodge, and, in the First Degree Initiation, is guarded by the Guardian of the Temple, while any other entrance to the Lodge is guarded by the Secretary or Deputy Master.

The Threshold should never be crossed after or between convocations or lectures, without due reverence being shown by the trespasser, standing upon the Threshold and making the Sign of the Cross, while facing the interior of the Lodge.

It represents the Passage from Darkness to Light, and from finite life to infinite life.

THE TEMPLE

The word is derived from the Latin *tempus—time.* To us, the true Temple of which we hope to be Masters, is the body of man, finding its counterpart in the Universe, which is the Temple of God.

The term Temple is applied to our buildings, devoted to the worship of God and God's laws, wherein are Chambers for study, work, and meditation. Because of the sacredness of such study, work, and meditation, our Temples are sacred, and must be so considered and regarded, passively and actively, by all Members. "As above, so below." The Temple of God is universal, non-sectarian, charged with Cosmic powers and vibrating forces, and designed by the Master Architect to continue His creative work in love, goodness, and justice; so our Temples should represent a place where universal minds, regardless of creeds or dogmas, may abide, attuned with such vibratory forces within as make for love, goodness, justice, and peace, that Nature may continue her creation without interruption or interference.

THE LODGE

Within our sacred Temples there are many Chambers, the principal one being the Lodge. The Lodge is the Central Chamber of all Temples, devoted to the general convocations and formal study of God's Works. It is, therefore, the "inner" or "middle" Chamber, the *Soul* of the Temple, the first circle within the great circle—the Holy Sanctum, the "abiding place of the Presence of God."

Our Lodges also represent the surface of the earth, with four cardinal points or horizons—East, South, West, and North, with earth, fire, and water beneath our feet, and air and "Nous" overhead, beyond which are the "stars and sky"—the immaterial world.

The Lodge is arranged so that it serves its purpose and performs its functions symbolically and practically. Its appointments are such as make for *efficiency* in the Work to be done, and *regularity* in practices performed therein. These arrangements and appointments are explained hereinafter.

The Furnishings of a Lodge of our Order are standardized, and serve the excellent purpose of providing the necessary articles and means for Work and Worship. These, too, are explained hereinafter.

THE "EAST"

The "East" of the Lodge is the *first* point on the horizon, and, therefore, the *most important* point of direction in the Lodge to all Rosicrucians. It was in the East that man first saw the "Symbol of Life," and knew, by what he saw, that God's Laws were mechanically and mathematically perfect. The diurnal rising of the Sun, with such infinite exactness, after a period of transition from ebbing life at the West, to its dismal darkness of the North, likewise teaches man that life is *continuous* and *immortal,* rising again and again in the East, the South, and the West.

In the East is the new life begun. From the East comes forth the Glory of God, "which is of God." Therefore, in our Lodges, the East is the point in which all Brothers and Sisters seek that Dawn of Illumination and Divine Resurrection, from the "dismal darkness of the West," as will make them free from the superstitions of darkness (ignorance) and the fears of night (evil).

For this reason, the East is always respected and saluted, as the "place of Divine Illumination and Resurrection." It must be so regarded at *all* times, and must never be occupied by the profane (unilluminated, uninitiated) or the unworthy.

THE "SOUTH"

The "South," in our Lodges, is that point where the Sun (source of illumination) shines in the greatest glory and strength, and finds the culmination of its ascendency in the realm of Heaven (spirituality). Therefore, this point is where the Divine Mind finds fullest (spiritual) expression, and is occupied in all Lodges by the Chaplain, the spiritual representative of God in His Temple.

From the "South" shall come words of prayer and holy blessings, in all matters of our Work and Service for God and Man.

THE "WEST"

In the "West," the Sun of life slowly resigns itself to the close of its journey, and, in radiant splendor, goes to rest in the "arms of the Mother" (peace and quiet).

The "West" in our Lodges is that point where the Brothers and Sisters seek peace, rest, and attunement with the Cosmic, through silent prayer and meditation. It is where the Matre (mother) of the Lodge awaits the coming of her children, and welcomes them ever to "rest awhile and tarry in Communion with God."

THE "NORTH"

The place of "dismal darkness," where the Sun sheds not its glorious light. It is the abyss of evil, the valley of death (stagnation), the realm of darkness (ignorance), the hours of night (evil).

It is "the place from whence cometh naught but desire to come hither," hence it is the place or point in the Lodge, where the Seeker for Light (applicant) dwelleth, and the Neophyte (now Initiate) enters the Lodge in search of more light.

THE ALTAR

In the East of the Lodge is situated the Altar of the Master, who represents the Greater Light, and is, in fact, the Lesser Light in all Lodge convocations, except when the "Vestal Light may more symbolically represent the rising of the Greater Light in all its glory."

Sacred and Holy shall the Altar be, that from its bosom may come Intellectual and Spiritual Illumination, equal to the physical illumination given by the Sun.

THE SHEKINAH

In the *center* of the Lodge, where lines from the four points of the horizon would meet, is the Heart of the Soul of the Temple.

This point—the *fifth* point of the Lodge—is occupied by the Sacred Triangle, called the Shekinah (pronounced she-ky-nah, with accent on the middle syllable).

The Shekinah is the Symbolical Place, representing "the Presence of God in our Midst."

It is "the point within the inner circle." (The outer circle is the Temple; the inner circle is the Lodge.)

Thus, it is "the triangle within the two circles."

It indicates, therefore, that God is in all *places* (Lodges—meeting places), in all *times* (Temple—time); therefore, He is *omnipresent.*

The Shekinah is illuminated at all convocations, to symbolize the "fire and fervor, flame and light" of the Divine Presence.

Three candles are used upon the Shekinah, to remind us of the law that with no less than three "points" can perfect manifestations exist.

The Shekinah is placed with its third point (having the shortest candle) toward the West, so that the "Presence of God" may manifest in the West, where dwell the Children of Light in peace, love, and meditation.

The outer two points of the Shekinah are toward the North and South.

The Shekinah receives its power through the Sacred, Mystical Vibrations generated in the East of the Lodge, and which radiate through the Sanctum toward the Shekinah, which is the focal point for such Vibrations. Thus, the "Presence of God" is carried in Vibrations from the East to the "Heart of the Soul of the Temple."

THE SANCTUM

In each Lodge there is a place, a condition, called the Sanctum. It is located between the Shekinah and the Altar. The Holy Place occupies all the space between the Eastern edge of the Shekinah and the Western line of the Altar, but does not reach to both sides of the Lodge. The Southern and Northern boundaries of this space are determined by leaving on each side of the Lodge sufficient walking space—about two and one-half to three feet—for reaching either the Northern or Southern sides of the Altar. The remainder of the space between the Altar and the Shekinah forms the Holy Sanctum.

In the Sanctum, at its Easterly end, in front of the Altar, is the Vestal Stand, and the "station" of Colombe.

The Sanctum is kept holy, and reserved exclusively for certain points or parts of sacred Ceremonies or Convocations held in the Lodge, and must not be used for other purposes.

It is also the place where Neophytes and Members stand for the taking of Sacred Oaths and Obligations, and where Brothers and Sisters are Knighted or Titled.

Trespassing between the Altar and the Shekinah, or in other words, "crossing the Sanctum," is not only forbidden to all but the Master or Colombe, but is a "serious and grievous error, bringing a lesson from the Cosmic upon the Lodge, and more especially upon the trespasser."

The foundation for such a solemn warning is in the statement previously made (see Shekinah), wherein it is explained, that from the Altar comes forth " Life, Light, and Love," and the Shekinah receives its power (the Presence of God) from the Vibrations passing from the Altar to the Shekinah. This would make the Sanctum a place always charged with sacred Vibrations, and trespassing between the Altar and the Shekinah would interrupt the flow of such Vibrations, and disturb the Harmony established there.

The Master has the authority, in fact, command, to reprimand one who will defile the Sanctum by trespassing upon it from North to South or South to North. When the Sanctum is entered for any legitimate purpose, he who enters it may pass only to the *center* of it, and must leave it from the same point by which he entered it. Likewise must each who enters it immediately face the East, from the center of it, and make the "Sign of the Cross" before doing that act or performing that function which necessitated entrance into the Sanctum.

In leaving the Sanctum, he who entered it must not only leave by the same point of entrance, but the exit must be made by stepping *backward,* and always facing the East.

THE MASTER

"For he who is greatest among you, shall be the greatest Servant unto all."

The Master of every Lodge is the Master-Servant. That title and position has been bestowed upon one because of ability, character, worthiness, and willingness to *serve*.

The Master of each Lodge is, by virtue of the Constitution, the autocratic executive of the Lodge, limited in his acts only by the Constitution and the Decrees of the Imperator, the Supreme Grand Master, or the American Supreme Council.

Symbolically, he is the Greatest Light of each Temple and each Lodge. He is the Imperator's representative in each Temple, and the Supreme Grand Master's representative in each Lodge.

His place is in the East, from whence all Knowledge comes. He stands in the East at all convocations and lectures, to act as a medium —the Master Messenger—for the Radiation of Light and the Dissemination of Knowledge.

The Supreme Grand Master shall be addressed as: *The Most Worshipful Supreme Grand Master.* During all convocations he shall be saluted as hereinafter explained (see *Salutations*), and in all ways shown that respect, consideration, and honor due his noble, unselfish, and autocratic position.

In Subordinate Lodges the Master shall be addressed as: *The Worthy Master.* He shall be saluted and respected like unto a Grand Master, so far as form and ceremony are concerned, although amenable to the Grand Master of his Jurisdiction and its Grand Council.

THE MATRE

The mother of each Lodge holds therein a position akin to that of the Master. Her station is in the West, where the Sun retires in glory, and life closes its material activities and finds sweet repose.

She is *Mother* in a material and spiritual sense to the children of each Lodge (the Brothers and Sisters), and to her should be confided those intimate personal problems of life which none but a mother can understand. Then she, in turn, may secretly and in strict confidence seek the help of the Master of her Lodge and such Brothers and Sisters as can render the material or spiritual help necessary.

How often are there small problems, delicate and intimate affairs which burden our hearts and tax our greatest endeavors to overcome. And—how many of these often roll away into insignificance or become *nil,* when once we confide them to *Mother!* Mother who *understands,* mother who *sympathizes,* mother who *knows* and *trusts* and *loves* and *sacrifices* that we may be happy.

Let us ever keep the name, the spirit, the holy God-purpose of *Mother* sacred and sweet; and never may we be too proud to kneel before the warm heart and kind smile of our Matre, and find in her sweet repose and Peace Profound at any time.

THE VESTAL FIRE

This Symbolical furnishing of all Lodges of our Order occupies a place directly in front of the Altar in the East. The stand, on which the Vestal's Urn is placed, should be at least two feet from the edge of the Altar, to permit room for the Vestal (Colombe) to stand between it and the Altar.

In the days of old, every Lodge was furnished with a Vestal Altar, on which a Holy Fire burned continuously day and night and was attended by a caretaker, or a blue light, burning during all convocations in Lodges.

In our Lodges of today, the Vestal Altar may be replaced by a Stand of some kind, appropriate in design, and surmounted by a metal Urn, in which Incense is burned to represent the ancient "Vestal Fire," and wherein the "Lesser Light" is demonstrated at Initiations.

The soft "blue light" of medieval times may be used also, by having a light with a blue globe burning on the Vestal Stand in the Lodge.

THE VESTAL COLOMBE

The Vestal of each Lodge is the ritualistic "Colombe." Aside from her ritualistic work, she should see that the "blue light" or incense fire, or both, on the Vestal Stand are lighted for each convocation.

She should have a permanent seat, at the right side of the Vestal Stand, and this must never be occupied by any other Officer or Member of the Order. A visiting Vestal should be seated at the left side of the Vestal Stand.

The Colombe of each Lodge represents "Life, Light, and Love," also the *Conscience* of each Brother and Sister of the Lodge.

In all convocations, ceremonies, lectures, Council hearings, or discussions, she should have precedence over all others, excepting the Master, in voicing any sentiment or directing any act of Ceremony or Rite. "When Colombe speaks, all shall be silent!" says an old law of the Temple; for from the Mouth of a Child comes Wisdom, and from the Bosom of Conscience comes Truth.

Colombes must be less than 18 years of age, when appointed to their office, and not younger than 13 years of age. Each *must serve until 21 years of age,* during which time they must retain their virtue (remaining unmarried). They are retired with honor on their 21st birthday, when a successor is installed with fitting Ceremony. Colombes are, in fact, "Brides of the Order" during their term of office. They shall be initiated and attend one of the regular classes for instruction.

TO THE VESTAL COLOMBE

By CHARLES CLINE HUBBARD

Beautiful Character, True Herald of the Cycle's New Progression—
The New, Pure Womanhood of a Newer, Purer Race—before
Thy Heart's Most Holy Shrine in solemn-toned Confession
My thoughts, true-homaged all attend, Thy Pureness to adore!

Sweet Vestal, the worldly masters scoffed at Thee, Thy garments sought to mar,
Jeered at Thee, and laughed at Thee; but with forgiving sweetness,
Ensconced with Rose and Cross, Thou sought that ever Perfect Land,
Wherein Thy God awaited Thee with the Crown of His Completeness!

And now, Sweet Dove of Purest Womanhood, the Temple Bells soft ringing
Their mellow tones of Holy Gladness, pause, whilst there surround Thee
Friends whose faces all familiar are, Thy entrance gladly singing,
For thou art, Thyself, the Cycle's Evolution—its own Eternity!

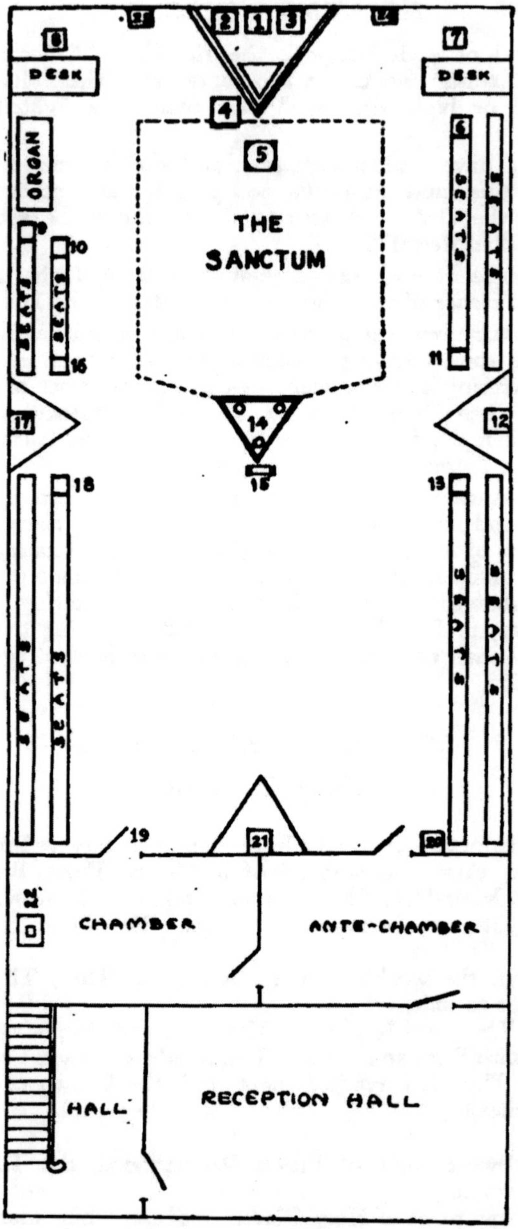

DIAGRAM OF R∴ C∴ TEMPLE AND LODGE

EXPLANATION OF THE DIAGRAM

▽ ▽ ▽

The diagram represents a typical Rosicrucian Temple with its stations and appointments. When Lodges plan their own Temples this diagram should be as closely adhered to as possible.

The figures on the diagram have the following indications:

1. The Master's Chair on the triangular dais in the East—with triangular lectern in front of his chair.

2 and 3. Seats for Visiting Masters.

4. The Vestal Chair.
5. The Vestal Stand.
6. The Deputy Master's Chair.
7. The Secretary's Chair at a desk.
8. The Treasurer's Chair at a desk.
9. The Precentor's Chair.
10. The Organist's Chair.

(Note: If the organ is placed on the opposite side of the Lodge, then the chairs numbered 6, 9, and 10 should be changed likewise.)

11. The Conductor's Chair.
12. The Chaplain's Station and Chair.
13. The Herald's Chair.
14. The Shekinah with Candles.
15. The Stool.
16. The Medalist's Chair.
17. The High Priestess' Station and Chair.
18. The Torch Bearer's Chair.
19. The Threshold.
20. The Guardian's Chair at Temple Entrance.
21. The Matre's Station and Chair.
22. The Rosy Cross in the Chamber.

23 and 24. Seats for Visiting Officers.

For a description of the other parts of the Temple and Lodge read the definition of various terms in the Manual herewith.

THE SIGN OF THE CROSS

Reference has been made many times in the preceding pages to the sign of the Cross. An explanation of this term and Sign is necessary.

Briefly written, in ancient manuscript and in Official papers, the term is expressed or indicated by "S. C." Again, the term and sign is expressed by a cross (+), while often words, "Sign of the +," are used.

The Sign itself is made as follows: Starting with the left hand at the side of the body, hanging in a natural position, the right hand is brought up to a place on a level with the chest, but about six to ten inches in front of the body. The fingers of the right hand are closed, except the thumb and first and second fingers, which are extended and brought together at the finger tips, the fingers pointing outward from the body.

Then the right hand, with fingers held as described, starts to make the *Sign,* by moving the hand upward, in a perfectly *perpendicular line,* until the hand is about opposite the throat. Then the hand is brought downward in a *curved line,* to a place about opposite the *left breast;* then straight across in a *horizontal line at right angles* to the *perpendicular line,* to a place opposite the *right breast;* then, on a *curved line* like *an arc,* to a level with the *throat,* where the Sign began, and downward on another *perpendicular* line to the *navel.* Then drop the right hand to the side.

These perpendicular and horizontal lines cross each other opposite the *heart,* at which place on the Cross the Rose is placed. At no time should the hand and fingers come nearer the body than six inches. The Sign is not made toward one's body, but *from* it, and away from the person making the Sign.

It should be made *slowly* and with *dignity* and sincere *reverence.* It represents the Obligation and Oath, taken by all Initiates at the time of the First Degree Initiation, and at other times in Ceremonies and Convocations. The various lines formed in making this sign contain many ancient symbols and signs.

It is used by Masters, Officers, and Members, when taking or indicating a solemn Obligation to the Order or its Members. It should never be supplanted by any form of pledge. Even in courts of law, and elsewhere, when one is called upon to pledge to an oath or statement, by placing the hands upon the Holy Bible, or by raising the hand, the Sign of the Cross should be used in preference. In America, one is privileged to use whatever form, for taking an oath, that is the most sacred to the maker of the oath; this permits the Rosicrucians to vow their allegiance to an obligation or *swear* to any statement, in court or out of it, by making the Sign of the Cross, in preference to any other form. And this preference should always be shown, explaining, if called upon to do so, that to you "The Sign thus made is the most sacred and binding of any." FOR IT CALLS

UPON THE MAKER TO TELL THE TRUTH REGARDLESS OF ALL COSTS AND ALL CONSEQUENCES, mindful of the Terror of the Threshold and warning of your Conscience.

SALUTATIONS

The following Salutations shall be used by all Members, under the circumstances indicated:

Entering the Lodge. Whenever a convocation is being held in a Lodge or a lecture is to begin, and the Lodge is open to Members, all Members must approach the door of the Lodge, and, in a whisper, give the regular Password for such Degree as may be working in the Lodge, to the Guardian at the door. If demanded, the Member must submit to an examination (see *Examination* hereinafter). Unless the Password can be given, admission to the Lodge will be denied by the Guardian.

After entering the Lodge, the Member must make a Salutation to the East. This is done by the Member walking quietly to a point just West of the Shekinah, facing the East, and, with the left forefinger, making that Sign which was made in the First Degree Initiation, when all Initiates faced thusly in the First Solemn Obligation of Service. The purpose of such Salutation, when first entering a Lodge, is to indicate that the Member *renews,* or *signifies his remembrance of,* the Obligation taken in the First Degree Initiation. After such Salutory Sign the Member may take his seat. This is the general Sign of Salutation in all Jurisdictions.

Saluting the Master. If, during any convocation or lecture, a Member shall await the first opportunity to interrupt the Master, and then shall rise in front of his or her seat and face the East, then, when the Master observes this, make the Sign of the Cross. The Master will then say: "How may I serve my Brother?" (or Sister). Then the Member shall say: "Most Worshipful Grand Master," or "Worshipful Grand Master," or "Worthy Master," and proceed to ask the question, make a plea, ask for permission to leave the Lodge, etc. While thus speaking, the Member must face the East, and speak with *dignity.* When finished speaking, the Member must take his or her seat quietly, or do that thing which was desired, without interrupting the convocation or lecture.

THE OBLIGATION OF SERVICE

All Initiates in the First Degree Initiation are called upon to stand in the Holy Sanctum of the Lodge, and, facing the East, make a certain Sign and at the same time repeat after the Master the following sacred Obligation, which is *voluntarily* taken, and is forever binding upon all Members:

"Before the Sign of the Cross, and in the name of our God, I promise to forever do my utmost to restore to the world the light which is gone and the Secrets which are best for Man to know."

This *Obligation of Service* makes it imperative for the Members to study and practice, to test and try the secret Laws taught in our

Order, and TO APPLY THEM AT EVERY OPPORTUNE TIME, so that the *LIGHT* which is gone may be restored and darkness (ignorance and evil) dispelled.

LODGE DECORUM

It should not be necessary to speak on this subject to a Rosicrucian; for all appreciate the Sanctity and goodness of the Temple and the Lodge.

Once within the Lodge Room, the Members must refrain from loud conversation or unnecessary walking about. Bear in mind that some within the Lodge may be in deep meditation, *requiring silence;* others may be conducting silent and sacred convocations. Entrance into the Lodge should not disturb these silent workers.

LEAVING THE LODGE

At the close of all convocations or lectures, after the Master has properly closed the Work and bid the Members depart, they shall remain standing before their seats, facing the East, until the Master has stepped from the Altar in the East and slowly proceeded down the Lodge and out of the door, into the Ante-Chamber. Then the Members may quietly move toward the door, or hold their informal meeting until the Lodge is finally closed by the Guardian, by announcing that all must leave, and the Lodge room be closed for the time.

LECTURES

The principal teachings of the Order are given to the Members in the form of lectures, either orally at the regular convocations of each degree in the Temple Lodge, or, in the instance of the National student, in manuscript form. In fact, each Degree of our Order consists of an Initiation and from twelve to fifty or more lectures. In the Higher Degrees the lectures for each Degree increase in number.

These lectures are given by the Master to the Members, by reading and illustrating the definite lesson for the day. These lectures are prepared by the Imperator's Staff at the Supreme Grand Lodge, and sent in typewritten form, sealed and protected, to the Masters of all Lodges of our North American Jurisdiction.

All Lodges receive identically the same lectures. In the West Indies, the lessons are translated (after being received) into Spanish and so given. In New York, in an Italian and a French Lodge, the lessons are translated by the Masters into Italian and French, and so given. Nothing is added to the Work or Teachings by the Masters, as personal opinion, unless so stated to the Members at the time.

The teachings given to the Members at the Supreme Grand Lodge are likewise the same as those given to other Lodges. The Imperator instructs only one Degree at the Supreme Grand Lodge—the highest Degree. The other three or four degrees meeting there weekly, on different nights, receive instructions from Brothers who have been selected for such work and who are Members of a special class in Oratory and Reading, preparing themselves, under very competent instructors, to become excellent speakers and readers for National Work in our Order.

The teachings are modified or added to, from time to time, according to new findings here or abroad. Such changes or additions will be sent to each Lodge, to be given to the Members.

There is no particular advantage in attending the lectures in the Supreme Lodge in preference to other Lodges. In all Lodges there are those who do Research Work between lectures and are prepared at each lecture to ask intelligent questions or enter into the discussion of the lecture. Therefore, it behooves every Master to encourage the asking of questions and the discussion of points contained in the lectures.

When questions are asked of the Master which he cannot answer from *our* point of view, he will frankly state so, and may then write to the Supreme Grand Lodge for the answer.

When questions are asked which the Master believes call for answers pertaining to Work covered in higher Degrees, the Master shall properly refrain from answering the question and defer it to a later Degree.

"ROSAE CRUCIS"

This is the Latin form of the name, and is generally used in all countries because it lends itself very readily to use in all languages and at the same time is a complete explanation of the true meaning. The words, translated into English, mean: "Of the Rosy Cross." Therefore, the words "of the" should never precede the words "Rosae Crucis." The name of our Order is Ancient and Mystical Order Rosae Crucis. *Order Rosae Crucis* is a shorter way of writing the name, and it means: Order *of the* Rosy Cross. The Official abbreviation of the name, however, is, as given in the American Constitution, A. M. O. R. C.

The words Rosae Crucis are never translated when used in other languages. For instance: Our Grand Lodge in West India, conducted in the Spanish tongue, translates the name Ancient and Mystical Order Rosae Crucis as follows: *Antigua y Mistica Orden Rosae Crucis.*

ROSY CROSS

This term is not used officially by our Order, except as an explanation of the term Rosae Crucis. The reason for this is two-fold. By using Rosae Crucis instead, we adhere to the foreign custom. And we likewise keep from identifying ourselves with any of the commercial propositions in America, using the term Rosy Cross as titles for written-to-sell books which have nothing to do with our work, or as the name for colonization schemes, classes, etc.

THE ROSE AND THE CROSS

A book might be written upon the subject of the Symbology or Mystical meaning of the Rose and the Cross. The most popular explanation of these two symbols—the one which writers in encyclopedias love to use with great show of seeming authority—is that the Cross and the Rose have much to do with *dew* and other alchemical terms. This is simply a fanciful, though satisfactory, explanation for the casual reader. It is not the Truth, however.

So far as legend is concerned, we are informed in our own records that man first used the Symbol of the Cross when, in Egypt, or possibly Atlantis, a Mystic stood at sunrise upon a plane, and, looking toward the East, he raised his arms to a level with his shoulders in adoration of the Sun—the giver of life. Then, turning to face the West to salute the place where life ended, symbolically, he found that his arms and body, while in the act of salutation, formed a shadow on the ground before him, cast by the rising sun. The shadow was in the form of the *Cross,* and to him it meant that life was but a *shadow*—the *shadow of the Cross.*

An explanation, often offered by the wise, is that the origin of the Cross was in the *crux ansata* of the Egyptians—the cross with the oval opening at top, often seen in Egyptian designs and used symbolically in Egyptian and mystical Eastern writings. The crux ansata, called the *cross of life,* was designed by the Egyptians and Mystics to represent the continuity or immortality of life. The statement that in time the oval, or upper part of the crux ansata was closed into one perpendicular piece, thereby giving the original of the Cross we use, is a mistake, for in our records we find, as will others find, on the oldest Egyptian records of Mysticism and history, *both crosses used in the same period.* They seemed to come into existence about the same time—at that time when the Master Minds of the Orient were originating and creating symbols which would have definite meanings in the minds of the learned students. If the Cross and other symbols confuse and perplex the wise today, it is not to be wondered at that in the days gone by there were many who saw naught in these symbols but arbitrary marks of indefinite character.

The Rose, on the other hand, offers little trouble to the student of Symbology. Its fragrance, its cycle of budding into life, maturing into full bloom and sweetness and then dropping to decay and dust, represent the Cycle of Life—even human life. That the seed of the disintegrating Rose should drop to earth and in earth find again the opportunity to be reborn, typifies the Mystic's understanding of the *continuity of life,* or reincarnation.

In our Work, the Cross represents many things esoterically; likewise the Rose. But exoterically, the Rose represents *Secrecy* and Evolution, while the Cross represents the Labors and Burdens of Life and the karma which we must endure in our earthly existence.

In our ritual of the First Degree Initiation, there is this reference to the Cross and the Rose: "Life is represented by Light, Aspiration by the Rose and the Cross, and Death by Darkness." From this we would learn that Aspiration—the desire to do, to serve, to accomplish, and to Master and finally *attain*—is possible through the *karma* (cross) we must endure and the *evolution* (rose) we attain thereby.

THE TRIANGLES

There has been much discussion as to why we use as a Symbol the *Inverted* Triangle. Just why the triangle with point downward is called inverted, has not been explained to us. There is no reason, except Mystically, why a triangle, such as ours, should have any definite position. A triangle is always a triangle, regardless of position, and to use the word *inverted* is to presume that the triangle has a *proper* position of some kind which can be inverted

We are not unaware of the fact that certain organizations in America have used the triangle with the point upward as a Mystical Sign, but this did not give to that position of the triangle any proper or *just* position which should not be varied.

But the very best—and truthful—explanation for our use of the triangle in this fashion is the fact that it was used by the old Mystics of Egypt and possibly Atlantis, to represent the Divine (or so-called spiritual) creations of the Universe, while the triangle with the point upward was used to represent the material creations of the world. (The pyramids of Egypt typify the *material triangle*.)

The *doctrine of the trinity* is an after-creation of the old Mystical law of the triangle. By comparing the laws given in our Temple lectures regarding the two triangles (in the First Degree Temple Lectures) with this doctrine, one will find at once the similarity, as well as an explanation of why the triangle with the point downward represents Divine or Spiritual Creations.

Throughout the Work of the higher Degrees, the triangle or the "law of three points," helps to solve many problems. In fact, in the work being done at the Supreme Grand Lodge in the laboratory or out of it, in chemistry, electricity, healing, music, and even in the more subtle manifestations of nature's laws, the triangle in one of its two positions is used and always becomes the final or grand *Universal Solvent*.

The Cross within the Spiritual Triangle is one of the Official Symbols of *our Order* and is a very sacred Symbol. In one form or another it is to be found on every seal of every Lodge. It is an identifying mark not used by any other organization or society in the world.

SECRECY

There seems to be some doubt in the minds of many of our Members, as to what is *Secret* in our Work and what is not. This doubt may be removed by the following explanation:

The principal object of Secrecy in our Order, is to prevent those who do not belong to our Order (those who have not been examined, tested, tried, initiated, and instructed), from entering our sessions and convocations, and enjoying those privileges or rights which our Members enjoy, by virtue of their Obligations and Service.

Therefore, the Principles of Secrecy are associated with all that transpires in each Initiation Ceremony, or immediately preceding or following. In other words, those things which every Member is bound by Oath to keep Secret are: The *features* of each Initiation Ceremony, including what was said by the Master and each Officer, as well as the Member, in the Temple Ceremony; and what was *done* by the Master, Officers, and Member during, preceding or following the Ceremony. This includes the methods of opening and closing such Ceremonies, the terms, words, phrases, signs, symbols, etc., used in the Temple, Lodge, or Outer Chambers on the evening or day of such Initiations, as well as the *Grips, Passwords, Salutations, and Signs of Recognition.*

The foregoing things are to be held sacredly *Secret* by the members. The first Oath, taken by every Initiate, taken before being Initiated and signed by the Initiate's name in the Official Black Book of each Lodge, is as follows: "Before the Sign of the Cross, I promise, upon my honor, not to reveal to any one but a known Brother or Sister of this Order, the Signs, Secrets, or Words which I may learn prior to, during, or after passing through the First Degree." This Oath, being taken prior to Membership, is considered binding upon the Member for *all* Degrees. However, each Degree has its own Oath, similar in substance to the foregoing, so far as Secrecy of Signs, Words, and Symbols are concerned.

WHAT IS NOT SECRET

There is no obligation upon the Members of the Order, however, to keep Secret all the laws and principles which they learn in our lectures and teachings. It is not the *purpose* of the Order to educate men and women in vital fundamental laws which they *can never efficiently and properly use for the benefit of others.* To say that none of our laws or principles should be given or used outside of our Membership, would defeat the very purpose of our Order.

Discretion must be used, however. Our Members are taught certain vital laws, so that they may USE and apply them for the avowed purposes of the Order. It will not generally help a man or woman outside of our Order, who needs help, to explain to him or her the workings of Nature's laws. What is needed most in the average case is to set into *operation* such laws and principles as will bring about the results desired. Therefore, explanations which convey our laws and principles are unnecessary, *and sometimes defeat the purposes in mind,* and may, in other cases, cause trouble, worry, or ill effects.

But, there are cases where one will find it advisable, if not absolutely *necessary,* to explain to one outside of our Order the working of some of Nature's laws; for such an understanding may do all that is necessary to relieve a condition, or enable a troubled heart or sick body to find Health, Happiness, and Peace Profound.

Certainly, no Member will find in this privilege a reason to take all the lectures or teachings of our Order, or even part of them, and use them for a basis of another school or system, and either sell the instruction or publicly publish or teach it. The privilege which each Member enjoys, in giving some principles or laws to those who need them, makes *discretion necessary,* and when discretion is *not used,* and wilfully cast aside, the Member violates sacred Obligations, and will be forever cast outside the pale of the Great White Lodge. This is why the true teachings have never been published in books.

Those who are sincerely interested, *and worthy of Membership,* at some time, are easily recognized. To them the Order should be spoken of *carefully,* and only *casually,* until they are discovered to be anxious to unite in the *Work* and *Purposes* of the Order. Then, and only then, should they be invited by a Member to *make application,* as described herein.

In all ways, and in all things, maintain the *dignity* and *austerity* of the Order, and always be watchful for the seeker for knowledge who will greatly appreciate your bringing to his attention the existence of the Order and the means of entering it.

Part Four

GENERAL INSTRUCTIONS FOR ALL MEMBERS

The real benefits of membership in the AMORC—whether in the regular Temple Lodges or in the National Lodge—are many, and the most important are:

(1) Association with a body of men and women of like mind and purpose, ever ready to assist and cooperate, as true Brothers and Sisters;

(2) Association with a national and international staff of Officers and Directors controlling an organization of wide-spread interests, unusual facilities, and distinct powers for the carrying on of personal and practical work in behalf of mankind generally and the Brothers and Sisters especially;

(3) The privilege of direct and immediate advice in personal problems relating to health, business, social, financial, and ethical matters;

(4) The very special benefit that comes through the gradual and proper change of one's view-point of all the essential things of life, thereby eliminating the mysterious and perplexing matters which hold many in poverty, ill-health, and discontent;

(5) The awakening and development of certain latent or dormant faculties within each of us which will enable us to improve our position in life, increase our ability to do and accomplish, and bring greater success;

(6) The Cosmic and spiritual attunement with the Universal Mind and Master Minds so that we may live in co-operation with the constructive Divine Laws and Loving Divine Mind;

(7) The careful instruction and guidance in the attainment of such knowledge as will make us mighty and keen in the understanding and mastering of life's duties and obligations; also the complete instruction in the fundamentals of those arts and sciences which will make each student, each Member, strong in intellect, masterful in his daily occupation, perfect in his understanding, broad in his comprehension, and magnetic in his influence over the lesser minds of the world.

Our members will see, therefore, that of the seven points of benefits, outlined above, only one, the SEVENTH, pertains to the course of instruction, and that, therefore, to look upon membership in AMORC as being simply a student of a school, is to ignore many of the more important benefits.

And, it is a fact that the average member, or fully seventy-five out of every hundred, have need every month for many of the other six points of benefit, *and in times of emergency, sorrow, distress, perplexity, or serious complications in personal affairs,* the members find more need for the first six benefits than for the seventh.

In many foreign lands where the members have been students for ten to twenty years, and where they have long since completed the regular courses of study included in the seventh benefit, they retain active membership in the fraternity solely because of the other six benefits.

The GREAT AIM of the Rosicrucians has ever been to assist all mankind in evolving to the highest degree of earthly perfection, and to render aid to every living being "to the Glory of God and the Benefit of Mankind." This is covered in point number two in the above list. But, to do this, the organization INCLUDES the very complete courses of study.

Therefore, our members will see that the payment of their monthly dues is not for the purpose of supporting the COURSE OF STUDY or the WEEKLY LESSONS, but for the entire list of benefits, and many others which are of such a personal nature and so diverse that they could not be listed here without consuming many pages. The real SECRET BENEFITS of association with the Rosicrucians have always been the outstanding LIGHTS which have brought thousands to the portals of each branch of the Order yearly, humbly seeking permission to make the acquaintance of those who would invite them to unite with the Order.

The course of study may be set aside at times through changes in one's daily routine of living, or through temporary changes in environment, and for other reasons, but the other benefits of membership continue at all times, so long as a member remains in active membership.

On the other hand, as we have said, the mere payment of the monthly dues, without giving any thought to the studies, without attempting to render service to others, and live the progressive, constructive life of a true Rosicrucian, WILL NOT CONSTITUTE GOOD STANDING IN THE ORDER.

For this reason, members of the Order are urged to make regular reports of their studies, their experiences, or their activities in connection with their membership. These reports, whether from the Correspondence Members of the National Lodge or the members of the Temple Lodges, should be sent to their Lodge Secretaries at least once a month. And, to make progress from one grade of study to another, certain examinations are to be sent in by each student after each of the lower grades are completed.

One important point should be perfectly plain to all who read this Manual: The AMORC will NOT accept into membership those who wish to enjoy its benefits but DO NOT want to pursue its course of study and become trained to assist in the general advancement of mankind. Hundreds of inquiries are received each year from men and women who believe they have sufficient knowledge of the occult and mystical sciences and who want, therefore, only the benefits of association with the Rosicrucians. Regardless of the fact that these persons offer to pay their yearly dues in advance or make other financial inducements, they are never invited to join the AMORC and cannot become members.

SOME OF THE OFFICIAL SEALS OF THE AMORC OF NORTH AMERICA

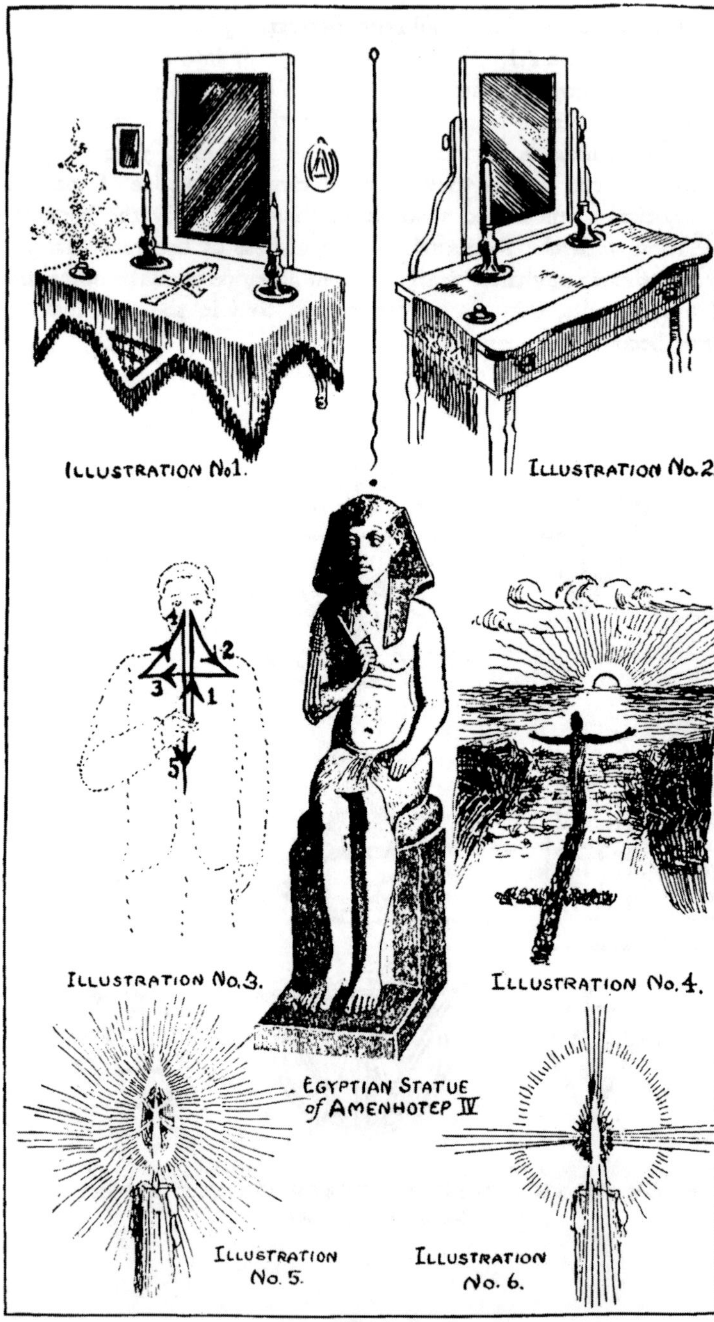

ILLUSTRATION No. 1.
ILLUSTRATION No. 2.
ILLUSTRATION No. 3.
ILLUSTRATION No. 4.
EGYPTIAN STATUE of AMENHOTEP IV
ILLUSTRATION No. 5.
ILLUSTRATION No. 6.

Part Five

SPECIAL INSTRUCTIONS FOR NATIONAL LODGE MEMBERS

The following pages contain information for members who receive the PRELIMINARY GRADES OF STUDY, later followed by the higher Temple Lectures, through the National Lodge, by mail.

The work of the National Lodge is unique. It consists of the most complete course of home-study of metaphysics and occultism ever offered, in addition to the other benefits of membership.

Members of the National Lodge do not pay for the instruction. The lessons are not sold, and membership in the National Lodge does not consist of simply reading the weekly lessons and trying the experiments. Nor does the mere payment of the monthly dues constitute good membership.

To be in good standing in the National Lodge the members must not only meet their monthly obligations—which are nominal—but they must live up to the rules and standards of Rosicrucian adeptship—and the careful study and practice of the teachings are but two points of the system.

The lectures, lessons, and experimental work of the National Lodge were especially designed to meet the requirements of members of the AMORC who *cannot* attend regular Temple Lodges or who wish to pursue the special study in the privacy of the home.

The lessons are arranged in two divisions, one division containing seven preliminary lectures and the other division containing three grades, with twelve lectures each. Additional talks, many experiments, and a number of practical systems, are included in each grade. Each grade also has an Initiation Ritual for a simple ceremony to be performed by the candidate at home, which illustrates and demonstrates some of the important teachings.

The Preliminary Division and Three Grades are outlined in the next few pages. The lessons of these Grades are constantly being improved, amended, and extended, and members receive additional instruction in accordance with their personal requirements, advancement, and psychic development. The lessons and lectures are NOT made in quantities for use for several years, as with correspondence courses, but made only in such groups of classifications as will meet the special needs of the various grades of standing of the members. The instructions, therefore, are practically PERSONAL and DIRECT, and when coupled with the advice and instruction sent separate from the lessons in letters, form a very personal system of instruction.

Furthermore, these lessons and lectures, rituals, and experiments of the National Lodge are different from the graded Temple lectures of the work conducted by the Temple Lodge. They are NOT ELEMENTARY, but are preliminary to the higher Temple Lectures, which you may receive, if you qualify in these first three grades.

Part Six

OUTLINE of the SYSTEM of INSTRUCTION OF THE NATIONAL LODGE

For six weeks the new members receive personal, private communications from an especially assigned Master of the highest work in the organization, who carefully analyzes the needs and requirements of the new member and instructs him in those fundamental principles and laws of nature which will enable the student to qualify himself in the most rapid time and perfect manner possible. These instructions are in the form of Secret Mandamus lectures, discourses, and other matter sent under seal by mail to the member. The member studies these preliminary instructions and tries certain experiments of a fundamental nature which are highly illuminating and intensely interesting, and reports to the Masters at the Supreme Lodge his comments, results of the experiments, and understanding of the points involved. In this way for six weeks the new member and an officer of the organization are in intimate contact by correspondence and in psychic contact through the Rosicrucian methods. At the end of the sixth week, if the member is properly prepared, he is admitted into the First Grade of the Neophyte studies and is given other confidential instructions. If the member is not properly qualified, further and more complete instructions are given by a special department of instruction so that the member may became prepared and ready for the First Grade work in the shortest time possible.

The instructions, lessons, laws, and principles given to the member in these preliminary lessons contain many astonishing ideas and do more to inculcate the true Rosicrucian art in the consciousness of the member than any preliminary steps that have ever been devised.

First Grade:

After the proper preparation and the development of certain psychic faculties and functions during the six weeks or more of preliminary preparation the member is ready for the personal initiation of a psychic and spiritual nature whereby he becomes acquainted with some of the highest principles in his own home.

The first papers sent to the new member after his admission into the First Grade include not only the beautiful and symbolical initiation ceremony which he or she is able to perform easily and quietly in the privacy of some part of the home, but many other papers of important instruction and guidance are also sent to the member.

Thereafter, the member receives twelve weekly sealed envelopes of a large size containing the secret and private lectures, lessons, and instructions of the First Grade, including many fascinating tests of Cosmic laws, many experiments of astonishing principles and scores of practical, helpful principles which the member can demonstrate and apply in his daily life for his own benefit and self-evolution. The lessons and lectures of the First Grade covering twelve weeks include complete information on the following subjects:

Objective and Cosmic Consciousness, The Brain and Mind, Mystic Symbolism, The Triangle, The Meaning of Numbers, Spirit Force, Soul, Experiments in Developing Psychic Consciousness, Breathing Exercises, Manifestations of Spirit, Manifestations of Vibrations, The Law of the Triangle, Mental Vibrations, Universal Force, The Mortal Existence of Matter, The Form of Matter, The Existence of Evil, The Positive Existence of Good, True Knowledge, The Changes in Matter, Delusions and Illusions, Experiments to Prove the Difference, Psychic and Material Seeing, Dreams, Mystical Comprehension, Protection Against Error, False Theories, The Cosmos, Man's Relation to the Cosmos, The Strange Nervous System in Man, The Secret Workings of this Nervous System, The Effects of Light, Color, Music, and Temperature, Mystic Vibrations, The Danger of Untrue Books, Some Mystical Experiments, Health Vibrations, The Nature of Life, The Life Force, Demonstrations With Thought Vibrations, Mystical Demonstration with Thought Vibrations, How to Direct Thought Vibrations, Demonstrations with Colors, Mystical Centers of the Brain, The Secret of Concentration, Concentrated Thought Waves, Meditation Experiments, Producing Manifestations, How the Blind Can See, Mystical Sight, Experiments with Seeing, The Mystery of Sleep, Demonstrating Cures Through Normal Sleep, Bible Miracles, Mental Treatments During Sleep, Self Treatment, False Terms, Mystical Consciousness, The Conscience, The Akashic Records, Intuition, Cosmic Attunement, Attunement with the Masters, Attunement with Others in Distant Places, and General Review of Rosicrucian Laws.

Second Grade:

Initiation Ritual, including demonstration of some Laws. Then twelve weekly lessons, including personal talks and lectures on the following subjects:

The Ego, The Elimination of the Ego, The Elevation of the Psychic Self, Divine Rights, Divine Blessings, Cosmic Gifts, The Oriental Secrets of These Principles, Nirvana, Personal Psychic Development, Help from Visible and Invisible Masters, The Holy Assembly, Jesus and His Work, The Work of Other Great Teachers, The Development of Psychic Aura, Interesting Experiments, Practical Methods of Cosmic Attunement, New Breathing Exercises, Mystical Sounds, The Law of Incantation, Experiments with Vocal Sounds, Developing Increased Life Force, The Mystical Meaning of Letters and Sounds, The Mystery of the Lost Word, How to Seek For It, The Purpose of Other Secret Organizations, The Good Points in Many Schools, Why Mankind Needs Help and Instruction, The Relation of Body, Mind, and Soul, The Divine Trinity, The Earthly Trinity in Man, Experiments to Prove the Statements, Man a Wonderful Organization, The Secret Parts of His Organization, Nature's

Secret Forces in Man, The One Mystical Force in Man's Body, The Control of This by the Mind, The Nature of Pain, The True Way to Relieve It, Several Mystic Methods for "Curing" Pains in Various Parts of the Body, Giving Treatments to Others, The Oriental Methods, American Methods Including Christian Science, Health and Hygiene, The Oriental Rosicrucian Health Principles, The Occidental Race and Its Special Needs, Demonstrating the Mystic Currents of Life Force in the Body, Many Experiments to Increase This Life Force, The Eye and Its Abnormal Conditions, Secret Methods for Treating the Eyes, Various Forms of Diseases, The Real Cause of Diseases, Experiments for Treating Some Diseases, How to Establish Harmony in the Human Body, The Duality of Life and Disease, The Two Secret Elements for Obtaining Health and Prolonging Life, Simple Methods for Attracting These Elements to the Body, Classification of Simple Diseases, Treating Oneself and Others with Simple Methods, The Secret of Life Cells, The Effect of Thought and Action on the Body, The Constructive and Destructive Periods of Life, Simple Laws About Eating, Rosicrucian Dietetics, The Use of Affirmations, The Use of Medicine, Experiments for Increasing Mental and Physical Strength, The Truth About Vegetarian Diet, The Relation of Spiritual and Mental Development to Diet, Important Instructions in Regard to Food Values, Methods for Preventing Disease, Practical Experiments and Demonstrations, What Prominent Scientists Say, Experiments with Water, Further Rules for Treating Others, Treatment at a Distance, Contact Treatments, Rosicrucian Secret Method, the Rhythm and Cycles of Life, Mystical Period of Years, The Cycles of Incarnations, The Law of Reincarnation, Old Age and Death, Rebirth and Regeneration, A Summary of New Rosicrucian Principles, and Important Personal Reading Matter and Instructions.

Third Grade:

Initiation Ritual covering three weeks, during which the Students prepare for Cosmic Attunement and Psychic Demonstrations before proceeding with the Lessons which include the subjects of:

The Four Principal Manifestations of Matter, The Mystery of Alchemy and Chemistry, Experiments with the Mental Control of Matter, Directing Mind Vibrations Into Matter, Mental Alchemy, The Mystic Magnetism of Man's Body, The Source of this Magnetism, Its Rapid Development, Rosicrucian Metaphysical Laws, Affecting the Blood of the Human System, Personal Advice in Regard to Health of Each Member, The Solar Plexus, Demonstrations With It, The Psychic Centers of the Human Body, Exercises for Developing Them, Controlling the Nervous System, Controlling the Organs of the Body, Improving Their Functioning, The Psychic Body of Man, Experiments for Proving Its Existence, What the Ancients Taught, What the Modern Rosicrucians Know, The Mystery of Fire, Its Place in the Universe and the Human Body, Some Mystical Experiments with Fire, Some Simple Alchemical Experiments, Experiments with Vibrations, Affecting Matter with Thoughts, The True Nature of the Soul, Its Relation to the Mind, Manifestations of the Soul, Higher Mystical Symbolism, Symbolism in Christianity and Oriental Philosophy, The Use of Symbols in Mental Experiments, Symbolism in the Human Body, Symbolism in the Cosmic, The Development of Religion, Religious Consciousness, God Manifesting Through Man, Proof of the Existence of God, God's Mysterious Ways, God's Methods of Creation and Evolution, The Truth About Spontaneous Generation and Artificial Creation, The Creative Powers in Man's Mind and Body, Man's Ability to Create Mentally, The Control of Natural Forces, Directing Desires to be Fulfilled, Making Thought Forms Become Realities, Experiments Which Show How Thought Forms are Materialized, The Development of God's Creative Powers in Each Member, The Value of Suggestions, Mistaken Ideas About Hypnotism, The False Beliefs About Black Magic, The Real Power of White Magic, Experiments to Test These Principles, Exercises for the Development of Personal Magnetism, The Development of Harmony in the Human Body, The Establishment of Harmony Between the Human Body and the Cosmic, The Rosicrucian Methods of Diagnosing Inharmony and Disease, Contacting Personal Masters, Receiving Illumination and Instruction from Cosmic Masters, Transmitting Cosmic Pictures and Thoughts, Telepathy and Universal Attunement, Methods for Contacting the Secret Chambers of the Cosmic and the Higher Chambers of the Order, Exercises for Perfecting the Psychic Development of the Individual Member, Special Instructions for Reaching the Higher Teachings, and General Summary of the Three Grades, followed by a series of Personal Letters from the Masters of the Order and the Imperator to assist the Individual Members to be qualified for any higher work offered by the Order.

AT THE END OF THE THIRD GRADE

It requires practically from nine months to one year to complete the foregoing three Grades of National Lodge study. But as one can see, the lessons are so arranged that after the first few weeks the Student is able to experiment and demonstrate a great many principles, and after the first twelve lessons is capable of extracting from the lessons such principles and exercises as should enable him or her to make many important changes in business and social affairs and improve in health and mind while being able to help others also. The average Student who has studied and read from many books in the past finds that these weekly lessons and lectures and personal letters of these three Grades supply all the information that a sincere Student can properly take care of in each week, and very few are ever anxious to go any faster in the work than our system provides for.

Bear in mind that with this Manual the lectures contain everything that is required for study except the use of a common dictionary, at times, or an encyclopedia when a student is anxious to hunt up some subjects that are of special interest to him. There are no textbooks of any kind that must be purchased and the Student will find in "The Rosicrucian Digest" (our own Monthly Magazine) many articles of help and practical application in his material worldly affairs.

"THE ROSICRUCIAN DIGEST MAGAZINE"

I mention also, at this time, that besides your interesting weekly lessons, lectures, the charts and diagrams, and other services, you receive a copy of the publication, issued by the organization, called "The Rosicrucian Digest." This magazine is sent to you free, and is very helpful, because it contains interesting articles of a constructive nature on subjects in which you are interested. It is really the leading metaphysical and occult magazine of this country. "The Rosicrucian Digest" contains no outside advertising and every page is filled with helpful information. This you receive as part of your membership.

ADVANCING TO HIGHER TEACHINGS

When members have completed the three Grades outlined above and have been found fully qualified by the Masters of the Order and the Imperator, they have two Paths open to them. The first is to unite with some Temple Lodge near them and, at the hands of Masters and Assistant Teachers, receive the Higher Teachings of the twelve Temple Grades after Initiation with Egyptian Ceremony in such Temples, and enjoy the association with hundreds of other sincere Students and Workers. The Second Path is open only to those who, for various reasons, and under certain circumstances, find it impossible to attend a Temple Lodge with regularity, or who live where there is no Temple Lodge within convenient distance.

Such Members may, by special dispensation, receive the discourses of the Teachings, beginning with the first Temple Grade, by correspondence; also there is included, in modified form, the Initiations and Rituals of the Temple Lodges or the Temple demonstrations. Furthermore, they will find all necessary charts and diagrams sent to them, and will find it possible to conduct many of the experiments and demonstrations equally as well in the privacy of their own homes.

▽ ▽ ▽

A FEW SPECIMENS OF THE MANY LODGE SEALS. EVERY LODGE MUST ADOPT A SEAL COMPOSED OF TRIANGLE, CIRCLE, AND CROSS.

PART SEVEN

Mystic Symbols

And Their Meanings

ESPECIALLY PREPARED FOR THIS MANUAL

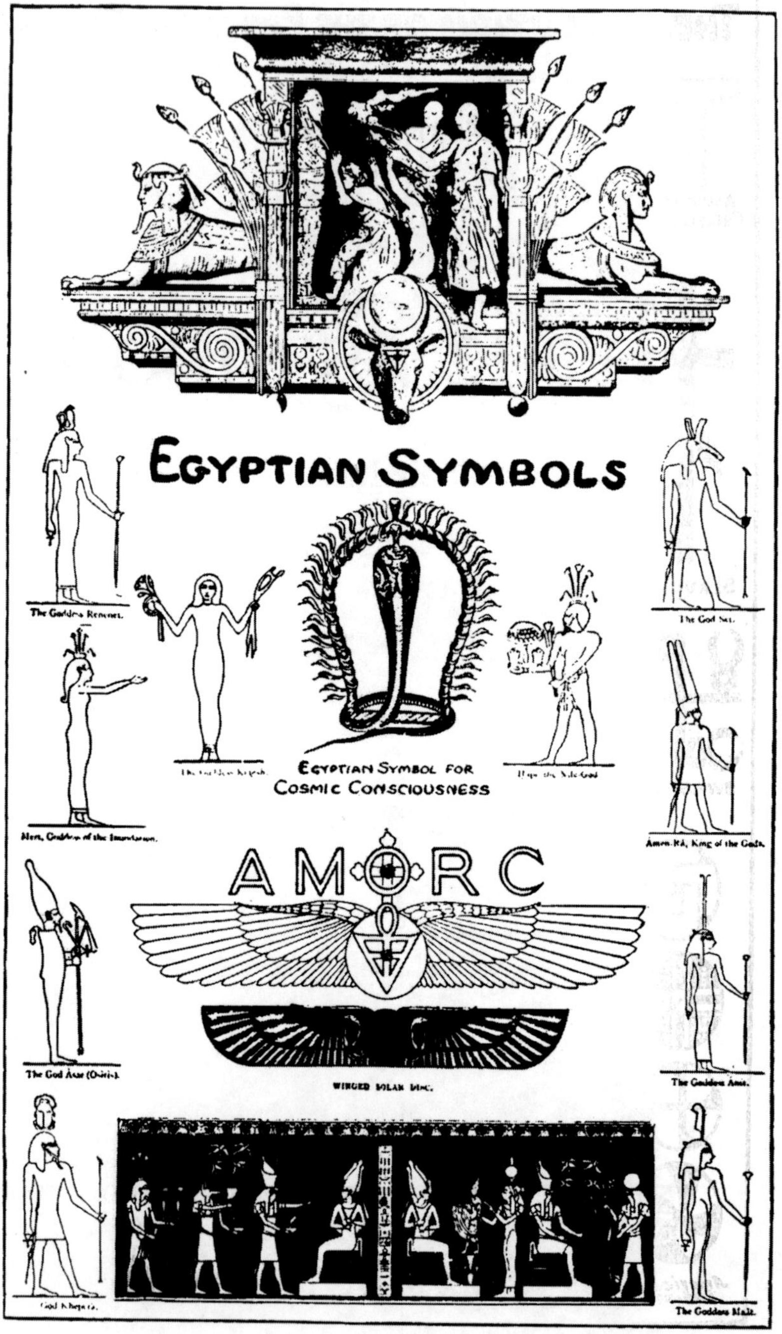
EGYPTIAN SYMBOLS
The God Set.
EGYPTIAN SYMBOL FOR
COSMIC CONSCIOUSNESS
Amen-Rā, King of the Gods.
AMORC
WINGED SOLAR DISC.
The Goddess Maāt.

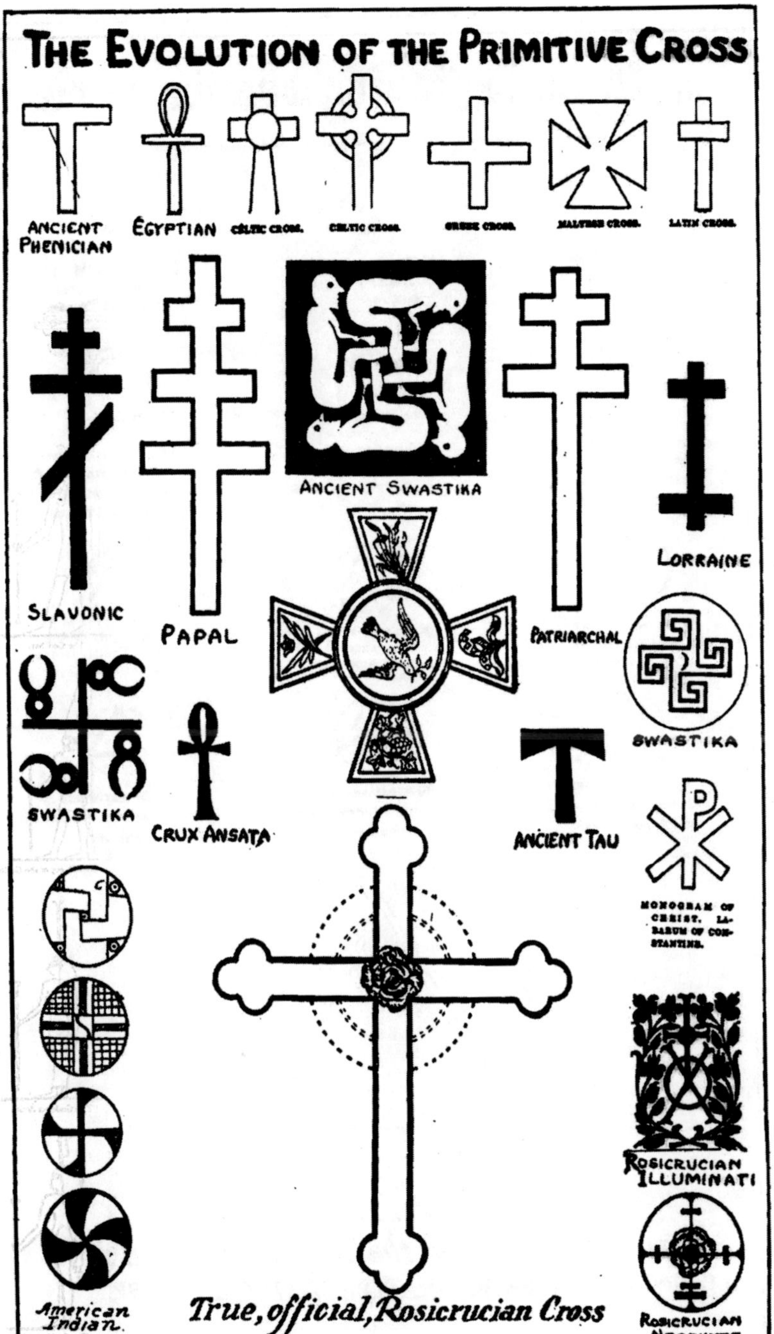
THE EVOLUTION OF THE PRIMITIVE CROSS
ANCIENT PHENICIAN
ÉGYPTIAN
CELTIC CROSS.
CELTIC CROSS.
GREEK CROSS.
MALTESE CROSS.
LATIN CROSS.
ANCIENT SWASTIKA
SLAVONIC
PAPAL
PATRIARCHAL
LORRAINE
SWASTIKA
SWASTIKA
CRUX ANSATA
ANCIENT TAU
MONOGRAM OF CHRIST. LABARUM OF CONSTANTINE.
ROSICRUCIAN ILLUMINATI
American Indian.
True, official, Rosicrucian Cross
ROSICRUCIAN NEOPHYTE

"In the beginning was the word:"

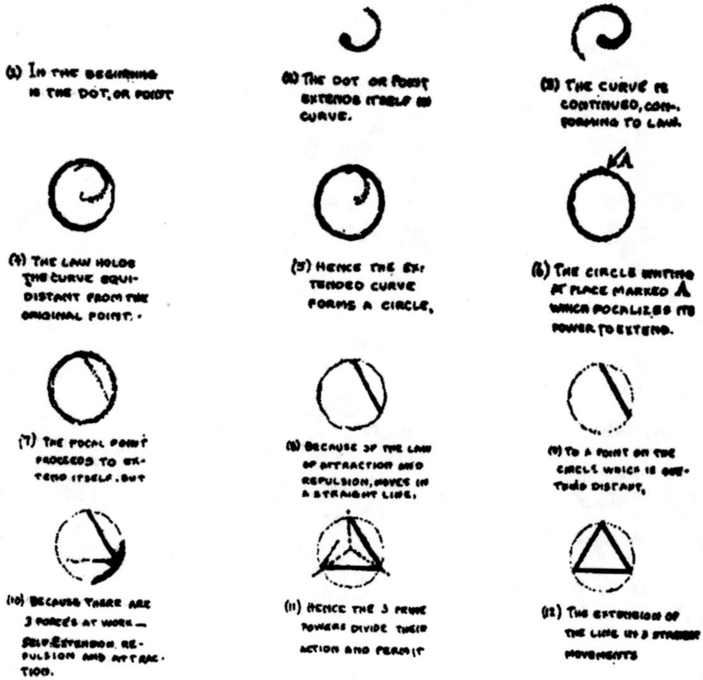

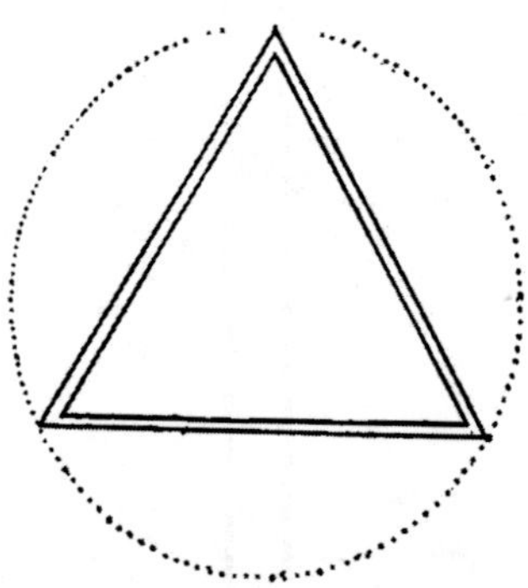

And in this wise was the TRIANGLE *of 3 equal sides, called the* TETRAGRAMMATON, *produced by Law.*

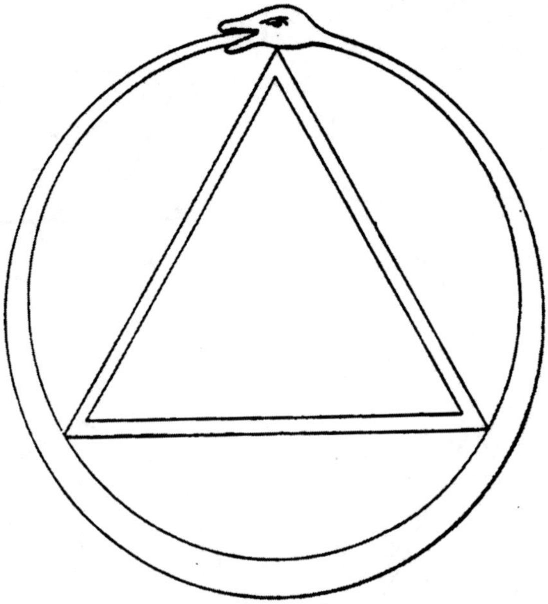

FIGURE 1.

HERE WE SEE THE OUTLINE AND ORIGIN OF ONE OF THE EARLIEST MYSTICAL AND PHILOSOPHICAL SYMBOLS, BASED UPON THE SYMBOL OF CREATION AS SHOWN IN DIAGRAM (6) ON PAGE 1 AND DIAGRAM (12) ON PAGE 1. THE SERPENT HERE REPRESENTS EARTHLY CREATION MADE MANIFEST, WITH THE POWER TO PERPETUATE ITS OWN BODY AND EXISTENCE. THE HEAD IS THE FOCAL POINT.

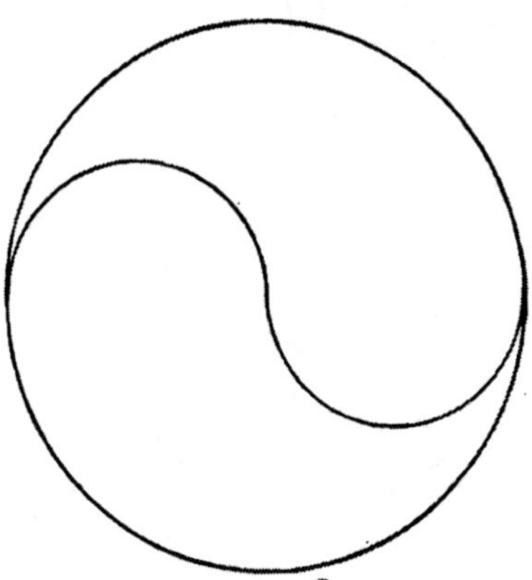

FIGURE 2.

ANOTHER OLD SYMBOL BASED ON DIAGRAM NO. (4) PAGE 1.

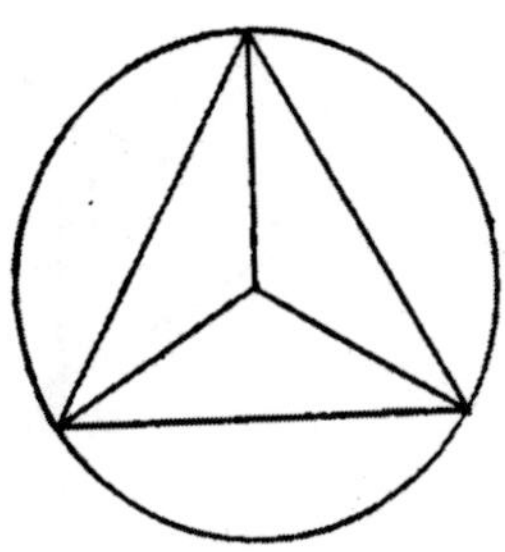

FIGURE 3.

HERE WE HAVE AN OLD MYSTICAL SYMBOL REPRESENTING THE ELEMENTARY GEOMETRICAL LAWS USED IN ALL MYSTIC SYMBOLS. THIS ONE IS BASED ON DIAGRAM NO. (11) ON PAGE 1.

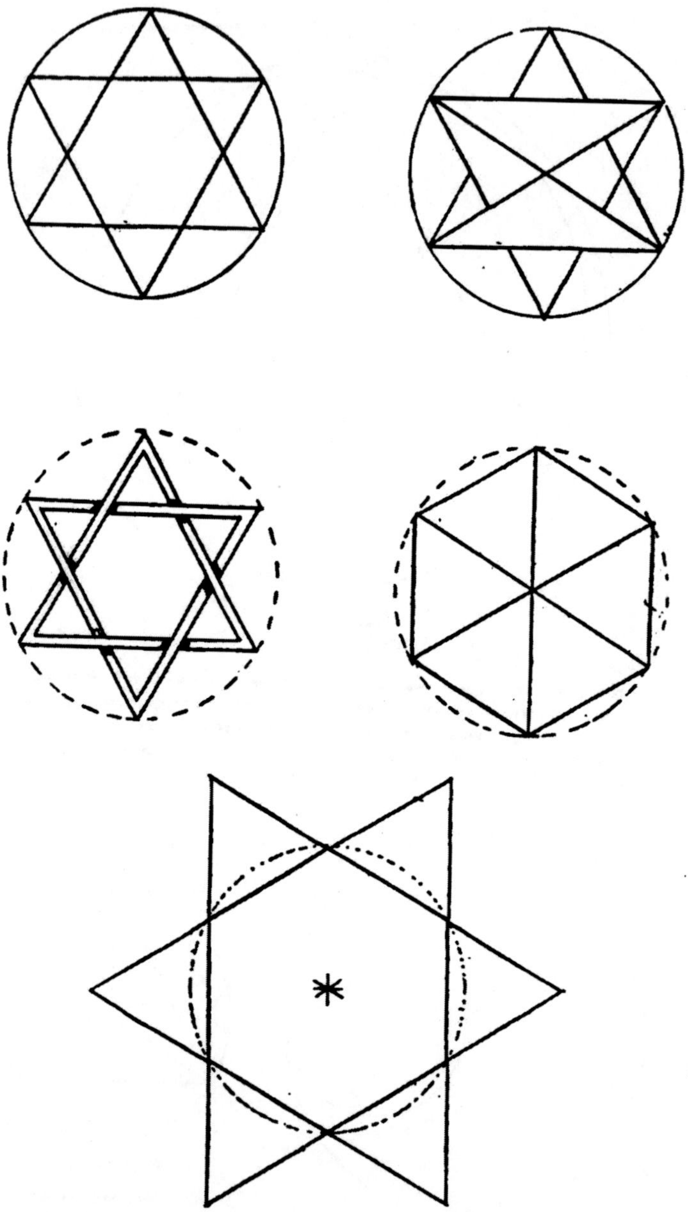

FURTHER DEVELOPMENTS OF THE TRIANGLE

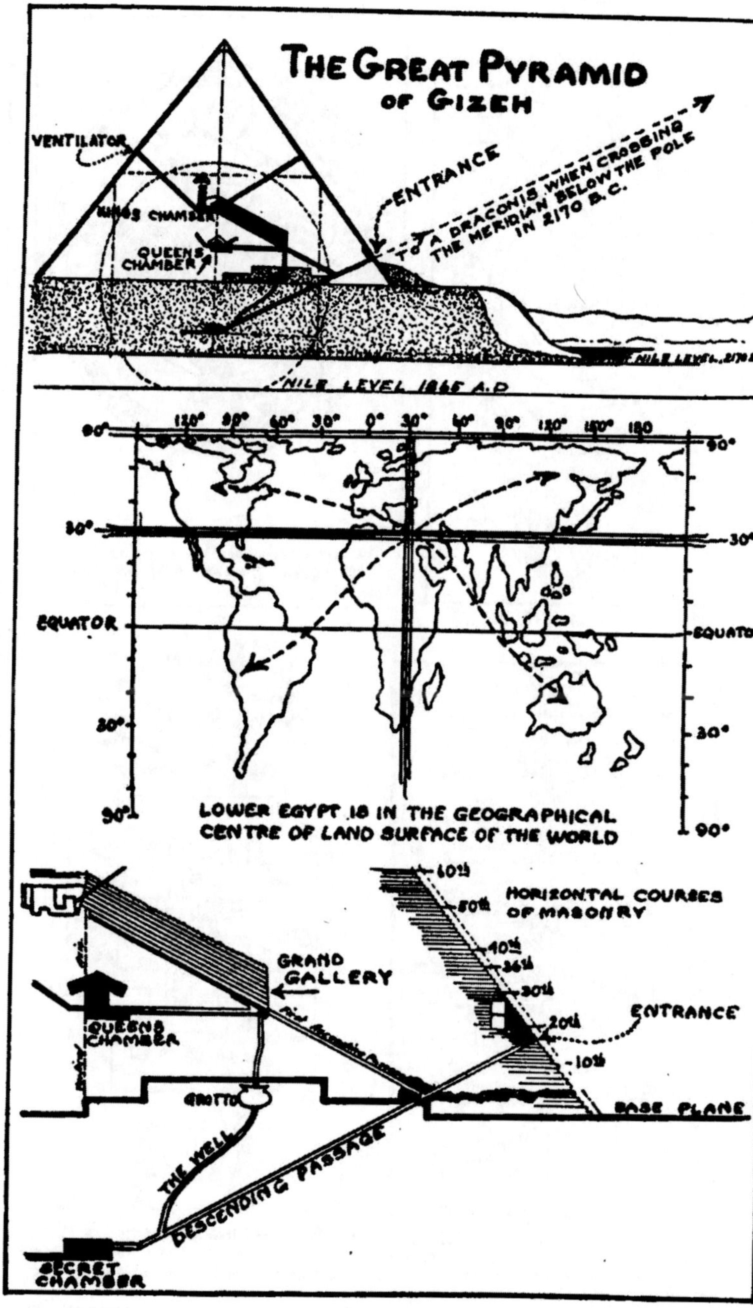
THE GREAT PYRAMID
OF GIZEH
VENTILATOR
KINGS CHAMBER
QUEENS CHAMBER
ENTRANCE
TO α DRACONIS WHEN CROSSING THE MERIDIAN BELOW THE POLE IN 2170 B.C.
NILE LEVEL 2170 B.C.
NILE LEVEL 1845 A.D
EQUATOR
EQUATOR
LOWER EGYPT IS IN THE GEOGRAPHICAL
CENTRE OF LAND SURFACE OF THE WORLD
HORIZONTAL COURSES
OF MASONRY
GRAND
GALLERY
QUEENS
CHAMBER
ENTRANCE
GROTTO
THE WELL
DESCENDING PASSAGE
BASE PLANE
SECRET
CHAMBER

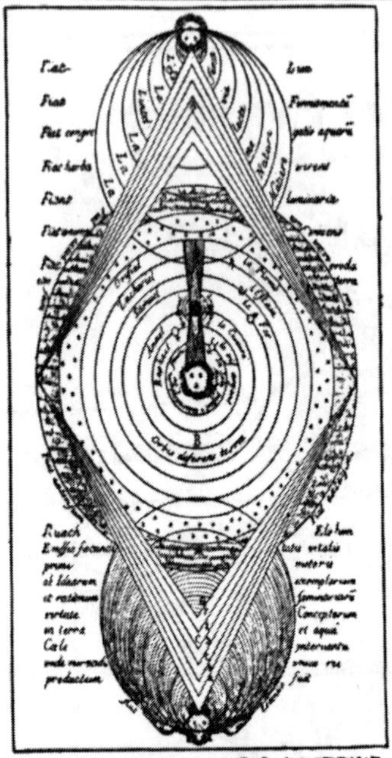

PLAN OF KABALISTIC DOCTRINE

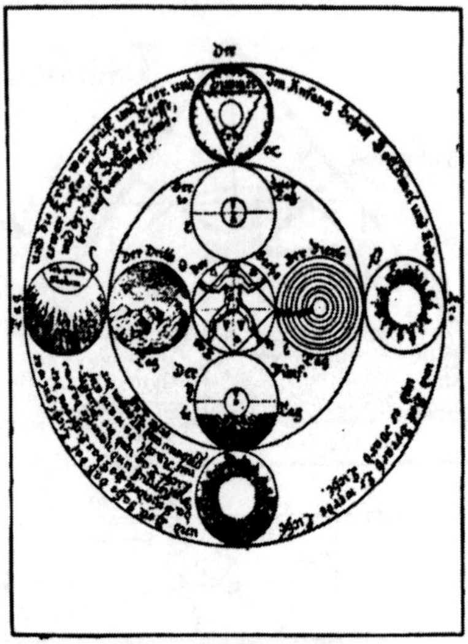

THE INTERCHANGE OF "MACROCOSM" AND "MICROCOSM" (FROM AN OLD GERMAN BOOK)

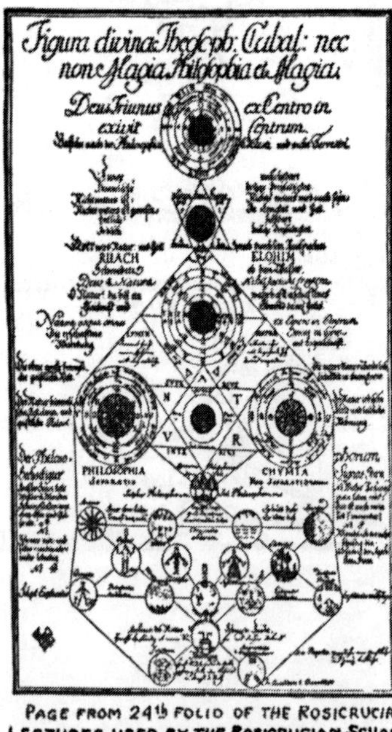

PAGE FROM 24th FOLIO OF THE ROSICRUCIAN LECTURES, USED BY THE ROSICRUCIAN SCHOOL ESTABLISHED NEAR PHILADELPHIA, U.S.A., 1694

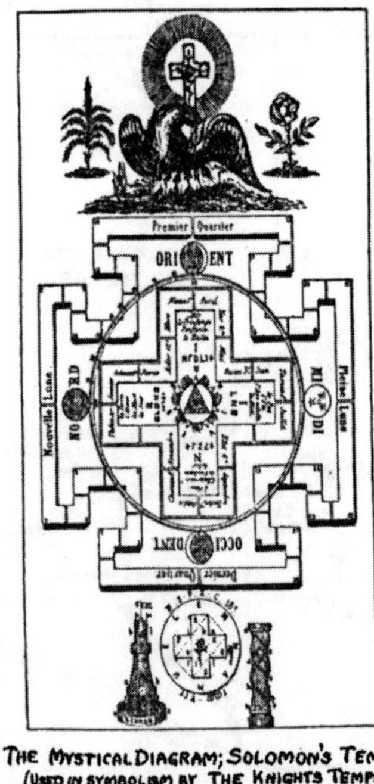

THE MYSTICAL DIAGRAM; SOLOMON'S TEMPLE (USED IN SYMBOLISM BY THE KNIGHTS TEMPLAR) NOTE CROSS WITH ROSE AT TOP AND BOTTOM

THE GREAT SEAL OF SOLOMON

THE PENTAGRAM OF FAUST

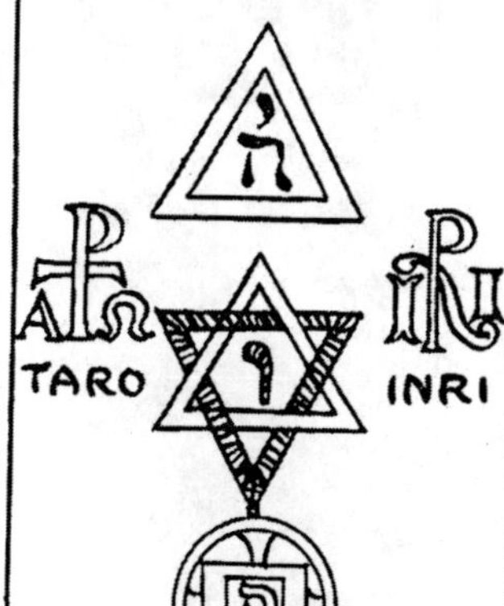

FOUR GREAT KABALISTIC NAMES

THE CHARIOT OF HERMES (SEVENTH KEY OF THE TAROT)

SOME ANCIENT MAGICAL INSTRUMENTS

THE SEVEN SEALS OF ST. JOHN

ANCIENT SIGN OF EXCOMMUNICATION

Part Eight

THE TEMPLE LECTURES

The Higher Teachings of the Order are those which were especially designed and compiled by the Higher Masters of the Order for delivery in the Secret Temples of our Order by the appointed Masters and Officers in Tiled Lodge Rooms and under the Seal of Secrecy and Sincerity. Such lectures contain the most complete presentation of all the occult Laws and Principles handed down through the Ages and amended by the modern Masters in all countries, so that today they are of practical value in these modern times. Naturally, they cover all of the points, Laws, and Principles touched upon in the three correspondence grades of the National Lodge, but present each Law and Principle in more complete and demonstrable form, and include hundreds of subjects and mystical Laws which could not be put into the three grades of the preliminary National Lodge work; but, as explained before, they can be received by National Lodge Members after they have made certain preparations, which are not difficult if they are sincere students. In addition to the lectures given in the Temple Lodges the Members have the benefit of Temple demonstrations performed by the Masters and most advanced Members, and the valuable discussions with questions and answers which follow each Convocation.

Those members who cannot attend Temple Lodges and who are carefully selected and deemed worthy of receiving the discourses of the Temple Lectures by correspondence under Oaths of Allegiance and Secrecy will receive the same private lectures by mail each week as the Masters of the Temple use in their Lodges in delivering the teachings to the Members assembled. These lessons and lectures are the same throughout the AMORC of North America, and the only difference between the lecture work as given in the Temples and the study of the lessons at home by correspondence is the absence of the discussions and the modified form of Rituals.

The correspondence Members are able to make their own demonstrations at home, in most cases, and, therefore, do not miss the important part of this phase of the Temple work; and, of course, all of the exercises and demonstrations to be made in their personal affairs are the same and just as efficient with the correspondence Members as with the Temple Members.

Nevertheless, all National Lodge Members are urged, at some time or another, to visit one of the Temples of the Order throughout the country, and especially to attempt to attend some special session at the Grand Lodge in San Jose, California. They will not be inconvenienced because they cannot attend the sessions regularly; their studies will be found to be complete, in the manner in which they are especially prepared by the Imperator's staff.

OUTLINE OF THE TEMPLE LECTURES AND SYSTEM

First Grade:

Initiation Ritual, constituting the famous "Crossing of the Threshold" ceremony, which is ever the goal of all Seekers for Rosicrucian Illumination. The initiation is followed by a series of weekly or semi-monthly Temple lectures and lessons covering the following subjects:

The Ethics of Rosicrucianism, The Meaning of Initiation, The Search of Ancient Mystics for the Portals, The Secrecy of Its Higher Teachings, The Mystery of Mysticism, The Law of Symbolism, Ancient Secret Alphabets, Numerals and Symbols, The Meanings of Numbers, Matter and Its Existence, The Law of the Triangle, Crystallography, The Laws of the Universe, The Material World and Its Composition, The Physical Composition of Man and All Animal Life, First Laws of the Rosicrucian Ontology, The Difference Between Living and Non-Living Matter, What Makes Man a Living Being, The Elements of Physiology, The Place of Spirit in Man, Distinction Between Spirit and Soul, The Manifestations of Spirit Energy, Spirit Vibrations, Electrons and Atoms, The Natural Law of the Composition of Matter, The Law of Motion and Rhythm, Polarity and Magnetism, Demonstrations of the Action of Electrons in Forming Matter, The Hidden Principles Regarding the Nature of Matter and Its Manifestation, The Law of Vibrations and the Cosmic Keyboard, A Summary of the Principal Laws of the Universe Regarding Matter, and Man's Material Body and All Forms of Existing Things.

Second Grade:

Initiation Ritual illustrating the Member's advancement in the work and mental development. Series of lectures covering the following subjects in detail:

The Rosicrucian Alphabet of Mystical Subjects Covered by the Future Lectures, The Mind of Man and Its Faculties and Functionings, Its Objective and Subjective Divisions, The Scale of Operation, The Mind's Relation to Cosmic and Mundane Consciousness, The Voluntary and Involuntary Functions in Man, An Analysis of the Mind and Brain in Action, The Dual Consciousness in Man, Disorders of the Mind and Brain, Various Forms of Reasoning, The Improvement of Reasoning, Will Power, Its Development, Its Relation to Health and Disease, The Memory, Its Origin, Location, and Development,

Using the Memory, The Purpose of the Memory with the Soul and Cosmic, The Secret Inner Chief Engineer of Each Being, Subjective Conditions of the Body, Objective Functionings of the Body, The Nature of Habits, How they Are Formed and Suspended, The Power of the Subjective Mind Over the Human Body, Mental Suggestion, The Art and Science of Suggestion, The Living Soul Within the Body and Its Reason for Being Incarnated in the Human Body, Whence IT Came and Whither IT Goeth, and a Review of the Mental and Psychic Parts of Man.

Third Grade:

Initiation Ritual, including demonstration of Alchemical principles and mental phenomena, followed by a series of lectures covering the following subjects in detail.

The Laws of Motion and Change Throughout the Universe, The Laws of Devolution, Evolution and Involution, The Evolution of Consciousness in Life, The Nature of Consciousness and Its Attributes, The Reason for Life, The Purpose of Living Organisms, Sensations of Consciousness, The Coming and Going of Consciousness, Individual and Group Consciousness, Intelligence, Intellect, Imagination, Imaging and Mental Creating, The Perfection of Mental Action, Ideality, Mystical Alchemy, Rosicrucian Mental Methods, Objective Sensing, Psychic Sensing, The Actuality of Things and Our Realization of Them, Realities Created, Actualities Made to Disappear, Actualities May Not Exist, Demonstrations of Actuality and Reality, Psychic Products, Mental Products, Illusions, The Effect of Environment, The Effect of Thoughts, Soul Memories, Exercises for Awakening the Memory and Developing Psychic Consciousness, Man's Association with the Cosmic, The God and Master Within, Contacting the Psychic Minds of Others, The Psychic Man Separate from the Physical Man, How They Can be Made Visible at the Same Time, and General Review of the Mental and Psychic Duality of Man's Consciousness.

Fourth Grade:

Very elaborate Initiation Ceremony introducing the Member into the next stage of the Higher Teachings and illustrating to him the mysteries of Life; followed by a long series of lectures covering the following important subjects:

The Origin and Nature of the Life Force in Man, Its Source, Its Form of Manifestation, The Secret Knowledge of the Rosicrucians Regarding the Life Force, How the Life Force Enters the Human Body, How to Control It in the Human Body, How to Direct It to All Living Matter, The Rosicrucian Method for Increasing the Life Force, The Prevention of the Breaking Down Process in the Human Body, The Complete Presentation of the Ancient Secret Manuscript Written by Nodin Explaining the Nature of the Life Force in All

Living Cells and How It May be Directed and Controlled, Methods of Directing This Life Force from the Human Body for Treating Others, The Development of a Strong Aura and the Secrets of Long Life and Perfect Health, and General Review of the most important knowledge regarding Life Force ever given to Man.

Fifth Grade:

Interesting Initiation Ritual followed by a series of lectures introduced at this stage of the Student's progress so that he may have time for Psychic development through the many experiments he is conducting night and morning, and at other spare times, without taking up any new metaphysical or psychic subjects. Therefore, the lectures of this Grade include a complete review of all the Ancient Philosophies showing the development of mystical and philosophic thought and leading up to the modern philosophies and religious doctrines so that the Student will be well versed in Philosophy, Religion, and Ethics.

Sixth Grade:

A very impressive Ritualistic Ceremony conferring honors upon those who have progressed properly to this degree, followed by a long series of lectures and lessons with charts, diagrams, illustrations, and exercises explaining, in the most simple and fascinating manner, the secret methods of the human body in the digestion of food, the principles of dietetics, the making of blood, the entering of the vital Life Force into the blood, the real purpose of Rosicrucian breathing exercises, the true cause of all disease and suffering, the diagnosis of disease, and the secret Rosicrucian methods of directing the healing Forces of the Universe to the different parts of the Body to those who may be suffering; including quick methods of bringing about rapid changes in serious conditions and explaining all of the functions of the organs, nerves, and plexuses of the Human Body in their relation to the Psychic and Cosmic Forces of the Universe. This is the most complete course of study in metaphysical healing ever given to students of mysticism and is exclusively Rosicrucian.

Seventh Grade:

Very impressive Psychic Initiation illustrating some of the highest mystical teachings of the Order, followed by a series of lectures and lessons dealing with the metaphysical and psychic existence of Man, and leaving aside the material and earthly matters covered in the first six Grades. This Grade fully explains the real purpose and nature of the psychic body of Man within the physical body and contains exercises for strengthening the vitality and power of the Psychic Body with its Psychic Consciousness; and then proceeds to explain how the Psychic Body may be temporarily separated from the Physical Body and both be made visible at the same time. After these experiments are completed the Student is instructed in the Rosicrucian methods of projecting the Psychic Body out into space to any point or place and there made visible to others without affecting the continuous functioning of the Physical Body. Other exercises assist in the development of the Aura, so that it may be made very visible in a darkened room and sufficiently strong to cause illumination and to make the hands magnetic. Also other exercises are given in connection with the highest mystical vowel sounds with methods for pronouncing them so as to produce psychic manifestations at will. Also the Lost Word, sought for by the ancients, is further explained in this Grade and the Student begins to realize that he has been gradually acquiring the Lost Word and gaining very unusual occult powers. This is the most mystical Grade of study in the principles of Rosicrucian Teachings ever given in the Occidental World.

Eighth Grade:

Another impressive Ritualistic Ceremony or Initiation for those who have succeeded in the work of the previous Grade, followed by twenty-nine lectures in the higher metaphysical principles whereby the Student is gradually revealed in his proper incarnation as related to God and the Cosmic, and is instructed with definite lessons and exercises in the possibility of projecting his psychic body through all matter and space to any person or place and there making himself visible as he is in this incarnation, or as he was in a previous incarnation, with the further ability to cause certain material things to move or respond as he directs, including the production of sounds from musical instruments, from his own voice, or from things he may psychically touch. He is also instructed in the principles taught by the old Rosicrucians whereby he can give treatments to others during such projections or carry on humanitarian activities without revealing himself, and attend sessions or convocations or branches of the Order in foreign places by projection and attunement, and in other ways, carry on the experiments described by the Masters of the Far East and heretofore only taught by Rosicrucians in the Temples of Tibet, where the Masters of the Great White Lodge hold their Sacred Convocations. This Grade also reveals the Laws regarding the real personality in each of us and many facts about our past incarnations. True facts regarding so-called spiritualistic principles and phenomena are revealed, and many other important Rosicrucian Teachings, including the Keys to the Ninth Grade.

Ninth Grade:

Another highly impressive Temple Ritual whereby the Members who have properly reached this Grade and duly qualified for it are given titles and honors of the highest standing in the Order, so far as Temple Ceremonies are concerned. Serious obligations of Secrecy and devotion to Rosicrucianism are required of those who take this Initiation in the Temple and receive the highest Passwords and methods of recognition in the Temple Grades.

This is followed by a series of forty very complete lectures and lessons dealing with subjects, many of which cannot be described in a Manual of this kind, that include revelations regarding Man's relation to God and the higher Forces of the Cosmic and the development of the highest metaphysical powers within his own body. He is enabled to use some of these forces of Nature to blot out and make hidden material things as well as eliminate mental and psychic things which may be obstacles in his life, or direct or change the course of natural events in their relation to him so as to bring about certain results in his own affairs or in the affairs of others. This is the last Grade in which the Student receives Initiation on the Material Plane in Material Temples, and from this point he receives further instruction and Psychic Initiation as he is ready for them. In this Grade, also, the Student receives the last vowel sound of the Lost Word and learns how to use this word for instantly affecting Laws, Principles, and Manifestations throughout Nature.

Tenth Grade:

Eleventh Grade:

Twelfth Grade:

The Initiations into these Grades are given Psychically to the Worthy Members who have advanced to the preceding Grades and very often these Initiations occur Psychically in the Temples of the Order in the Orient. The lessons and lectures of these Grades will be received by the Members and Students in a mystical manner which cannot be explained here, and they will, from time to time, assemble with others in the same Grades for the exchange of knowledge and experiences while carrying on their mystical activities in all parts of the world without interference with their regular business and social routine. No Master or Officer of the Order determines when Members of these Grades are ready for advancement into the next, for this information is received by each Member psychically when he is ready.

AT THE CLOSE OF THE NINTH GRADE

Members who attain and complete the psychic instruction of the Ninth Grade or those above it may enter the ILLUMINATI, which is a higher organization of the Order wherein the worthy Members continue to carry on specialized work and studies under the direction of the Imperator of their Jurisdiction and the personal Cosmic Masters. Members cannot ask for admission to the Illuminati but must wait until they have been found ready and invited to share in this additional work.

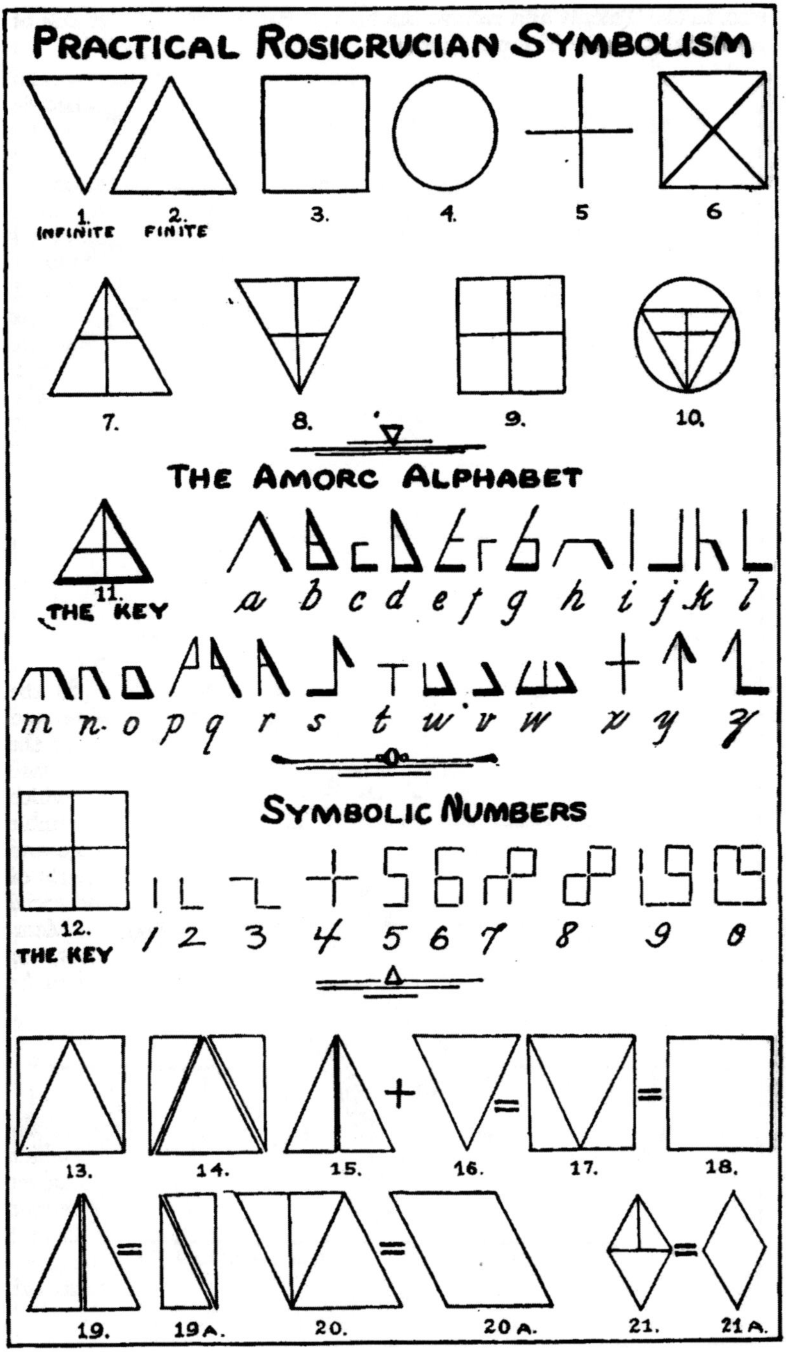
PRACTICAL ROSICRUCIAN SYMBOLISM
1. INFINITE
2. FINITE
3.
4.
5
6
7.
8.
9.
10.
THE AMORC ALPHABET
11. THE KEY
a b c d e f g h i j k l
m n o p q r s t u v w x y z
SYMBOLIC NUMBERS
12. THE KEY
1 2 3 4 5 6 7 8 9 0
13.
14.
15.
16.
17.
18.
19.
19A.
20.
20A.
21.
21A.

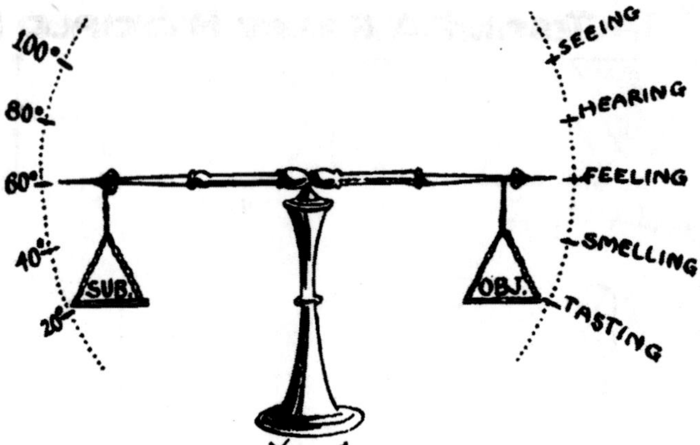
100°
80°
60°
40°
20°
SUB.
OBJ.
SEEING
HEARING
FEELING
SMELLING
TASTING

No. 1

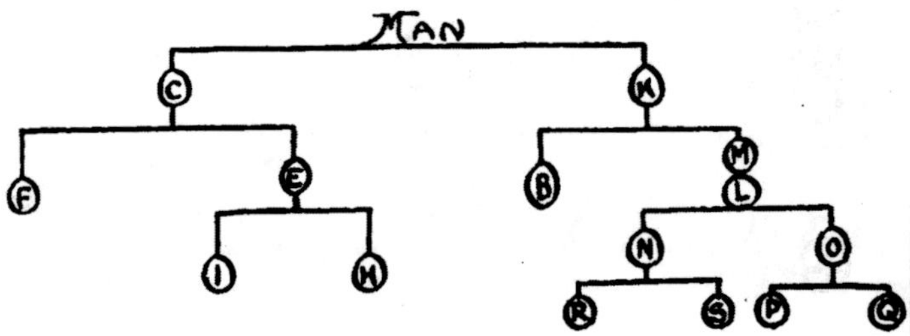
MAN
C
K
F
E
B
M
L
I
H
N
O
R
S
P
Q

No. 2.

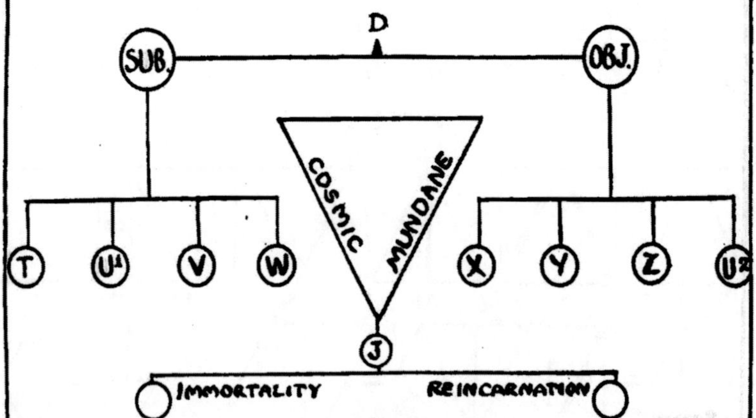
D
SUB.
OBJ.
COSMIC
MUNDANE
T
U1
V
W
X
Y
Z
U2
J
IMMORTALITY
REINCARNATION

No. 3

TESTING A GREAT PRINCIPLE (b)

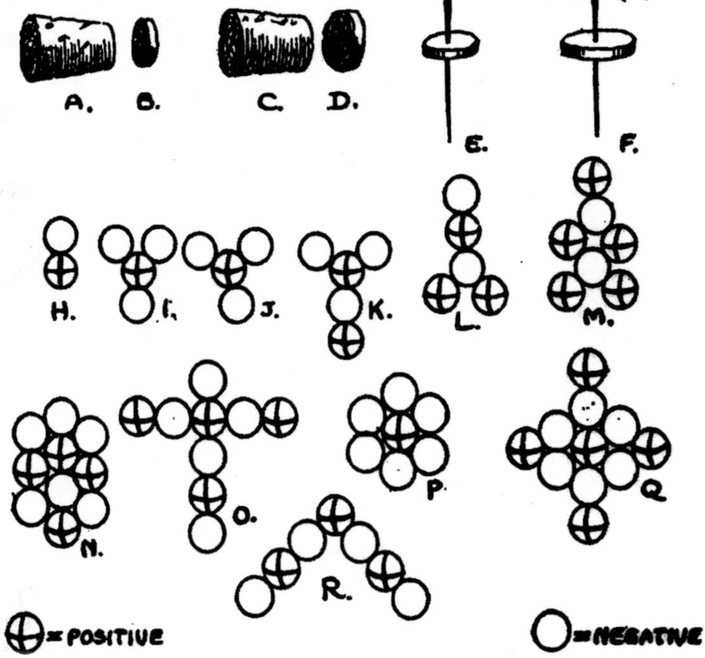

DIAGRAM No. 1

SCIENCE'S HYPOTHETICAL STRUCTURE OF THE RADIUM ATOM

Part Eight

(Continued)

CHARTS, EXPLANATIONS, *and* SPECIAL SUBJECTS

FOR STUDENTS OF

TEMPLE LECTURES

Prepared Especially for This Manual

Creative Principles (a)

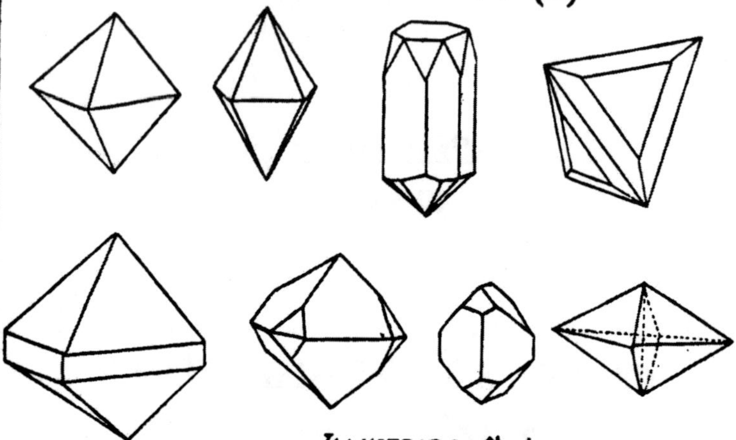

Illustration No. 1

Illustration No. 2

Snow Crystals

Ice Crystals

Mineral Crystals

Acid Crystals

CRYSTALLOGRAPHY

In various parts of our lectures reference is made to the *law of the triangle* in the composition of matter, the manifestation of matter and the manifestation of spirit energy and psychic energy. And in other places reference is made to crystallography, or the law of crystal formation in matter.

Crystallography so beautifully illustrates the *law of the triangle* in all nature that we urge the student to hunt up the subject in encyclopedias or other reference books. For those who cannot do this, we append here a short article on this subject. Before reading that article, however, let us call your attention to the chart shown on the opposite page.

Illustration No. 1 shows some of the typical forms of crystals as known to science. These are but a few of a very great many, and attention is called not only to the very evident working of the *law of the triangle*, but also to the beautiful grace in form.

In illustration No. 2 we see how the *law of the triangle* shows itself in connection with a demonstration of vibrations. By placing a piece of glass on a pedestal and sprinkling sand on the glass, one can manifest the vibrations by drawing a violin bow on the edge of the glass and cause the vibrations to flow across the surface of the glass and thereby arrange the sand in various forms, as shown in the seven black squares of illustration No. 2. In the lessons of our higher grades where the metaphysical principles are taught, we learn that *thought* vibrations can be directed into designs and "forms" just as with the sand and the physical vibrations on the glass.

The rest of the chart shows how nature adheres to the *law of the triangle* in the formation of snow crystals, ice crystals, mineral crystals, and acid crystals. Nature is truly an artist in her great work, but solely because she uses SYSTEM and Order.

CRYSTALLOGRAPHY

The Science Which Treats of Crystals

A crystal is a portion of inorganic matter with a definite molecular structure and an outward form bounded by plane surfaces called "crystal faces," and conforming to the angles of a triangle. These crystal faces result from the regular arrangement of the particles of the substance undergoing solidification, every addition of matter to the crystal in the process of formation being piled upon the particles already solidified as cannon balls or oranges are built up into a pile. All of which reveals the "Law of the Triangle." The reason for this is that every minute particle of a crystallizing substance, which we call a "crystal molecule," has certain lines of attractive force by which it gathers to itself other crystal molecules of the same substance, in the same way that a magnet attaches itself to a piece of iron or to another magnet. Crystal molecules of different substances generally have different lines of attraction, some being of different intensity; hence it follows that in most cases the solid formed by the piling together of the crystal molecules of a certain chemical compound has an outward shape characteristic of that compound. We also assume that the direction of attraction of the unit of crystal accretion (the crystal molecule) is dependent upon the structure of the chemical molecule of the substance crystallizing; that is, made up of a number of chemical molecules grouped together. Hence only elementary chemical substances and definite chemical compounds form crystals. So that the crystal molecules of a substance may come into sufficiently close proximity to admit of their being mutually attracted along their lines of crystallizing force, it is necessary that they should be crowded together by reason of the contraction of the space in which they are confined. This happens where a mass solidifies by cooling, or when by evaporation the amount of a substance dissolved in a liquid (such as water) exceeds in quantity the amount which the solvent can retain in solution under the conditions obtaining. Either condition results in the formation of crystals. A condition of formation more rarely met with is that in which crystals form directly from vapors, as in the case of iodine or chloride of ammonia.

The best means of studying the formation of crystals is afforded by the evaporation of a solution of some soluble compound, such as salt or blue vitriol, until it is supersaturated, when crystals of the dissolved substance will be thrown down. If two substances, such as salt and borax, are dissolved in the same solution, the result of evaporation will be crystals of both substances, each set of molecules building themselves up in distinctive forms. Solutions show considerable inertness, and it is often necessary to start the process of crystallization by introducing some solid substance (a crystal of the substance) to form a nucleus for the growing crystal. The outward form (the solid bounded by plane faces) is only an expression of the regular grouping of molecules which takes place when a substance crystallizes; consequently we may expect other evidences of the molecular arrangement. These evidences become apparent when we consider the physical properties, such as the transmission of light, heat, and electricity through crystals. A sphere cut from a quartz crystal does not expand equally in all directions when heated, as does a sphere of an uncrystallized substance, such as glass or amber; neither does a piece of beryl transmit polarized light in the same way as does a piece of glass of the same shape. This latter property of crystals is of great use in the detection of imitation gems. In the sphere of quartz we find that the action of heat pulls the molecules apart in one direction more than in other directions and the sphere becomes an ellipsoid. Substances like glass, showing no evidences of crystallization, are said to be *amorphous.* A substance in which the molecules have responded to crystallization but in which crystal faces have not been developed is said to be crystalline. Crystalline masses are often the result of the close crowding of crystals to the exclusion of the development of crystal outlines.

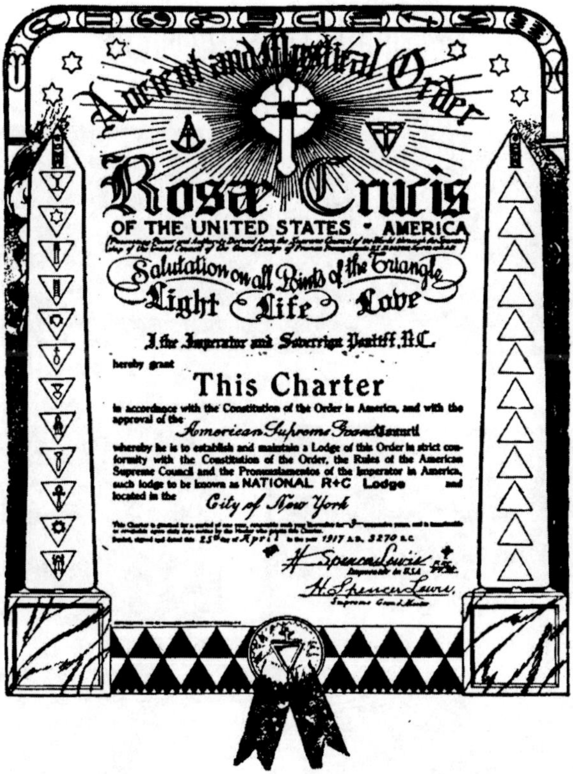

Ancient and Mystical Order
Rosae Crucis
OF THE UNITED STATES • AMERICA
Salutation on all Points of the Triangle
Light Life Love
I, the Imperator and Sovereign Pontiff, R.C.
hereby grant
This Charter
in accordance with the Constitution of the Order in America, and with the approval of the American Supreme Grand Council
whereby he is to establish and maintain a Lodge of this Order in strict conformity with the Constitution of the Order, the Rules of the American Supreme Council and the Pronunziamentos of the Imperator in America, such lodge to be known as NATIONAL R+C Lodge and located in the City of New York
Sealed, signed and dated this 25th day of April in the year 1917 A.D. 3270 R.C.
H. Spencer Lewis
Imperator in U.S.A.
H. Spencer Lewis
Supreme Grand Master

THE CHARTER GRANTED TO THE NATIONAL ROSICRUCIAN LODGE

Magnetic Chart

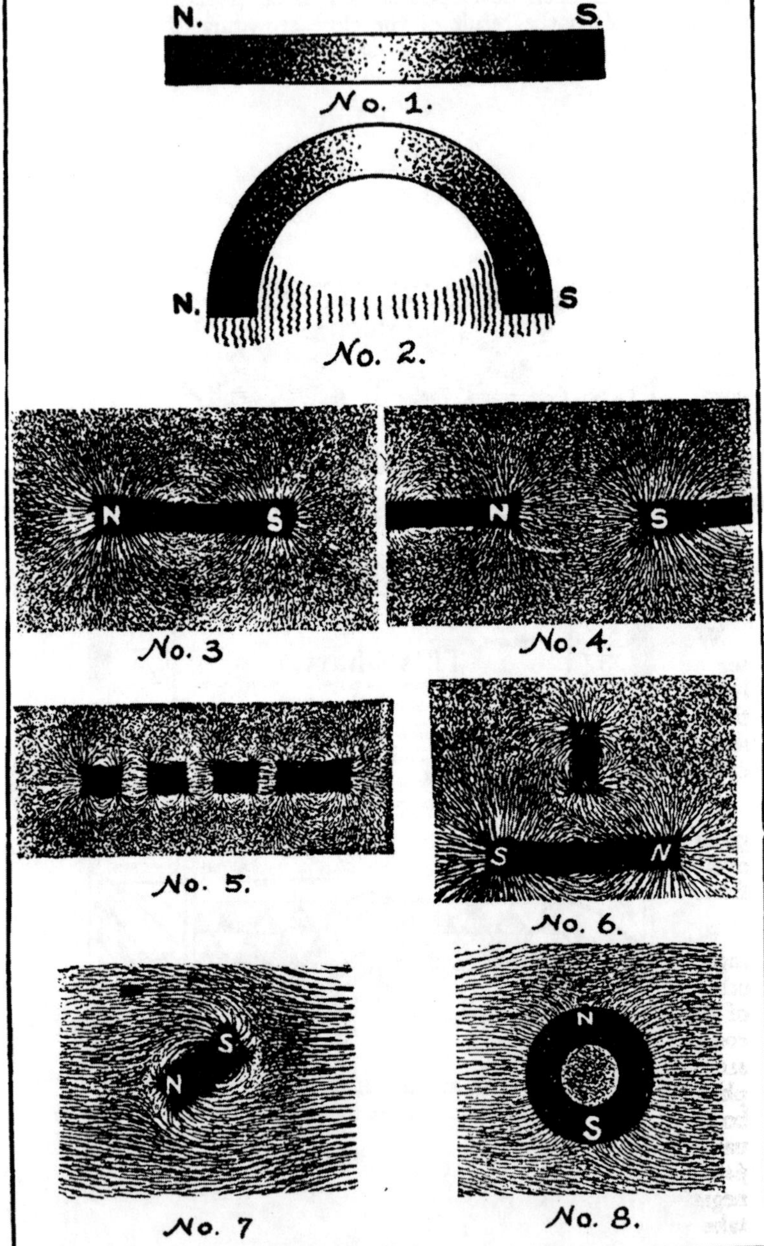

THE MAGNET

(In connection with the lessons of the First Grade of Temple Lectures)

In a number of lectures reference is made to the magnet, and the laws and principles demonstrated by the magnet are used to illustrate other laws.

Certain simple points about the magnet will be of interest to our members, and for this we will refer to the illustrations shown on the opposite page.

The magnet with which we are most familiar is shaped like a horseshoe, but it may be shaped like No. 2 on the opposite page. The purpose of such forms is to bring the two poles of the magnet close together; for every piece of steel or other mineral having magnetic qualities must have two poles or points of distinct polarity—*the north pole and the south pole,* marked N and S on the chart.

When the two poles come within a certain distance of each other, a magnetic effect is made manifest. This is because each pole has an *aura* or *field* of magnetic attraction around it. If we say that the north pole is negative, and the south pole positive, in polarity, then the north pole has a space around it in which negative magnetism radiates, and around the south pole is a field or space in which positive magnetism radiates.

We cannot see this magnetic radiation—any more than we can see any form of electric energy; but we can demonstrate it. By holding one end or pole of the magnet under a piece of paper and then sprinkling very fine steel powder on top of the paper, we will see the powder moving in certain lines, which plainly show the lines of magnetic attraction and repulsion.

In illustration No. 3 we see a small, straight magnet under a piece of tissue paper and the powder or grains of steel sprinkled over the paper. This enables us to see the radiations of magnetism from each pole.

When the north and south poles of a magnet are brought so close together that their fields of magnetism or auras begin to contact each other, there is a *stressed condition* set up which is greatest in the center of the space between the two poles. This magnetic field and *stressed condition* is used in many wonderful electrical inventions, and the same principle in nature is responsible for much startling, natural phenomena. Even in the most minute forms of cell life in animal bodies, the principles of magnetism are responsible for the continuance and reproduction of life. Illustration No. 4 shows the *stressed field* between the north (negative) and south (positive) poles. The negative is attracted to the positive and the positive reaches out to take the negative; combining, they form a magnetic field of dual, active potentiality. The greater the magnets, the larger this field and the more powerful the force.

If two north or two south poles are brought together or near each other, their lines of magnetism repulse each other. This shows the principle that "like repels like and attracts unlike."

In illustration No. 5 we have another interesting principle illustrated. If we take the piece of steel bar shown in illustration No. 3, which has its north and south poles and its neutral part in the center of the bar, and saw it into four short pieces, we find that we have four perfect magnets, each having a north and south pole like the longer bar.

In illustration No. 6 we see the peculiar, yet strictly logical effects of the magnetic fields when two bar magnets are brought into relation to each other at right angles.

In illustration No. 7 a short magnetic bar is held under the paper and turned around rapidly. We see that the revolving magnetic field pulls the steel powder around with it.

Even a steel ball or piece of pipe may be magnetized, in which case the inside of the ball may have one pole and the outside another, or the opposite sides of the pipe may be of different polarities. This is indicated by illustration No. 8.

Bear in mind that when we speak of polarities in our lectures we are referring to the magnetic polarities, such as are shown in these illustrations. All living, vital bodies, whether mineral, plant, or animal, have magnetic polarities, and all such living things are therefore magnets, with both positive (south) and negative (north) poles or polarities; but in one sense or another each of these has one of the polarities predominating through greater strength. Thus we speak of a body being of a positive polarity or negative polarity, referring to the predominating magnetism of its two poles.

EVOLUTION OF THE CROSS

Many who see the symbol of the Rosy Cross for the first time believe it to be a Christian symbol or very likely a Roman Catholic symbol, and most surely a religious symbol. We have found that we are called upon daily to make some explanation, not only about the Rosy Cross, but the Cross in any form, in our correspondence. We trust, therefore, that this explanation will anticipate many questions.

First of all, let us say that the Cross was not originally a religious symbol and is used by many organizations, in some form or another, as a symbol without any religious significance. Nor was there any such thing as a Christian cross during the time of the birth of the Christian doctrines as taught by the Master Jesus. It is a coincidence in religious matters that Jesus, like many others for centuries before Him, was crucified on a Cross—and not even on a Cross like that now used as the Christian symbol; and it was due to another coincidence that the Cross was adopted by the Christian Fathers, centuries after the Crucifixion, as a symbol of the Christian Faith. They might have adopted the exclusive use of a Golden Crown (which they do at times) or the Crown of Thorns, or many other symbols typical of some event in His life and works.

Those who are of the Hebrew race or Jewish religion justly feel that the Cross is a symbol to them of suffering in the form of persecution. One need only read the real history of the Hebrew race to note how it suffered needlessly and continuously through campaigns conducted by those who ever cried aloud: "Via Crucis!" *By way of the Cross* the Jew was ever made to be an outcast and a persecuted victim of the ancient systems which merely used the sacred symbol to hide their real purposes. For, truly, the Christian principles have naught in them to justify that which has been perpetrated in their name; but the same may be said of many other religious movements during their early stages.

However, we wish to assure Jews and Gentiles, Roman Catholics, and Protestants alike, that to the Orientals—who belong to none of these four classifications—the Rosy Cross symbol is sacred, not as a religious symbol, but as a Divine Symbol, because it represents the true Divinity in Man and all Nature.

The origin of the Cross is lost in antiquity—it is so old! Perhaps the first use of it was in drawing lines from the four cardinal points, North, South, East, and West. Such lines from such points—important indeed to the ancients—would form a cross. The first definite form of the Cross, however, as a mystical or secret symbol was that often called the TAU CROSS and used by the ancient Phoenicians. This Cross is shown in the first illustration on the chart of Crosses.

The next important development was the addition of a loop to the top of the Tau Cross. This formed what is often called the Egyptian Cross, because it became a very important symbol of their rituals. By them it was called the *Crux Ansata,* or Cross of Life, and was their symbol of Immortality or the *continuity of life.* It is often found in the hands of their Kings, Queens, Gods, and Goddesses as the "Key of Life." By some, who are entirely ignorant of the facts, it is claimed that the *Crux Ansata* was a sex symbol. That is due to the fact that to the early Egyptians the reproductive process *throughout all nature,* in all plants and animal life, was a great mystery. That the seed in the ground, or any cell of living matter, could reproduce its like and assist in maintaining a continuous line of its own specie, proved the continuity of all life, or in other words, demonstrated the principle of *immortality,* through birth, transition, and rebirth. This led them to the doctrine of reincarnation, and the *Crux Ansata* became the symbol of that belief in immortality. One will see at once that the relation to sex matters was remote and purely incidental, as must be the study of such physical processes in relation to the whole scheme of the continuity of life.

The Rosicrucians today use the *Crux Ansata* as a symbol of Immortality and Reincarnation *exclusively.* To them it has no other meaning.

In a study of some of the other Crosses we see arbitrary changes and additions so as to form unique symbols, and we find the Cross was common to nearly all ancient races, antedating the Christian era.

The Rosy Cross of the Rosicrucians is always a gold cross with the distinctive looped ends as shown in the illustration. There is always ONE red rose in the center of the Cross, and sometimes for purely decorative purposes a green stem may be attached to the rose; but there is never *more* than the one rose, and symbols composed of a Cross with seven, or three, or four roses in the form of a wreath around the Cross or over the Cross, is not a true Rosicrucian symbol, but a personal adaptation, counterfeit, or a deceiving imitation. The most ancient of all pictures of the Rosicrucian symbol, and all references to it in the most ancient manuscripts, describe it as a gold cross with a "ruby red rose." The symbol described herein as the true Rosy Cross is registered in the United States Patent Office as the official Rosicrucian Symbol, and such patent registration is held exclusively by AMORC.

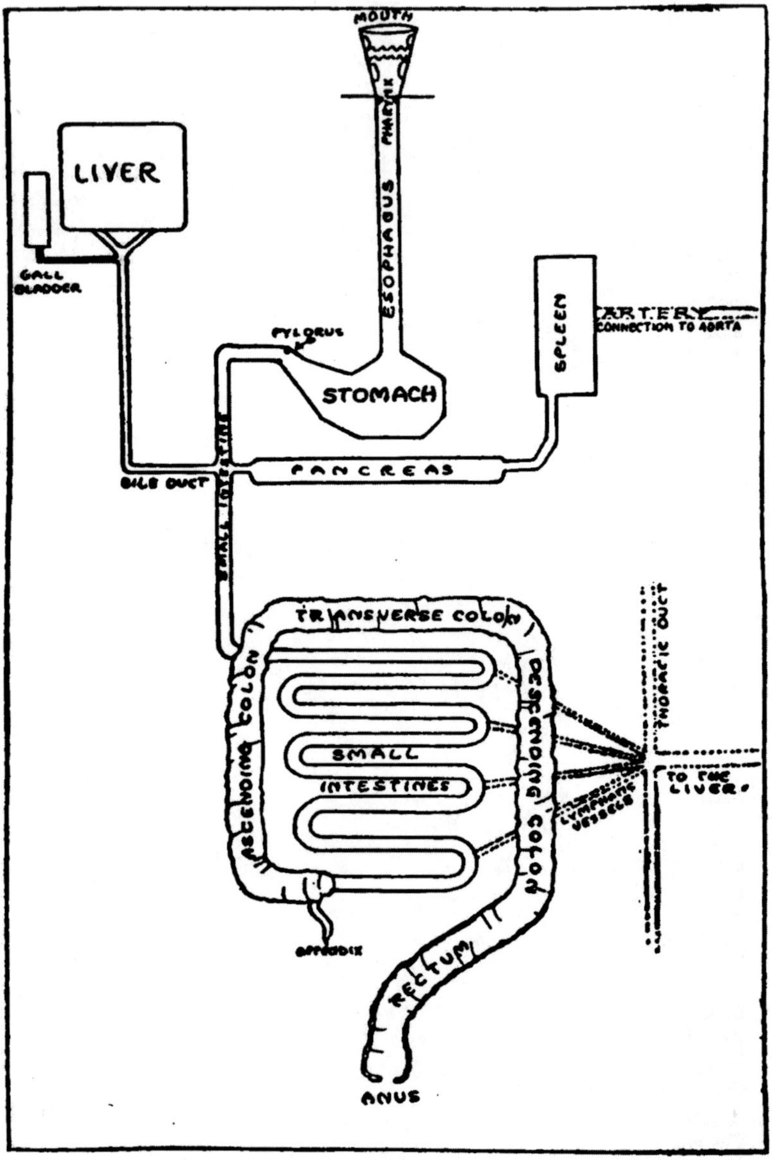
MOUTH
PHARYNX
LIVER
GALL BLADDER
ESOPHAGUS
PYLORUS
STOMACH
SPLEEN
ARTERY
CONNECTION TO AORTA
PANCREAS
BILE DUCT
SMALL INTESTINE
TRANSVERSE COLON
ASCENDING COLON
DESCENDING COLON
THORACIC DUCT
SMALL
INTESTINES
TO THE
LIVER
LYMPHATIC
VESSELS
APPENDIX
RECTUM
ANUS

Chart 1

SIXTH GRADE TEMPLE REFERENCES

EXPLANATION OF CHART 1

DIGESTION AND NUTRITION

The chart shown herewith is not to be considered as an anatomical drawing of the internal parts of the human body. The various organs and connections shown in the diagram herewith are arranged so that the mechanical action will be plain and understandable, and not in accordance with the true relations found in the human body. For instance, the position of the liver and gall bladder is not in keeping with the true condition. The same may be said of the spleen. And the connections from the intestines to the liver at the lower part of the page indicate where the liver should be located if we were going to be partly correct so far as the diagram is concerned. However, this mechanical drawing will serve a better purpose than any anatomical diagram you may find in any book.

It is well for our members to understand the mechanical process of eating and digesting food. We must keep in mind that food, whether in liquid or solid form, supplies the negative elements for the human body, just as breathing supplies the positive elements. It is when the positive elements in the breath of life come in contact with the negative elements of the physical body that there is a unit formed of the negative and positive polarities that constitutes life through the chemical action as well as the psychic action. This diagram and chart will help you to understand how the food is turned into the negative elements which release their negative electricity, or power, and thereby form one-half of the necessary vitality for life.

Food—and liquids—is taken into the mouth where, while being crushed, masticated, and rendered small in particles—like in a crushing device at the bottom of a grinder—a certain amount of saliva mixes with it to prepare it for digestion. It passes the pharynx in swallowing and goes down the esophagus (or throat) to the stomach.

In the stomach the work of churning takes place. The little valve or opening from the stomach to the intestines, called the "Pylorus," remains partly closed during the churning process. After the stomach has expanded and turned the food from side to side and mixed it well, the "Pylorus" automatically opens (and only when the proper time has come!) and the food passes into the beginning of the small intestines. On the way down the intestines there flows into the mixed food some bile from the gall bladder (through the bile duct) and also some "Pancreatic fluid" from the pancreas.

These two fluids, mixing with the food, help to "cut" the food and dissolve it into its primary "negative elements."

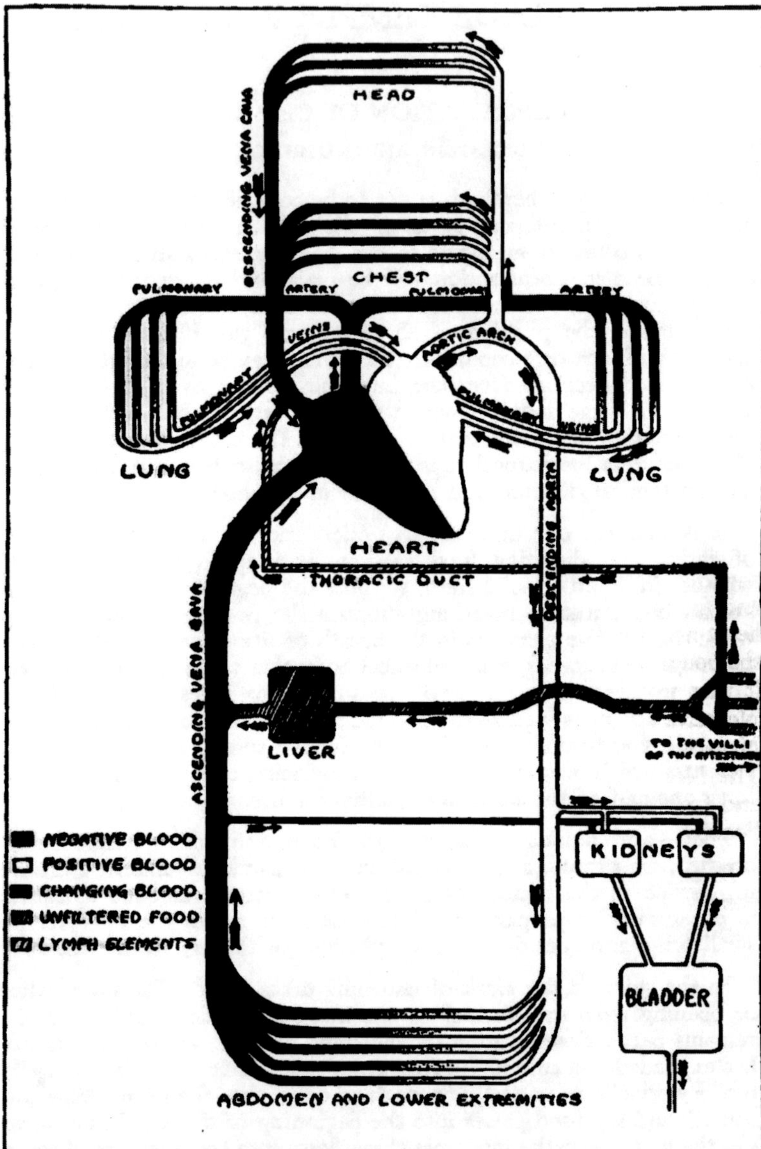
HEAD
DESCENDING VENA CAVA
CHEST
PULMONARY
ARTERY
PULMONARY
ARTERY
VEINS
AORTIC ARCH
PULMONARY
PULMONARY
VEINS
LUNG
LUNG
HEART
THORACIC DUCT
DESCENDING AORTA
ASCENDING VENA CAVA
LIVER
TO THE VILLI OF THE INTESTINES
KIDNEYS
BLADDER
NEGATIVE BLOOD
POSITIVE BLOOD
CHANGING BLOOD,
UNFILTERED FOOD
LYMPH ELEMENTS
ABDOMEN AND LOWER EXTREMITIES

Chart 2

EXPLANATION OF CHART 2

NUTRITION AND BLOOD CIRCULATION

The purpose of this diagram is two-fold. It is unusually clear and explanatory—especially for our work.

First of all, we see how the nutrition from food is taken into the circulatory system. At the side of the chart we see the vessels which lead from the intestines. These connect with the liver. In this way all nutrition from the food we eat passes to the liver. Here it is filtered, purified, and formed into what we call "Negative Elements" of the blood. From the liver these "Negative Elements" pass into the principal vein carrying the blood to the heart.

However, all fatty elements—which are separated from food in the process of digestion and assimilation in the intestines—do not enter the liver but pass through the so-called "Thoracic Duct" and go directly to the heart to form "Lymph Elements." This is plainly shown on the chart.

Now the "Negative Elements," forming negative blood, enter the right side of the heart and from there they are sent through the two "pulmonary arteries" to the lungs, to be made positive. That is, each negative blood cell is sent to the lungs to receive a Positive Polarity; and from the lungs this vitalized blood returns to the left side of the heart and there it is pumped out through the arteries to all parts of the body. As this Positive blood, vitalized, travels through the system it uses up its vitality or Positive Polarity and again becomes only Negative cells or Negative blood. Where it changes from Positive to Negative it does its greatest work in what are called "capillaries." The Negative blood must, therefore, return once more to the heart and from there be sent again to the lungs to be vitalized with a new Positive Polarity. This is a continuous process.

In our various breathing exercises we attempt to take more of the positive elements into our body than in the normal process of breathing. All the negative elements in the body will absorb, through the blood, as much positive vitality as we take in through breathing. In normal breathing, or what we should call subnormal breathing, we merely take in a small amount of the positive, which reaches the negative cells of the blood and charges only a small portion of the negative with the positive. By deeper breathing, or by holding the breath, as explained in our lectures, we cause more of the negative cells of the blood to become charged with the positive vitality of the air and thereby make our blood stronger or greater in its vitality. Other breathing exercises show us in our lectures how we can take on an additional amount of positive energy for psychic experiments and for special healing work. All of this, of course, is explained in detail in the lectures.

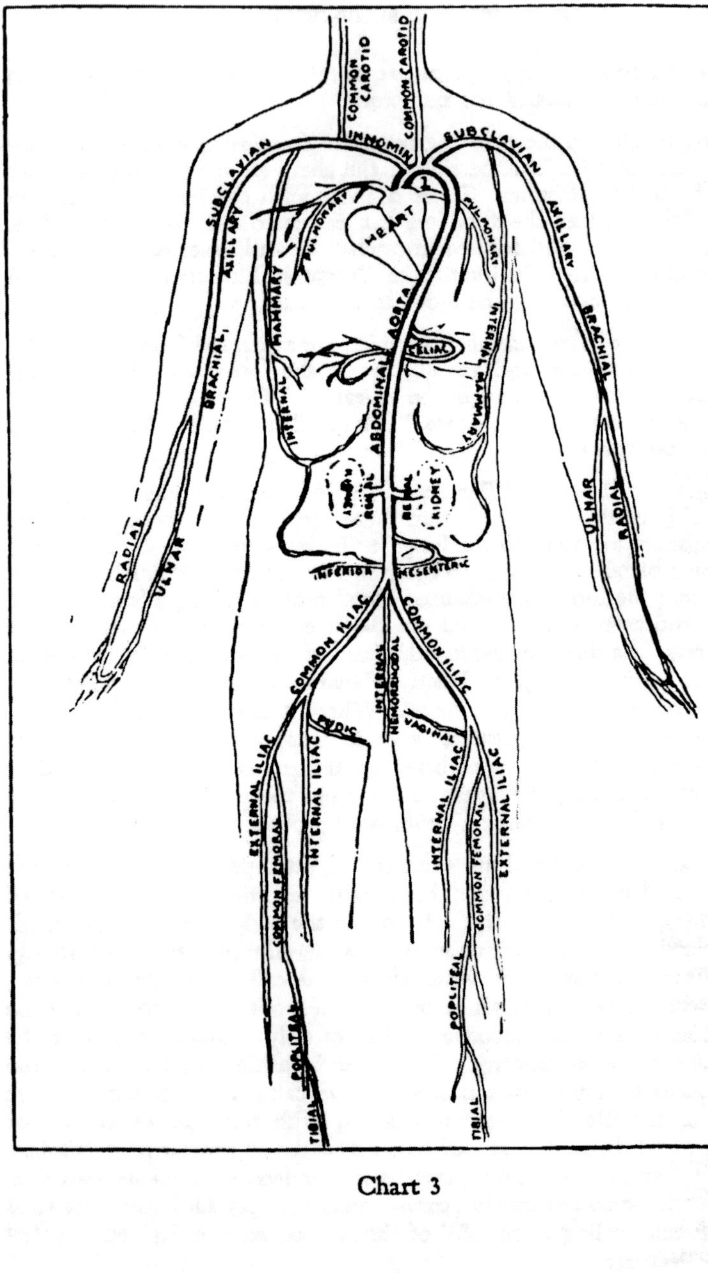
COMMON CAROTID
COMMON CAROTID
INNOMIN
SUBCLAVIAN
SUBCLAVIAN
AXILLARY
AXILLARY
PULMONARY
PULMONARY
HEART
MAMMARY
INTERNAL MAMMARY
INTERNAL
AORTA
ABDOMINAL
CELIAC
BRACHIAL
BRACHIAL
KIDNEY
RENAL
RENAL
KIDNEY
RADIAL
ULNAR
ULNAR
RADIAL
INFERIOR
MESENTERIC
COMMON ILIAC
COMMON ILIAC
INTERNAL HEMORRHOIDAL
PUDIC
VAGINAL
EXTERNAL ILIAC
INTERNAL ILIAC
INTERNAL ILIAC
EXTERNAL ILIAC
COMMON FEMORAL
COMMON FEMORAL
POPLITEAL
POPLITEAL
TIBIAL
TIBIAL

Chart 3

EXPLANATION OF CHART 3

PRINCIPAL ARTERIES

In our use of the blood for healing purposes, as well as for all mystic or psychic purposes, we deal with the vitalized or Positive blood. This is the blood which travels through the Arteries of the human body. Arteries carry the blood, the vitalized blood, from the heart to every part of the body to carry on the constructive work of nature. Veins, on the other hand, return the devitalized blood to the heart, and do not concern us so greatly.

The diagram on Chart 3 shows the principal arteries. From the upper part of the heart rises the great Aortic Arch (indicated by the figure 1. See also diagram on Chart 2). From this Arch, or large vessel, branch all the arteries supplying the great amount of vitalized blood to the body.

Every artery carrying blood to the most minute part of the body joins one of the principal arteries shown on this diagram. In our work, whenever it is necessary to know the source of blood for any small artery, one need only refer to any medical or anatomical book, or dictionary, and see what principal artery it connects with, and then trace it to the principal artery on this diagram.

The arteries throughout the body carry the positive blood of the system. Therefore, the arteries radiate the utmost vitality in a physical and also in a psychic sense. For that reason all healing work, where the hands are used, take advantage of the natural radiation of power from these arteries. In the hands of each person there are arteries as well as veins, and it is from the arteries that the hands receive their vitality as used in all healing work. Part of this vitality is the natural health and life of the physical body and part of it is the psychic power which is also in the blood and generated by the blood.

In the lectures and lessons of the Sixth Grade many references are made to methods whereby the blood can be stimulated or increased in vitality in certain parts of the body through certain secret methods known only to Rosicrucians. That is why this chart becomes very interesting and helpful in the Sixth Grade work. It is easy to understand how the vitalized blood in these arteries becomes weakened and less vitalized as it circulates around through the body and finally passes into the veins. But in some human processes it is necessary to keep the blood in these arteries weakened and less vitalized as it reaches the part or the section of the body which is diseased. Our methods show the members how this can be accomplished. It is one of the important secret methods of healing work known only to the Rosicrucians.

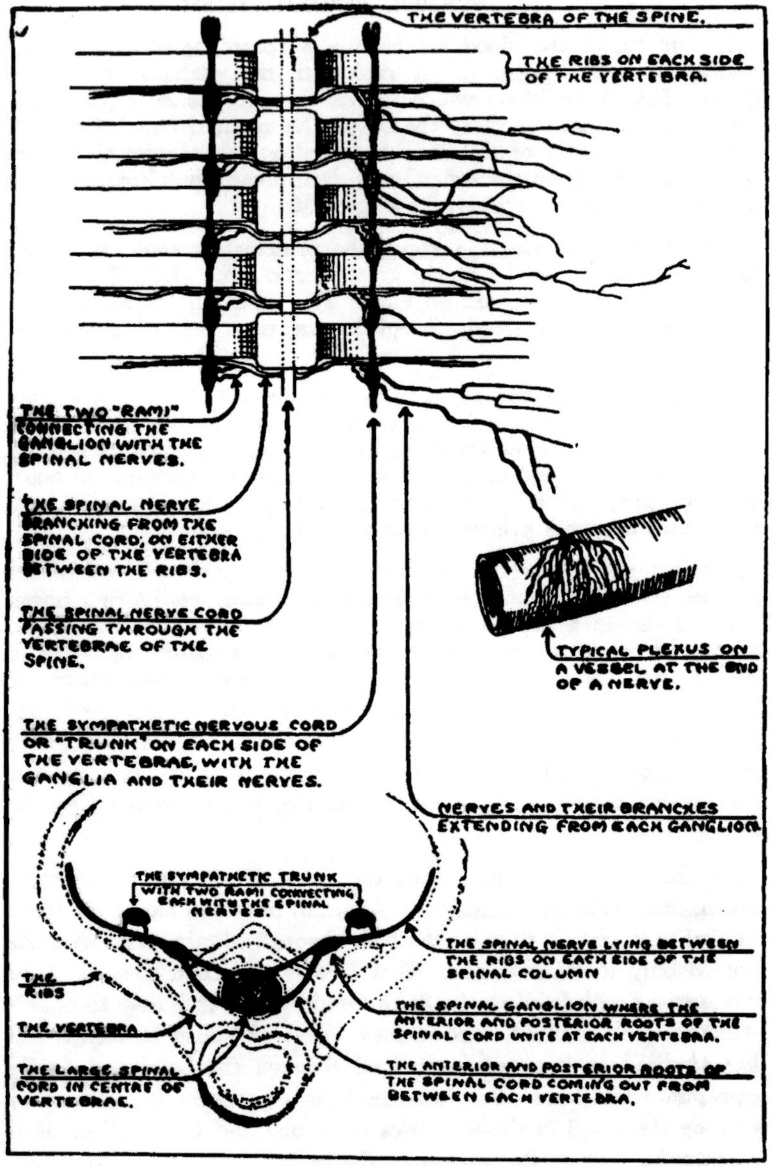
THE VERTEBRA OF THE SPINE.
THE RIBS ON EACH SIDE OF THE VERTEBRA.
THE TWO "RAMI" CONNECTING THE GANGLION WITH THE SPINAL NERVES.
THE SPINAL NERVE BRANCHING FROM THE SPINAL CORD, ON EITHER SIDE OF THE VERTEBRA BETWEEN THE RIBS.
THE SPINAL NERVE CORD PASSING THROUGH THE VERTEBRAE OF THE SPINE.
TYPICAL PLEXUS ON A VESSEL AT THE END OF A NERVE.
THE SYMPATHETIC NERVOUS CORD OR "TRUNK" ON EACH SIDE OF THE VERTEBRAE, WITH THE GANGLIA AND THEIR NERVES.
NERVES AND THEIR BRANCHES EXTENDING FROM EACH GANGLION
THE SYMPATHETIC TRUNK WITH TWO RAMI CONNECTING EACH WITH THE SPINAL NERVES.
THE SPINAL NERVE LYING BETWEEN THE RIBS ON EACH SIDE OF THE SPINAL COLUMN
THE RIBS
THE SPINAL GANGLION WHERE THE ANTERIOR AND POSTERIOR ROOTS OF THE SPINAL CORD UNITE AT EACH VERTEBRA.
THE VERTEBRA
THE LARGE SPINAL CORD IN CENTRE OF VERTEBRAE.
THE ANTERIOR AND POSTERIOR ROOTS OF THE SPINAL CORD COMING OUT FROM BETWEEN EACH VERTEBRA.

Chart 4

EXPLANATION OF CHART 4

GENERAL NERVOUS SYSTEM

The purpose of this chart is to show, in a mechanical fashion, the arrangement of the vertebrae of the spine and the location of the nervous systems.

In the upper diagram five vertebrae, with their ribs, are drawn mechanically as though they were sections of some metal frame work of a piece of machinery. The center squares represent the vertebrae, while attached to either side of these vertebrae are the ribs. The vertebrae represent the sections of a spinal column (See Chart 6).

Through the center of the vertebrae passes the spinal nerve cord—a heavy cord consisting of nerves—the top of which is the Medulla Oblongata (as shown in the upper diagram on Chart 8) and is connected with the brain. This cord is the center of the general nervous system.

Branching out from this cord, between each vertebrae, are smaller nerves, called spinal nerves, which connect on each side with the Sympathetic Trunks.

There are two Sympathetic Trunks, one on each side of the vertebrae of the spinal column (on the inside of the ribs) and running parallel with the middle spinal cord, as shown in the diagram.

Each Sympathetic Trunk consists of a heavy cord of many nerves with "Ganglia" opposite nearly every rib. From each Ganglion are two nerves, called "Rami," connecting the signal nerves to the Sympathetic System. And from each "Ganglion" are Sympathetic nerves going to various plexuses of organs, muscles, or vessels of the body.

The reader's attention is called to the fact that man has two nervous systems—the Spinal Nervous System and the Sympathetic Nervous System. Both of these systems are shown in the diagrams on the opposite page, which of course are not true to life so far as anatomy is concerned. Please note that the Sympathetic Nervous System is dual or double; a part of it is on each side of the vertebrae of the spine. The Rosicrucians were the first to realize the wonderful work of the Sympathetic Nervous System and its connection with the psychic body of man. Many systems of modern treatments deal with the Spinal Nervous System and any injury or pressure upon it; but the Rosicrucians alone give great attention to the Sympathetic, and point out in the easy, simple lessons of the Sixth Grade how the Sympathetic Nervous System can be used to cure disease or relieve conditions that cannot be treated in any other way. For this reason the student is asked to keep in mind the fact that he is dealing with new principles in our work and that he will find many revelations and startling laws not generally known.

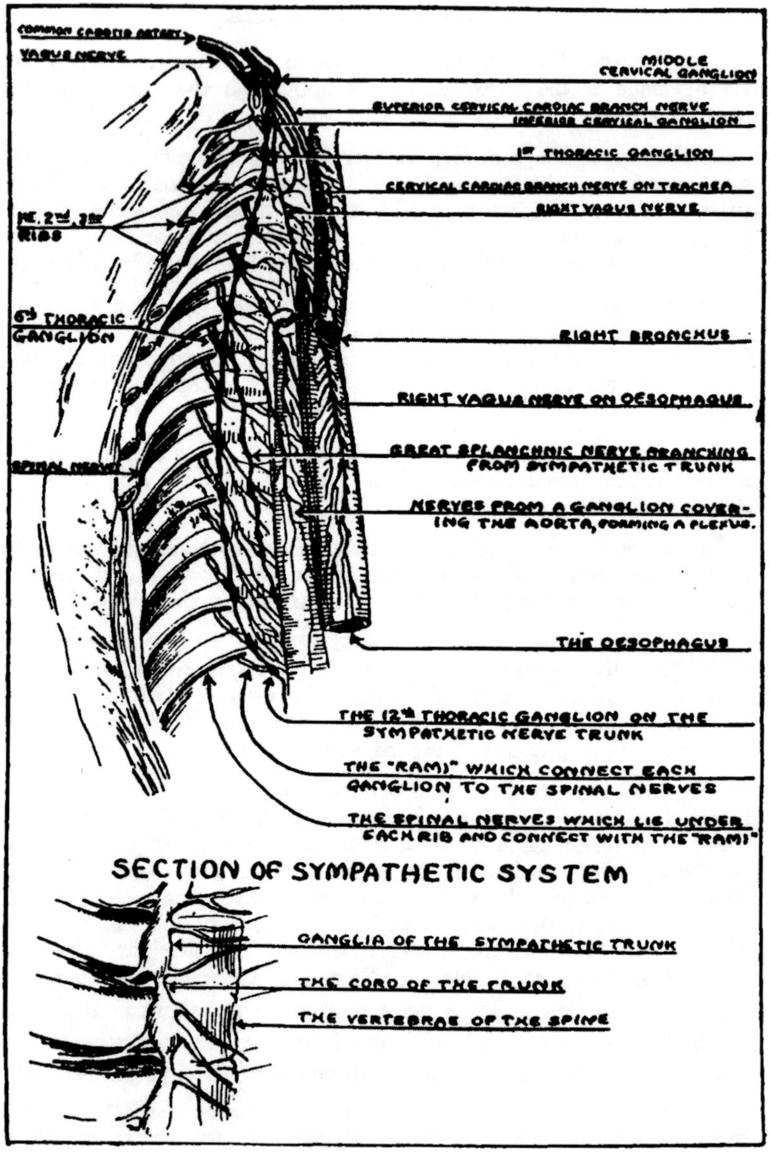
COMMON CAROTID ARTERY
VAGUS NERVE
MIDDLE CERVICAL GANGLION
SUPERIOR CERVICAL CARDIAC BRANCH NERVE
INFERIOR CERVICAL GANGLION
1st THORACIC GANGLION
CERVICAL CARDIAC BRANCH NERVE ON TRACHEA
RIGHT VAGUS NERVE
1st, 2nd, 3rd RIBS
6th THORACIC GANGLION
RIGHT BRONCHUS
RIGHT VAGUS NERVE ON OESOPHAGUS
GREAT SPLANCHNIC NERVE BRANCHING FROM SYMPATHETIC TRUNK
SPINAL NERVE
NERVES FROM A GANGLION COVERING THE AORTA, FORMING A PLEXUS.
THE OESOPHAGUS
THE 12th THORACIC GANGLION ON THE SYMPATHETIC NERVE TRUNK
THE "RAMI" WHICH CONNECT EACH GANGLION TO THE SPINAL NERVES
THE SPINAL NERVES WHICH LIE UNDER EACH RIB AND CONNECT WITH THE "RAMI"
SECTION OF SYMPATHETIC SYSTEM
GANGLIA OF THE SYMPATHETIC TRUNK
THE CORD OF THE TRUNK
THE VERTEBRAE OF THE SPINE

Chart 5

EXPLANATION OF CHART 5

DETAILS OF SYMPATHETIC SYSTEM

In the upper drawing we see a section of the human body opened and the organs and muscles removed to show the Sympathetic Trunk Cord on the right side of the vertebrae.

Just beneath each rib we see the spinal nerve running parallel with the rib. From these spinal nerves we also see the two "Rami" uniting with the Ganglia of the heavy Sympathetic Trunk.

A few vessels are also shown, and it will be noticed how the Sympathetic Nerves from the various Ganglia branch out over the wall of the esophagus, the right bronchus, and the aorta artery. This shows that a "plexus" covers the wall of a vessel or organ (as also shown on Chart 4).

The lower diagram shows an enlarged view of a section of the Sympathetic Trunk giving an exact picture of the Ganglia, their size, form, and location.

(It will prove interesting to the deep student to read in various text books on the "Nervous System" the diversified explanations and theories of the purposes and formation of "Ganglia" and "Neurones.")

The reason for the two forms of nervous systems in the human body will be easily understood when we say that the Spinal Nervous System conveys energy and power that is of a gross nature, to take care of the physical actions and functions of the human body. The Sympathetic Nervous System, however, belongs to the psychic part of man, and there is a place in the human body shown in our lectures and thoroughly explained, where the psychic power and energy is generated and sent into the Sympathetic Nervous System. This system, therefore, uses a higher rate of energy, which is almost a Cosmic energy, and this energy can be used for the healing of diseases and curing of conditions because its real purpose in the human body is to carry on the reconstructive actions in the human body. This function of the Sympathetic Nervous System was not known until the Rosicrucians explained it and even today it is only thoroughly understood by those who have the lectures and lessons of our work. It makes healing and the prevention of disease understandable and gives every one of our members a wonderful power not possessed by those who do not know the laws and principles.

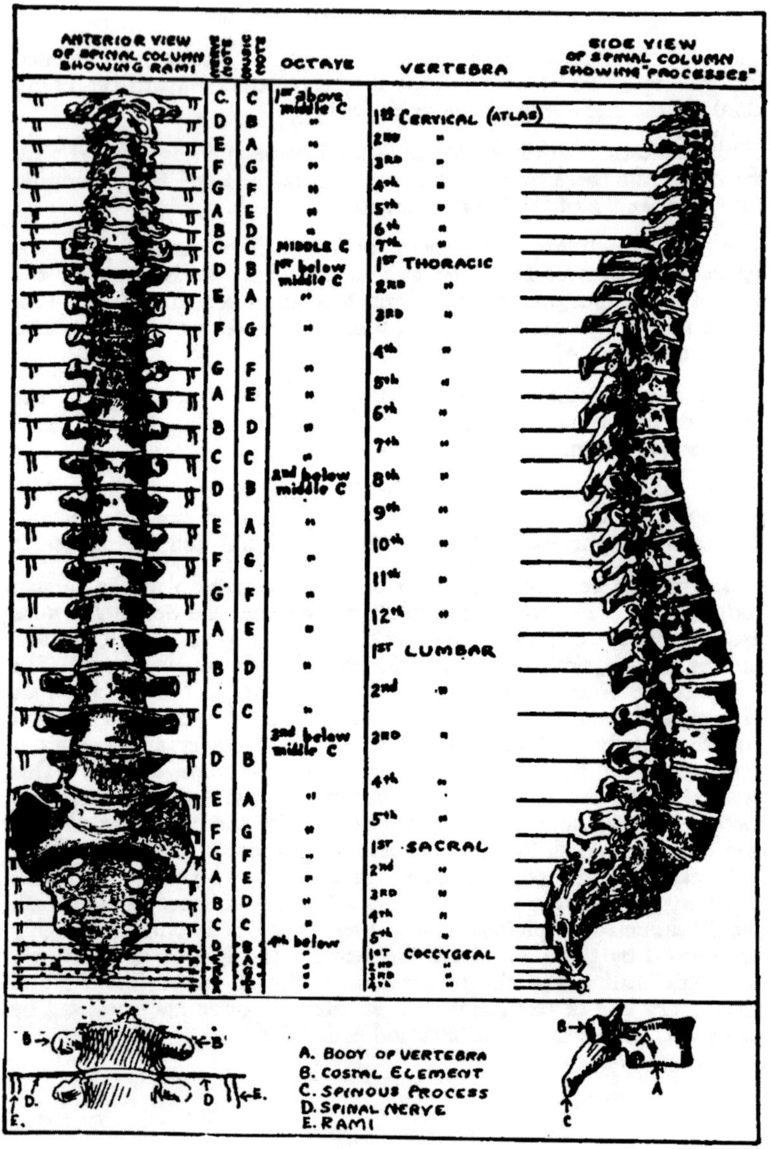
ANTERIOR VIEW OF SPINAL COLUMN SHOWING RAMI
VERTEBRA NOTE
MUSIC NOTE
OCTAVE
VERTEBRA
SIDE VIEW OF SPINAL COLUMN SHOWING "PROCESSES"
C C 1st above middle C
D B 1st CERVICAL (ATLAS)
E A 2nd
F G 3rd
G F 4th
A E 5th
B D 6th
C C MIDDLE C 7th
D B 1st below middle C 1st THORACIC
E A 2nd
F G 3rd
G F 4th
A E 5th
B D 6th
C C 7th
D B 2nd below middle C 8th
E A 9th
F G 10th
G F 11th
A E 12th
B D 1st LUMBAR
C C 2nd
D B 3rd below middle C 3rd
E A 4th
F G 5th
G F 1st SACRAL
A E 2nd
B D 3rd
C C 4th
D B 4th below 5th
1st COCCYGEAL
2nd
3rd
4th
A. BODY OF VERTEBRA
B. COSTAL ELEMENT
C. SPINOUS PROCESS
D. SPINAL NERVE
E. RAMI

Chart 6

EXPLANATION OF CHART 6

NAMES OF VERTEBRAE AND NERVES

The Spinal Column consists of 25 or 26 pieces, in the average body. The 25th piece—at the bottom of the column—may have the 26th section loosely attached to the end of it, or this 26th section may form part of the 25th. However, originally, at some time, the large 25th section consisted of nine definite divisions, each having the same purpose as each of the separate vertebrae above. Therefore, we continue to look upon the Spinal Column as consisting of 33 sections (that is, counting the so-called "Atlas" as the first section). Upon the first section—the "Atlas"—rests the skull, which, from one view-point, forms another section of the Spine, and would, therefore, make a 34th section.

However, using the plan or diagram of the Spine as usually adopted by all text books on Anatomy, we have, as shown in the two diagrams opposite, 33 or 34 sections or divisions. Through this Spine runs the Spinal Cord of the general or central nervous system. And branching out from between each vertebra, or section of the Spine, are two Spinal Nerves. These come from the Spinal Cord running down through the center of the Vertebrae, and pass right and left from the Spine. Joining to these spinal nerves are the two "Rami" on each side. (Refer to the lower diagram on Chart 4.)

In our work we have a "Nerve Note" and a "Music Note" for each of the Spinal Nerves between the Vertebrae. These are plainly shown on the diagram opposite, as well as the universally adopted name of each vertebra.

In the lectures of the Sixth Grade there are complete instructions as to how members may easily take advantage of the relationship between the various nerves and their association with colors, music sounds, and nerve energy. We show our members that music notes will arouse certain connections of the Sympathetic Nervous System into special activity and thereby cause the energy of these nerves to function more freely and completely. The same is true in regard to colors. And we show our members how even the mind, or thought waves, can reach the sympathetic connections and help in curing or relieving conditions. All of this is part of the wonderful secret system of the Rosicrucian teachings, laws, and principles.

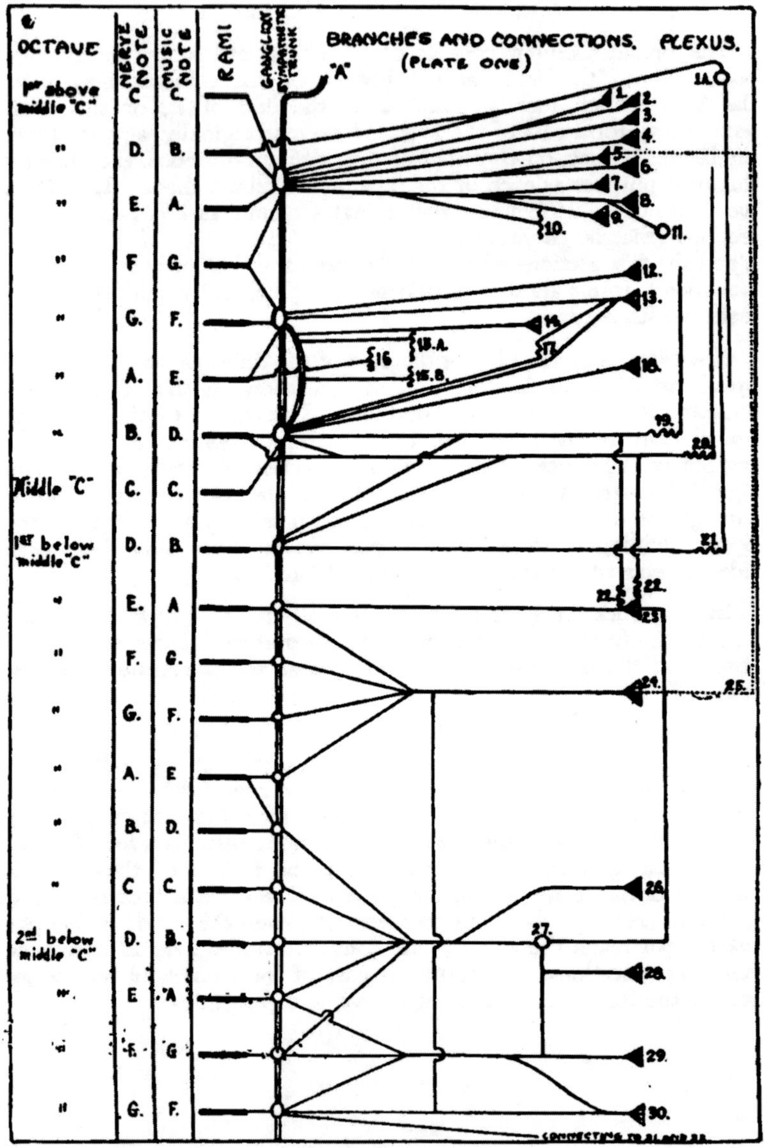

Chart 7 (Plate 1)

EXPLANATION OF CHART 7

Plate 1

FUNCTIONS OF THE GANGLIA

(Study first the Explanation of Symbols given at bottom of Plate 2 on next page.)

"A" is the Sympathetic Trunk running to the Brain and down through the body.

Connected to the first four Rami is the Superior Cervical Ganglion. Branching from this Ganglion are six Sympathetic Nerves with their extensions leading to Plexuses numbered 1, 2, 3, 4, 5, 6, 7, 8, and 9, and to two other Ganglia numbered 1A and 11, and to one Spinal Nerve numbered 10. We also note that from the second Rami one Sympathetic Nerve reaches out independent of the Ganglion and connects with the nerve ending at 1A.

The 4th, 5th, and 6th Rami connect with the Middle Cervical Ganglion and this Ganglion has two nerves extending from it leading to Plexuses Nos. 12 and 13.

The 7th and 8th Rami connect with the Inferior Cervical Ganglion from which 5 nerves extend leading to Plexuses Nos. 13, 18, and to Spinal Nerves Nos. 17, 19, and 20, and indirectly to spinal nerve No. 22, which connects with Plexus No. 23.

Between the Middle Cervical Ganglion and the Inferior Cervical Ganglion there is a nerve acting as a "loop" and connecting the two Ganglia as shown on the diagram. From this "loop" there are three Sympathetic Nerves leading to Plexus No. 14, and Spinal Nerves 15A and 15B.

From the 6th and from the 7th Rami we see Sympathetic Nerves extending independent of the Ganglia to Spinal Nerve No. 16, and Spinal Nerve No. 20.

The connections through the various parts of the body indicated by charts seven and eight form the most complete outline of this subject ever presented to any student. These charts and the references to them in the Sixth Grade constitute the work of many years of scientific research by the greatest authorities of Europe and America. The Rosicrucians were the first to have a complete outline of this system and to know exactly what part of the human body was connected with every other part. Therefore, our members will find in these charts and in the lectures of the Sixth Grade a complete system that is not the personal opinion of any one man or the result of some discovery. It means that thousands of experiments had to be made to test the principle of each idea as it was revealed through experimentation, and that only after tests and trials by many thousands of our members in many lands for many years were we ready to put this matter into the teachings for practical application. The subject

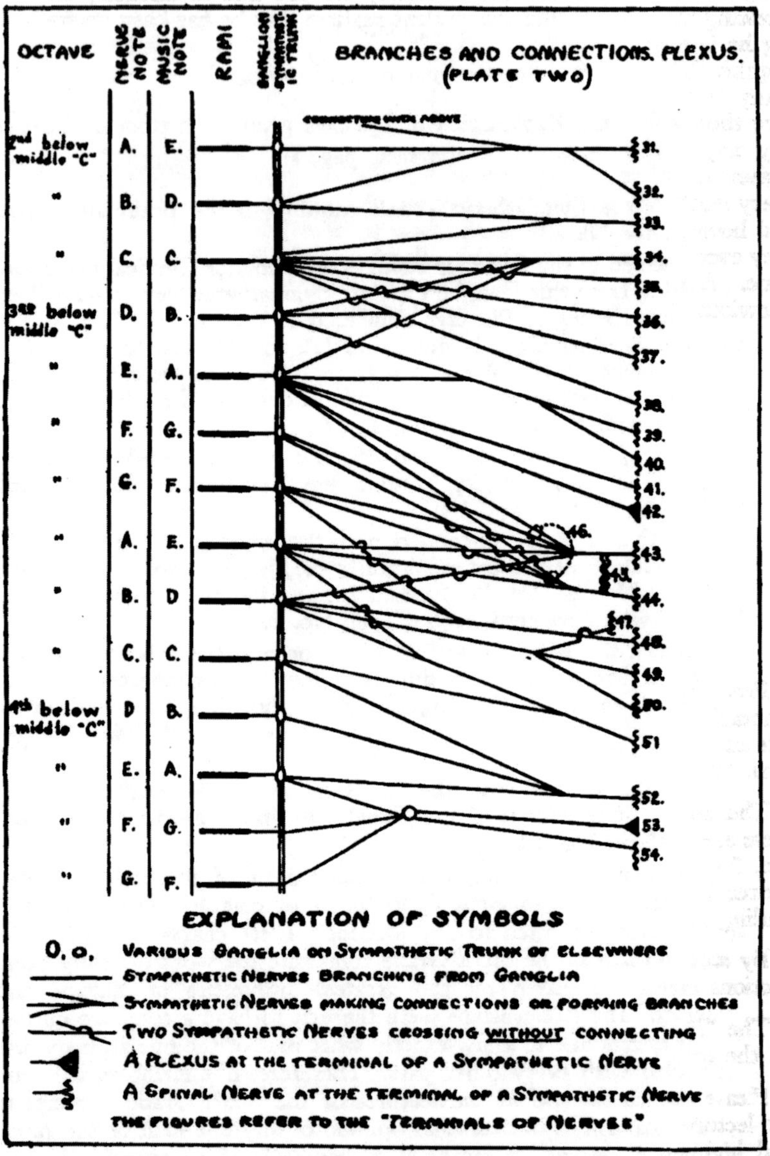

Chart 7 (Plate 2)

may look difficult when examining it from these charts, but the lectures in the Sixth Grade are so simply worded and so intensely interesting that long before the student realizes that he has been studying he is really absorbing knowledge that would take many years to acquire through any regular school of medicine or physiology. The many lectures of the Sixth Grade arranged in even steps gradually give the student a power of knowledge that cannot be measured in any way except from the Rosicrucian standard, and that means the highest standard of efficiency and power. Hundreds of our students every month tell us that they have learned more about their own body, and how to prevent disease and how to be strong and healthy, than they ever learned in any of the colleges or schools to which they have gone. Even physicians and scientists highly endorse the unusual knowledge contained in this Sixth Grade.

EXPLANATION OF CHART 7

Plate 2

FUNCTIONS OF GANGLIA

(Continued)

From the 9th Rami (which is located between the 1st and 2nd Thoracic Vertebrae) we have the First Thoracic Ganglion. From this extends three Sympathetic Nerves connecting with Spinal Nerves Nos. 19 and 20, and leading to Spinal Nerve No. 21.

The 10th, 11th, 12th, and 13th Rami have separate Ganglia, but these are connected by four Sympathetic Nerves which lead to Plexus No. 24, and connect indirectly by way of Nerve No. 25 with the Plexus No. 5. Connection is also made with Sympathetic Nerves leading to Plexus No. 30.

By studying the charts in this way one can easily figure the connections made by each Rami and each Ganglion.

The "Plate Two" of this chart continues "Plate One" and shows all the connections made by the other Rami.

Please note that each Plexus and Nerve ending is numbered. In the lectures given by the Masters in the work of the Seventh Grade, and higher, reference is made to the numbers given on these two plates. The numbers will refer to muscles, organs, tissues, and vessels affected by the Plexuses, so that by reference to these charts you can easily locate which Nerve and Ganglia affect every part of the body.

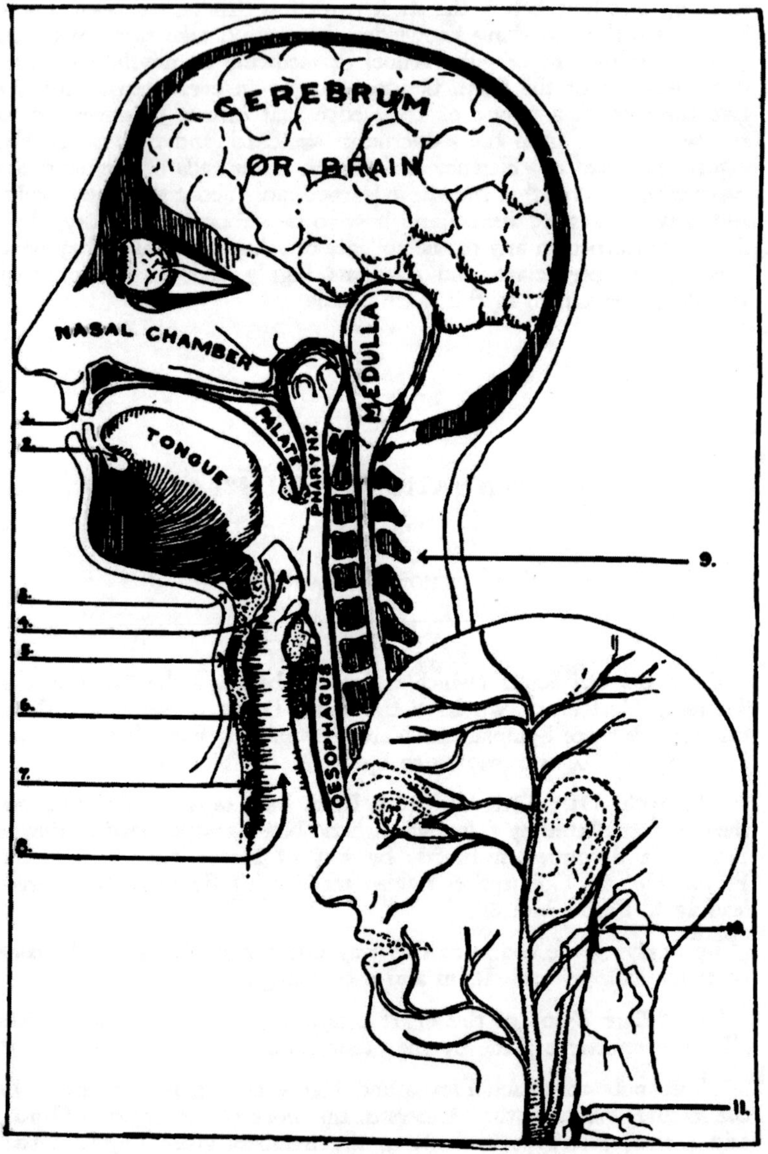
CEREBRUM
OR BRAIN
NASAL CHAMBER
MEDULLA
PALATE
PHARYNX
TONGUE
OESOPHAGUS
1.
2.
3.
4.
5.
6.
7.
8.
9.
10.
11.

Chart 8

EXPLANATION OF CHART 8

DETAILS OF HEAD AND NECK

Reference to the upper drawing on the opposite page will help the student to understand the location of the Vertebrae in the Neck. One should note that in the neck the vertebrae lie far from the surface and cannot be felt as is possible in the thorax of the body. The 7th and 8th Cervical Vertebrae are usually the first to come near the surface of the body. The one most prominent in its projection in the neck or just below the neck is the 1st Thoracic Vertebra.

1. The Oral Vestibule, between teeth and lip;

2. Oral Cavity;

3. Hyoid bone;

4. The Epiglottis;

5. Thyroid Cartilage;

6. Cricoid Cartilage;

7. Tracheal Cartilage;

8. The Larynx;

9. The Vertebrae of the Spine with the Spinal Cord running from the Medulla Oblongata down through the center of each Vertebra.

The lower drawing shows the principal arteries of the head connecting on each side of the neck with the Common Carotid Artery (see Chart 3). It also shows location of the beginning of the Sympathetic Trunk on each side of the neck.

10. The Superior Cervical Ganglion of the Sympathetic Trunk. (Just back of the ear, on a line with the mouth.)

11. The Middle Cervical Ganglion. (On a line beneath the Superior Ganglion, and level with the "Adam's Apple" of the throat).

Part Nine

The Mystery of DR. JOHN DALTON *and his* ALCHEMICAL LAWS

Reprinted from the
American Rosae Crucis
of November, 1916

DALTON'S LAW OF PROPORTIONS

THE STORY OF THE ATOM

(Especially Prepared for All Members of the Order)

By THE IMPERATOR

(Copyrighted and Fully Protected)

Brothers and Sisters, permit me to introduce Dr. John Dalton, the public expounder of the atomic laws, the mystic of his day, and the scientific puzzle of the scientific world.

And with this, Dr. Dalton steps upon these pages to give you those facts and those laws which prejudiced science and skeptical human nature have kept in the dark to decay and obliterate the name of one who has done much for chemistry, but now receives such belittling comments as: "crude and unpractical worker in science," "careless and indifferent observer of facts," "unskilled meddler in fields too profound for him," and "unscientific dreamer and propounder of alchemists' fallacies."

For several years I have had in mind an attempt to revive a serious interest in Dalton and Dalton's work. It has seemed to me that not only do the reference works slight him and chemistry now ignores him, but that, when chemistry continues to use his laws—and cannot do without them—and then wilfully, consistently, and with real, selfish purposes sees to it that his laws are kept from the searcher for truth, it is time to have the searchlight thrown stronger than ever upon those things which Dalton spent a lifetime in evolving from theory into fact and demonstrated.

And Dalton has a special interest for us, because he WAS a member of the Order and DID attend the lectures and worked in the laboratory of the Lodges in two different cities where he pursued his experiments and observations. The principles upon which he worked, and which formed the foundation of his Philosophy of Chemistry, he learned in our Lodges in the first three grades and in the 8th, 9th, and 10th grades. Every member of our Order today, who has passed through the First Grade and then through the Fourth, knows that Dalton's principles (as they are outlined here in his own words) are a logical result of the regular study of our teachings. The great mystery, which puzzles the scientists today, as to "where did Dalton get his first ideas, and did they come from Newton?" is easily answered by those who are in our Order; for Dalton and every other member MUST receive such principles in order to understand even the elementary work of our grades.

But let us consider the value of Dalton's work. Soon after he had made some important discoveries he was called upon to address certain scientific bodies, the most important in the country at the time, and so great became the interest in his work that he decided, like many an optimistic disciple of truth, to help the science of chemistry and physics by publishing some of his theories in such form as would be available to those very scientists who later condemned his work as "crude." Because Dalton was not one of their colleagues; because he was not of their school nor of their narrow view-point and narrow materialistic training, he was considered a "heretic" in science and unfit to enter their domain and show them that which they did not know. With the zeal of wanderers seeking for a guide they seized his theories, which are now admitted to be laws, and after having made them a stepping stone to the accomplishment of many greater discoveries, they ignored Dalton, and, up to the present hour, have succeeded in keeping his original papers and actual statements from the eyes of the true seeker for light.

Dalton's papers, as published by him in 1805 to 1808, contained not all the laws he had formulated by his researches and experiments. He knew well enough that to give all the laws, to explain all the workings of the R. C. Triangle in the composition of matter, as now explained to all our members of the First and Fourth Grades, would be to reveal that which would never be understood by the uninitiated and always misunderstood by his critics. But Dalton did refer to the triangle in some places of his manuscript and in some of his public speeches. In fact, the triangle was the key to his work, the use of it becoming an obsession with him. All in all, Dalton made many thousands—not hundreds—of observations of the workings of nature and kept them well tabulated and classified. He made many hundreds of laboratory experiments, and he had students and friends cooperating with him in making other experiments. He climbed mountains almost daily to register effects; he had certain instruments in his home and outside of it constantly attuned to register various manifestations and demonstrations of nature. He lived the life of a hermit in many ways; isolated from all pleasure, building his own instruments, devising his own methods, and accumulating facts which would take a dozen volumes to record. And all this because he searched for the triangle and its law in everything that was or seemed to be. And among all these trials he made 200,000 meteorological observations which are still preserved in records owned by a foreign scientific society.

In a letter to Jonathan Otley in 1796 (six years before he made public much of his discoveries) he said: "I may answer that my head is too full of triangles, chemical processes, and electrical experiments to think much of marriage."

In the matter which follows, I will attempt to make plain to our members the laws which Dalton evolved, based upon the working of the triangle. I will make plain to them that which may not be so plain to those not initiated into our Order. Furthermore, I have added to Dalton's original charts, reproduced herewith, those points and illustrations regarding Atoms which he did not make public. The charts, themselves, have not been published in this form, or complete in any form, since his transition, and no doubt students of chemistry generally, as well as research workers in the field of physics, will appreciate this rare treat.

The life of Dalton may be learned from almost any good reference book or encyclopedia. But what follows is taken from his own writings and from my own Rosicrucian manuscripts and Secret Mandamuses. It gives a fair example of how complete and replete with valuable, unpublished, and little known information are the papers possessed by the Masters of our Order.

Passing then from the generalities to the specific points of Dalton's work, we must make reference to the charts from time to time. I will quote Dalton's own words whenever his language is plain enough for our members (for it is often robed with symbolism which requires interpretation). But I shall use my own methods of presenting the facts more often and when statements are not directly quoted they are in my own words, giving the facts as I KNOW them and have had them demonstrated to me in the Order's work and in my own experiments in a typical R. C. laboratory.

It is difficult to approach a subject like this, for so much leads up to it which must be passed in a short magazine article. But, essentially, the first two lectures of the First Grade of our Order show that matter is composed of those particles which manifest the first distinction of material expression.

In other words, the particular things which make a book are the pages in size and number, the cover, and the title page. The pages alone do not constitute a book; the cover alone, regardless of its appearance as a book and having the distinction of being a book, does not constitute a book; nor does the title page of a book, alone and independent, constitute a book. Yet each of these things is necessary to a book; without them a book is not possible, and each must have certain qualities of its own in order to make it assist in composing a book. Thus it is with matter. Matter as a whole is a composite thing. But the elements which compose it may have the natural distinctions or qualities necessary to make matter, without being matter themselves. Therefore, the Rosicrucians start their study of matter with the nature and quality of that which enters into the composition of matter, and one of the particles thus studied is the ATOM.

Dalton did not discover the Atom, nor did he ever publicly or privately claim to have discovered it. But he did find that the Atom was subject to some wonderful laws, and these laws are unchangeable and universal in their application.

Starting, then, with the premise, the FACT, that matter in all its expressions, in all its classifications, is composed of molecules, and that these molecules are only a collection of Atoms united and held together by some force or power, we are at once ready to study the Atoms themselves. And our first conclusion is that there must be different kinds of Atoms in order to make different kinds of molecules of matter.

This conclusion is sometimes disputed by those scientists who have a different theory of the composition of matter, or by those who have no theory and will accept none. But we will waste no time in arguing the FACT in this case.

Dalton proceeded with the fact and determined that there was not only a definite quality to each Atom, but also a definite weight to each Atom, as he called the other distinctive feature of each Atom. And—right here I find myself in a quandary. I must explain what is meant by "weight," and to do so I would have to refer to terms which I do not care to put into public print. Members of our First Grade will recall that matter is made manifest by a certain condition, a certain attribute, which distinguishes one kind of matter from another. This feature of matter is according to numbers—and the difference in numbers makes a difference in the manifestation of matter. The particles which compose Atoms—as explained in the lectures of the First Grade—are a result of this distinctive condition which has different numbers of expression. Now, when Dalton referred to the "weight of Atoms" he did not refer to "weight" as it is usually understood by the world. Chemistry has always supposed he did mean "weight" in its physical and common sense, and gradually they have found that there is a difference between their observations and what they thought he meant. That has occasioned considerable criticism of Dalton's theories, and I do not suppose that chemists will give any credence to my explanations, so I will not explain to them but to our own members.

So Dalton began to classify Atoms according to their inner nature. When I say inner nature, I mean that nature which they have and which is the result of the smaller particles composing them. Our members will remember that matter is expressed by the triangle in our work, and that the three corners of the triangle are certain steps in the evolution or composition of matter. The Atom is at the second point. So I will call Atoms point TWO of the triangle, and the particles which compose them, point ONE of the triangle. Now point one is a result of certain numbers and these numbers assist in composing the Atoms. Therefore, Dalton worked to discover the NUMBERS COMPOSING EACH ATOM. He avoided the large figures and used a scale by calling one thousand, one; two thousand, two, etc., up to 200,000, which he called 200, etc. That made it easy to write brief notes.

The result of his years of work produced what is to be found on the upper part of PLATE ONE.

PLATE ONE

Here we have Dalton's division of Atoms into Elements. Let us consider first the "simple Elements," numbered from 1 to 37. These numbers do not refer to "weights," size, or nature. All numbers on the plates refer only to the matter in the text.

Dalton invented a series of symbols to represent the Atoms, each symbol based upon a circle with a definite mark or letter inside. Many of these symbols he took from the Rosicrucian work, especially that which pertains to Astrology, Alchemy, and the Triangle and Cross. (Note, for instance, symbols numbered 1, 5, 6, 7, 10, 11 20, 32, 34, 35, 36, and 37.)

These first 37 symbols show that there are 37 definite forms of matter which show their nature clearly and accurately WHEN COMPOSED OF ONLY ONE ATOM. Some forms of matter are not definite in nature until two, or three, or four, or possibly seven Atoms are united. But these first 37, or the "Simple Elements," are composed of only ONE ATOM EACH. Naturally the Atoms are different, different in size, in " weight," and in constitution, or there would be no difference in the matter they manifest. So Dalton listed these Elements as shown below and at the same time gave the weight of each Atom. Remember the "weight" is the number of the particles of "point one of the triangle," which composes the Atom, but each number should be read in thousands. Thus, the first Atom has 1 as its weight. It should be read 1,000. Number 4, Oxygen, has 7 as its "weight;" that should be read 7,000.

LIST OF SIMPLE ELEMENTS

No.	Nature	"Weight"
1.	Hydrogen	1
2.	Azote (nitrogen)	5
3.	Carbon or Charcoal	5
4.	Oxygen	7
5.	Phosphorus	9
6.	Sulphur	13
7.	Magnesia	20
8.	Lime	23
9.	Soda	28
10.	Potash	42
11.	Strontites	46
12.	Barytes	68
13.	Iron	38
14.	Zinc	56
15.	Copper	56
16.	Lead	95
17.	Silver	100
18.	Platina	100
19.	Gold	140
20.	Mercury	167
21.	Nickel	25 or 50
22.	Tin	50
23.	Bismuth	68
24.	Antimony	40
25.	Arsenic	42
26.	Cobalt	55
27.	Manganese	40
28.	Uranium	60?

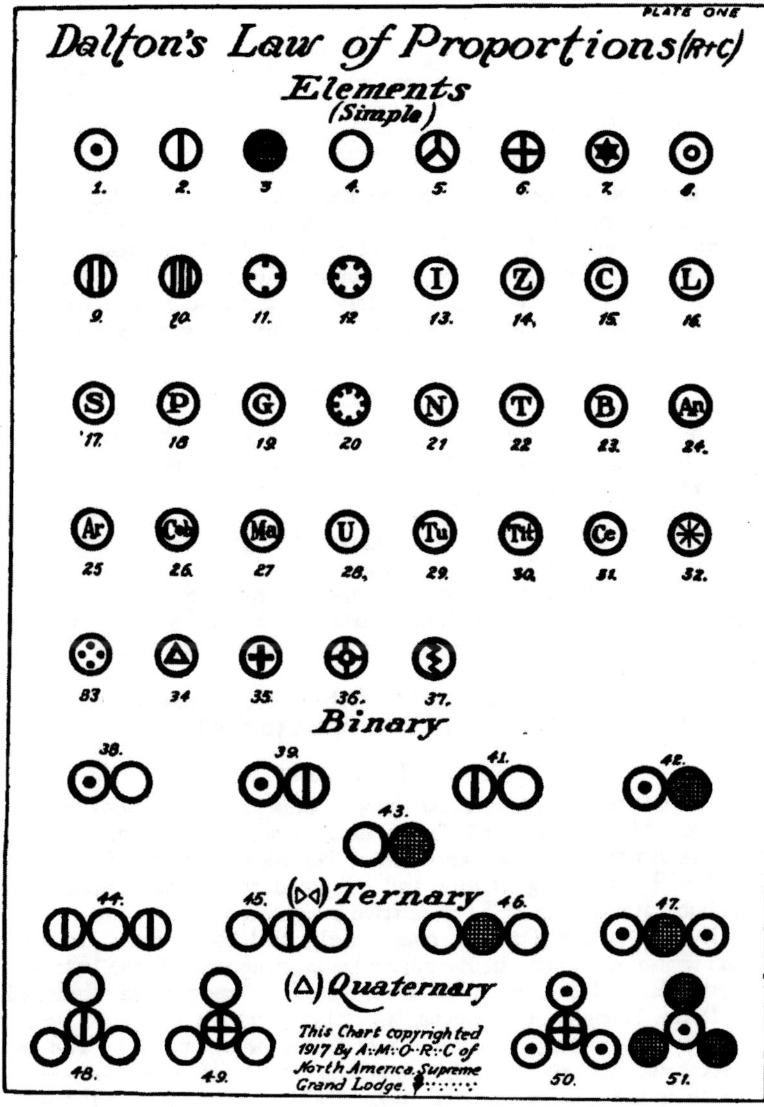
PLATE ONE
Dalton's Law of Proportions (RtC)
Elements
(Simple)
Binary
Ternary
Quaternary
This Chart copyrighted 1917 By A∴M∴O∴R∴C of North America, Supreme Grand Lodge.

Plate 1

29. Tungsten .... 40?
30. Titanium .... 40?
31. Cerium .... 45?
32. Magnesia? 17
33. Alumine 15
34. Silex 45
35. Yttria 53
36. Glucine 30
37. Zicone 45

The foregoing, as stated, are the simplest elements. Dalton's work was to demonstrate and prove that from these and a few other elements came all the known forms of matter. At the present time we have enlarged Dalton's number of simple elements to 92. But from the foregoing 37 a very great number of the best known forms of matter are evolved, so to speak, by combining several of the above simple elements.

DALTON'S LAW OF PROPORTIONS

It is in the combining of two or more Atoms to make another form of matter, another manifestation of matter, that Dalton discovered the workings of the triangle. He did not express it in the terms of the triangle as we do in our own Temple lectures, for his lectures were for the public, but he did express it in this wise: "One added to two to make one is equivalent to two added to one to make one; and in adding two to two to make one, or one to three to make one, the same law in its square is maintained by its conformity to the law of three; and every other multiple is a duplication of the original law."

This is beautifully illustrated in the charts herewith and as we come to each example I will call attention to this law.

BINARY ELEMENTS

One added to one to make one, is illustrated here with five examples. No. 38 represents "one Atom of water or steam, composed of one Atom of Oxygen and one of Hydrogen, retained in physical contact by a strong affinity and supposed to be surrounded by a common atmosphere of heat; relative weight is 8."

The above are Dalton's own words, and they mean just this: that water or steam, in its molecule, is composed of one Atom of Hydrogen and one Atom of Oxygen. The "weight" of Hydrogen is 1; the "weight" of Oxygen is 7; therefore, the combined weight of the two, making the molecule of water or steam, is 8. The two Atoms are held together by the strong affinity of ——————, which is the quality referred to by Dalton when he uses the word "weight" to symbolically represent this quality as explained in the 18th paragraph of this article. This strong affinity, or quality, or power, is explained further on by chart and words.

When Atoms unite as do Hydrogen and Oxygen and others, they do so according to a law. That law is the basis of the so-called affinity between certain elements. Briefly put, it is that LIKE ATTRACTS UNLIKE AND REPELS LIKE. In other words, two Atoms of a like nature repel each other and will not unite according to this law; but two or more Atoms of an unlike nature will attract each other. Therefore, if the Atoms on Plate No. 1 were marbles and were thrown together on a table, they would move toward each other and form into as close and solid a unit as possible. But if you added a few more marbles which were duplicates of those already on the table, they would be pushed away by those which were like them and pulled toward those which were unlike.

Another feature of this law is that when three, four, five, or six or more of these Atoms are put near each other, again like marbles on the table, they will unite and form, and these forms are based on the triangle, square, and circle, or a combination of them. Note these two features of the law in the following examples of atomic combinations:

No. 39. 1 Atom of Ammonia, composed of 1 of Azote and 1 of Hydrogen 6

No. 41. 1 Atom of Nitrous Gas, composed of 1 of Azote and 1 of Oxygen 12

No. 42. 1 Atom of Olefiant Gas, composed of 1 of Carbon and 1 of Hydrogen 6

No. 43. 1 Atom of Carbonic Oxide, composed of 1 of Carbon and 1 of Oxygen 12

The above five examples are of two Atoms united to form another element. Each thus formed has an Atomic "weight" equal to the total of the two Atoms composing it, as shown by the number at the end of the line.

You will note that the two Atoms in these examples hug each other closely. Whether one is above the other or beside the other in a diagram is unimportant; but always will two unlike Atoms touch each other in some relative position.

TERNARY ELEMENTS

Now we come to another form of elements—that composed of two Atoms of one kind and one of another kind. In such form, three Atoms composing an element, the three Atoms cannot be of the same nature, because in that case they would not unite, but would repel each other according to the law of like repelling like. Therefore, when an element is composed of three Atoms, two of them are alike and one is unlike, and THE UNLIKE ATOM IS ALWAYS IN THE CENTER. The reason is easily explained in this way. In the first place, the two similar Atoms, in their repulsion of each other, will separate as far as possible. That permits the dissimilar Atom to come in between them, for both of the similar ones are attracted to this single Atom, which, in turn, is attracted to them. Therefore, the single dissimilar Atom pulls the other two closely to it, while they try to push each other away. In this manner the two similar Atoms would be on the opposite sides. This is plainly shown in the diagrams Nos. 44, 45, 46, and 47 of Plate 1.

The diagrams represent elements as follows:

No. 44. 1 Atom of Nitrous Oxide, composed of 2 of Azote and 1 of Oxygen.......... 17
No. 45. 1 Atom of Nitric Acid, composed of 1 of Azote and 2 of Oxygen 19
No. 46. 1 Atom of Carbonic Acid, composed of 1 of Carbon and 2 of Oxygen 19
No. 47. 1 Atom of Carburetted Hydrogen, composed of 1 of Carbon and 2 of Hydrogen.......... 7

In each case of the above four Ternary elements, the "weight" of the element is given at the end of the line. It will be noticed that two of them, while totally different in nature, have the same "weight." Such an inconsistency may be difficult for science to understand or explain.

QUATERNARY ELEMENTS

Now we come to those elements composed of four primary Atoms. In fact, the four examples of quaternary elements given on Plate 1 are molecules composed of several Atoms.

First, note the manner in which these Atoms unite when there are three of one kind and one of an unlike kind. Here is another beautiful example of like attracting unlike and repelling like. Take No. 48, for instance: the unlike Atom remains in the center while the other three Atoms arrange themselves in perfect order around the unlike Atom. Each of the three outside Atoms is attracted equally by the unlike Atom in the center. That makes them hug, so to speak, the centre Atom as closely as possible, all the while pushing the other like Atoms away. Because each of the three outside Atoms pushes the other away from it, they keep equidistant, and the space between each of these three is always as mathematically equal as though it had been placed in its position by some carefully adjusted instrument—in fact more perfectly posited in this regard than any system of measurement we know of could do it.

Another law, demonstrated by this attraction and repulsion between Atoms, is that when there are more of one kind than of another, as in Nos. 48, 49, 50, and 51, the greater number of like Atoms will be on the outside.

Also, please note that four Atoms arranged in this way make the form of a triangle; thus the triangle on the "material plane, is used to indicate quaternary elements as shown before the word "quaternary" on Plate 1. Some of the most interesting and profound problems of chemistry are solved through a study of the composition of the quaternary elements, and this is what Dalton referred to many times when he said, as do many Rosicrucians in their works in chemistry, that he was "busy with triangles."

No. 48 is a molecule of Oxynitric Acid, composed of 1 Atom of Azote and 3 of Oxygen.. 26

No. 49 is a molecule of Sulphuric Acid, composed of 1 Atom of Sulphur and 3 of Oxygen.. 34

No. 50 is a molecule of Sulphuretted Hydrogen, composed of 1 Atom of Sulphur and 3 of Hydrogen.................. 16

No. 51 is a molecule of Alcohol, composed of 1 Atom of Hydrogen and 3 of Carbon.. 16

PLATE TWO

Let us examine now two other forms of elements, called Quinquenary and Sextenary. These are illustrated as Nos. 52 and 53.

In No. 52 we have a very different arrangement of five atoms. Three of them are alike and two of them are unlike. In this element, called Nitrous Acid, we have a combination of Nitric Acid and Nitrous Gas. By referring to No. 41 on Plate 1, you will find that Nitrous Gas is composed of one Atom of Azote and one Atom of Oxygen. The two combined make Nitrous Gas. By referring to No. 45 on Plate 1, you will also see that Nitric Acid is composed of one Atom of Azote and two Atoms of Oxygen. In other words, the difference between Nitric Acid and Nitrous Gas is a difference of one more Atom of Oxygen in the Acid. But to turn these into a Nitrous ACID we must combine the Nitric Acid and the Nitrous Gas. That means combining the five Atoms. Illustration No. 52 shows the only possible way in which these five Atoms of two different natures would combine. Four would unite, as shown, with the fifth Atom clinging to one side of the Azote Atom as far away from its companion Azote Atoms as it could be without severing the attraction that exists between it and the Oxygen Atom. The relation of these five Atoms to each other and the form they thus take illustrates one of Dalton's principles in his law of proportions—that in combining, the Atoms adhere to the law of the triangle, the square, or a combination of them. For in No. 52 we can see both the triangle and the square. Its "weight" is 31.

In No. 53 a different problem is presented. Here we have six Atoms of three different natures. It represents a molecule of Acetous Acid and is composed of two Atoms of Carbon and two of Water. But whereas Carbon is composed of only one simple element, water is composed of two Atoms (one of Hydrogen and one of Oxygen). The manner in which these six Atoms arrange is interesting, yet in no other way could these six be placed and still maintain their attraction and repulsion. The relative "weight" of this is 26.

And now we come to Septenary elements. No. 54 represents Nitrate of Ammonia. It is composed of one Atom of Nitric Acid, one of Ammonia, and one of Water, as will be seen by referring to Nos. 45, 39, and 38 of Plate 1. Its relative "weight" is 33. No. 55

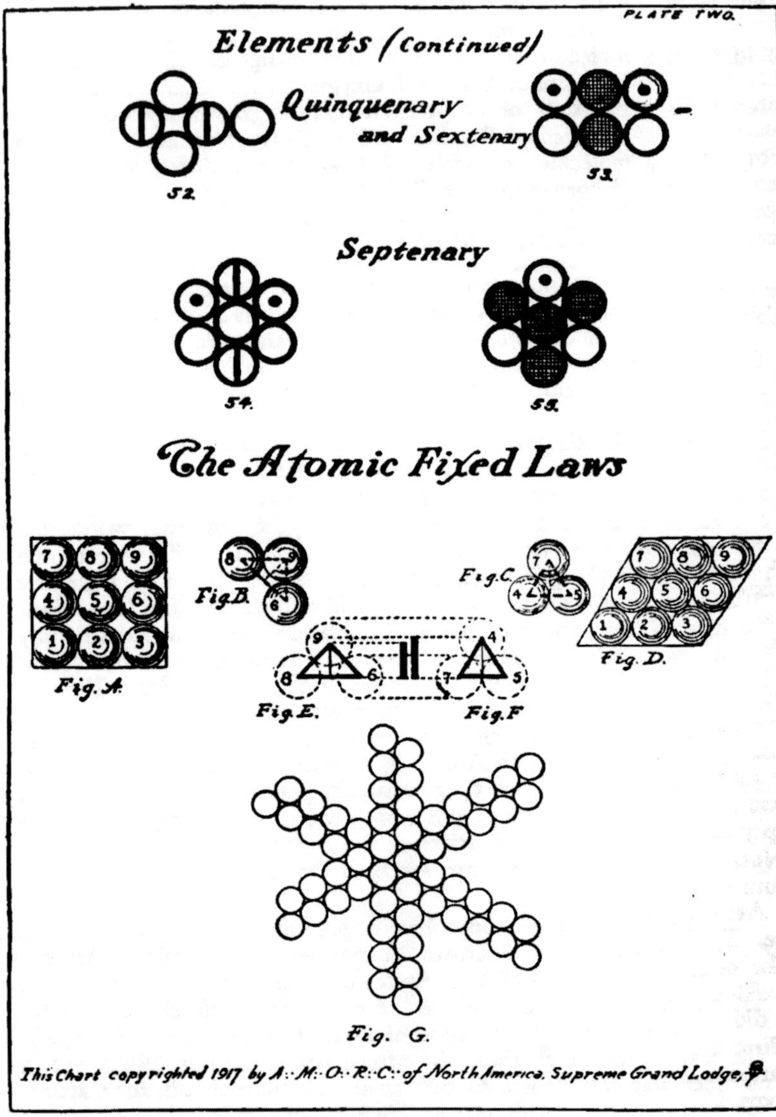
PLATE TWO.
Elements (continued)
Quinquenary
and Sextenary
52
53
Septenary
54
55
The Atomic Fixed Laws
Fig. A.
Fig. B.
Fig. C.
Fig. D.
Fig. E.
Fig. F
Fig. G.
This Chart copyrighted 1917 by A∴M∴O∴R∴C∴ of North America. Supreme Grand Lodge,

Plate 2

represents Sugar and is composed of one of Alcohol and one of Carbonic Acid as shown in Nos. 51 and 46 of Plate 1. Its relative "weight" is 35.

Both of these elements are composed of seven Atoms and in form they present the outline of a circle inside of which are three triangles, the center Atom being the vertex of each of the three triangles. Thus again we find the law of the triangle, square, and circle being demonstrated.

For the purpose of diagrammatic illustration the Atoms will be considered as perfect spheres. That they may at times be of different shapes is due to the fact that they may be compressed or flattened in places by contact with other Atoms. Of late, science has considered the Atom as like unto a rubber ball, which may be pressed so that it loses its perfectly spherical shape, but always retains a certain resemblance to a sphere.

The spherical shape of atoms accounts for much that could not be accounted for in any other way, and the shape also makes for many conditions and phenomena in chemistry and physics of a very interesting nature. In fact, the spherical form of Atoms, as well as their chemical nature, enables them to manifest in many different ways.

This latter fact Dalton illustrated by the diagrams shown on Plate 2.

Here we have in Figure A nine Atoms placed within a square so that we may study their relation one to another. We notice that by having the Atoms touch each other, as they do in this diagram, Atom No. 5 makes contact only with four other Atoms—Nos. 2, 4, 6, and 8. We note also that there is a considerable space between these nine Atoms.

If we consider each layer of Atoms in this square space as being a stratum, we have three strata in Figure A. Between these layers or strata we have the large opening or "air" space. This means that in any such arrangement of Atoms there will be a great amount of space between the Atoms, and this space is occupied by what we shall simply call "air."

Now if we take these nine Atoms and arrange them as shown in Figure D, we change the square to a rhomboidal form. By arranging the Atoms in this wise we do several things of considerable importance. Dr. Dalton, in his papers to the scientific bodies of his day, spoke only of one or two results attained by this arrangement of the Atoms, but I will speak of another result which he knew well but did not fully illustrate.

First of all it will be seen, as Dr. Dalton pointed out, that this arrangement of the Atoms causes Atom No. 5 to contact SIX other Atoms instead of only four as shown in Figure A. Thus, Atom No. 5 is in contact with Atoms Nos. 2, 3, 4, 6, 7, and 8. Furthermore, Atoms Nos. 2, 4, 6, and 8 now touch one another, whereas they did not in the arrangement in Figure A.

This different arrangement makes every Atom in the composition of anything a center of a mystic group, so to speak. For every such center Atom will have six other Atoms surrounding it, each making contact with the other. Thus each group consists of seven Atoms—the center one and its six companions. This is why such a group is called a mystic group. And the true power of such a group is usually determined by the nature of the center Atom. The result of such grouping, in a truly mystical way, is explained later on.

But the principal point which Dr. Dalton wished to bring forth by such an illustration of grouping was this: That when the Atoms were so arranged the amount of air space between the Atoms was reduced. By examining the grouping in Figure D one will see that there is considerably less air space between the Atoms than between those in Figure A. He held, and it has been demonstrated as true, that when the air is extracted from the matter by a rearrangement of its Atoms, the change or new condition is brought about by this law.

The most interesting point, however, which Dr. Dalton touched upon, though did not fully explain in his lifetime, is illustrated in Figures B, C, E, and F.

By changing the arrangement of Atoms as shown in Figure D, the strata of the Atoms are altered in a manner clearly shown by the diagrams. By taking any three Atoms in Figure A and grouping them in the same relation to each other as shown in Figure B, we discover another law. For example, we show Atoms numbered 6, 8, and 9 of Figure A. In Figure B we see these three Atoms in precisely the same relation to each other as they occupied in Figure A.

Now by drawing a line from the center of each of these three Atoms to the center of the others we have a triangle. If we consider the one Atom (No. 9) as resting upon two others, as constitutes a building of layers, or strata, we find in Figure E that the triangle has a certain height indicated by the dotted lines. We also note that the triangle is not an equilateral triangle. (And this is important to all Rosicrucians.)

If, on the other hand, we take three Atoms from the grouping in Figure D, we find another law. By taking any three Atoms, or in this example by taking Atoms numbered 4, 5, and 7, and placing them in the same relation to each other as they are in Figure D, we find that a triangle can be formed by drawing a line from the centers of the Atoms. But in this case the triangle is an equilateral triangle.

By comparing these two triangles as shown in Figures E and F we see that they have different heights (indicated by the dotted lines) and the height is shown by the two heavy lines in the center of the diagram.

This, says Dr. Dalton, shows the height of the strata of each group of Atoms.

He also calls attention to the fact that in the grouping shown in Figure D, the angles are always 60 or 120 degrees—a fact to be kept in mind by all Rosicrucians.

Therefore, we see that when the law of the triangle (the equilateral triangle) demonstrates or manifests itself in the composition of matter or the arrangement of Atoms, we have an entirely different and important demonstration of the Atomic laws.

The grouping in Figure D represents the grouping of Atoms in the formation of ice. By this arrangement of the Atoms the air space or "air" is eliminated to a great extent and thereby the liquid becomes more solid. This is accounted for by the two facts that since the Atoms fit more closely together the matter becomes more solid, and that the elimination of air takes from the water a great amount of its elasticity.

To further demonstrate the grouping of Atoms in this fashion in the formation of ice, Dr. Dalton points to another interesting fact. He calls your attention to the formation of ice. He asks you to note that when water freezes by sudden congelation (that is, when water is brought into an atmosphere below the freezing point and is suddenly chilled) certain forms of crystals or spiculae can be seen upon the surface of the water. Figure G shows one of these spiculae and it illustrates two points: That the Atoms are co-related to one another as shown in Figures C and D, and that the angles are very significant.

An examination of the designs shown in snowflakes will teach one many interesting facts regarding the laws embraced in the foregoing statements.

COMBINING ATOMS

Plate Three

Let us turn our attention to Plate Three. Here Dr. Dalton illustrates many other laws of the Atoms.

To understand what Dr. Dalton meant to convey—and to make plain to our Rosicrucian readers the laws they have been studying —we must bear in mind that all Atoms have a certain aura around them due to their vibrations. Considering the nature of an Atom and its composition from the Rosicrucian point of view, it is not surprising that we should speak of an aura surrounding an Atom. This aura of influence or magnetic quality has been recognized by scientists many years. David A. Wells wrote in his book issued in 1863 that Atoms possessed a *certain polarity* which gave them a certain magnetic force, and he said that "the action of these forces compels the Atom, in assuming its place in a crystal (of matter) to maintain a certain direction as respects the contiguous particles" (or atoms).

In Figures 1, 2, and 3, of Plate Three, Dalton shows Atoms in groups to form certain elastic fluids. Figure 1 shows Atoms forming Hydrogen. Figure 2 shows Nitrous Gas. Figure 3 shows Carbonic Acid. What he intends to show is that the aura from the Atoms composing these three causes the atmosphere around the Atoms to be charged with certain emanations from the Atoms, and that this atmosphere and the vibrations in it cause the composition or element

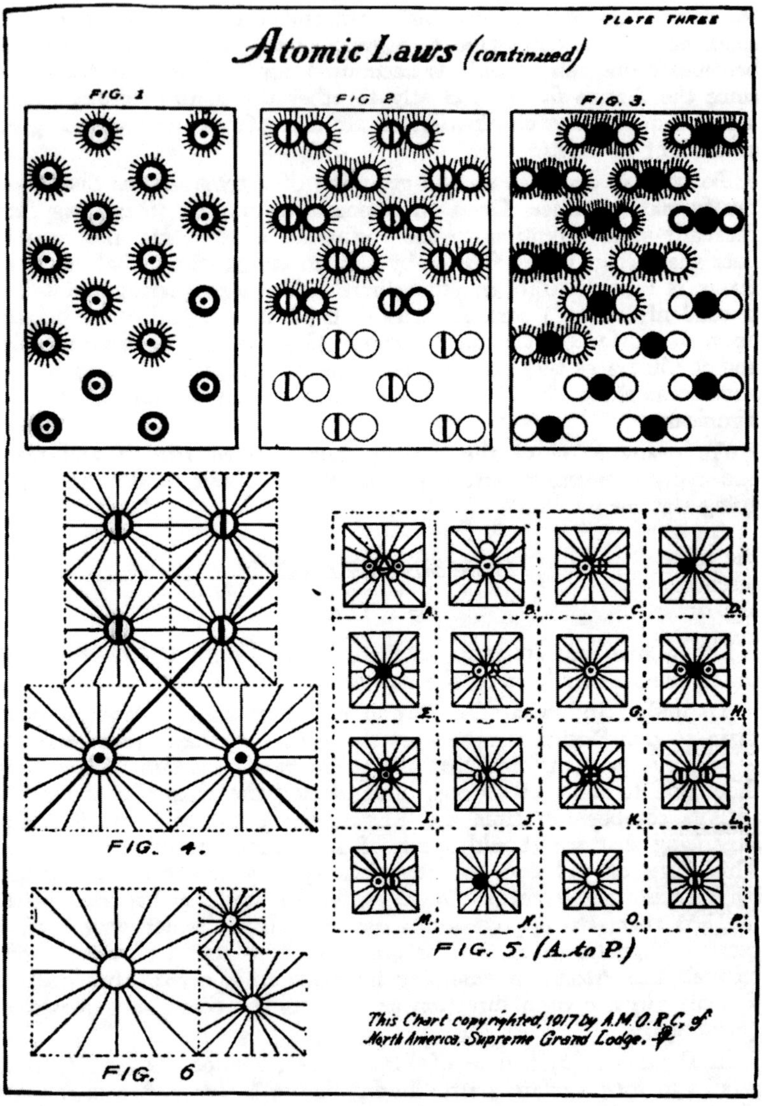
PLATE THREE
Atomic Laws (continued)
FIG. 1
FIG 2
FIG. 3.
A.
B.
C.
D.
E.
F.
G.
H.
I.
J.
K.
L.
M.
N.
O.
P.
FIG. 4.
FIG. 5. (A. to P.)
FIG. 6
This Chart copyrighted, 1917 by A.M.O.R.C. of North America, Supreme Grand Lodge.

Plate 3

formed by the Atoms to be "elastic." In this way, he says, are elastic fluids or gases formed.

In Figure 4, however, we come to one of the most interesting diagrams and illustrations of the Atomic law. In fact, the point which Dalton tried to present in a veiled way has not been fully offered to the workers in chemistry before; and it is only with the hope that some chemists or workers in chemistry may find in my more or less veiled explanations some help for their problems that I venture to elucidate one of our Rosicrucian laws.

Assuming (and this may not be an assumption at all) that the Atoms do have certain rays emanating from them, we can best illustrate these emanations by making them diagrammatic. Therefore, we will consider that the rays issue from the center of each Atom and go outward from the Atom in straight lines. For a very good reason we will assume that these rays from an aura around each Atom, and that this aura is in the form of a square. (I must repeat that this MAY NOT BE an assumption at all.) We find, however, that there are four emanations from each Atom which form diagonal lines in the square aura surrounding each atom. In other words, there are four definite rays from each Atom, stronger than the others, which leave the Atom at equidistant points, and these rays are called the POTENTIAL RAYS.

Another point to be remembered is that all Atoms are not of the same size. Figure 5 on Plate 2 shows a number of Atoms representing sixteen different elastic fluids, from A to P. The Atoms are drawn in their proportion to one another, and the square of aura surrounding each Atom is drawn in proportion to the size of the Atoms. Thus we can plainly see by the size of the square aura the difference in the aura of each of these sixteen Atoms.

Behind all the laws known to chemistry for the combining of certain Atoms, or the mixing of certain elements, is this law: That the rays from each Atom must meet and find harmony with the rays of other Atoms if they would blend or unite. This law is illustrated in Figure 4 on Plate 3. There are four Atoms of Azote (Nitrogen) in their square auras at the top of Figure 4. You will note that the rays from these four Atoms, forming the square auras around each Atom, unite or meet.

Because these rays join in this manner the four Atoms form a united element. You will further note that the POTENTIAL RAYS of each of the four Atoms meet and thereby form diagonals in the large square composed of the four smaller squares. At the bottom of the four squares of Azote there are two squares containing Atoms of Hydrogen. These latter squares are larger than the others above them, because the Atoms and auras of Hydrogen are larger than the Atoms and auras of Azote, as shown in the diagrams G and P in Figure 5.

However, the Atoms of Hydrogen unite well with the Atoms of Azote because the diagonal rays, or the POTENTIAL RAYS of all the Atoms in the combination of Figure 4, meet and unite perfectly. This is shown in Figure 4 by the HEAVY DARK diagonal lines running through four squares and which represent the Potential Rays.

To make this more clear, Figure 6 has three different Atoms and their auras enlarged. Here we find that because of the difference of the rays forming the auras of those Atoms, not one of the rays in one of those Atoms or auras meets with others. No matter how you may place or try to unite those three Atoms—whatever they may be—they will not make the perfect association desired.

By this we learn that when the potential rays of Atoms unite there is one form of mixture; and that when all the rays meet (as in the upper four squares of Figure 4) there is another mixture of a purer and unmodified nature. And—when none of the rays unite we find that the Atoms do not give a true mixture of any kind.

Thus we see that theoretically, at least, there is a great deal to study and learn about the potentiality of Atoms and the emanations of Atoms; for in the potentiality and in the rays lie the secret of the combination of Atoms and the formation of matter.

This, then, is the great work of Rosicrucian chemistry, and in our Order, as in no other teaching, are laws found making all those things plain which I have been able to refer to only in a veiled way in this interpretation of the work and discoveries of Dr. John Dalton.

CONCLUSION

Members are urged to study this carefully. Reference to any standard text book on chemistry will be helpful, but where contradictions appear, that is, where there are contradictions in the text books in regard to what is published in this article, you will naturally remember that such contradictions are errors which we are striving to overcome by establishing certain truths.

SIR FRANCIS LORD BACON

Baron Verulam, Viscount St. Albans, Eminent Imperator of the Rosicrucians

Because of the increasing interest in the life and works of Francis Bacon, we introduce his portrait (on page 9) and a few brief remarks about him.

He was born in London on January 22, 1561. He attained very high positions in the British government, and was a secret representative of many high officials, and was often forced to assume the responsibility and guilt of those whose reputations he would save. For years those unfriendly to him believed the evil that was said of him, and which he cared not to deny in order to save further explanations. But within the past fifty years certain unquestioned records have proved the Rosicrucian contention that he was one of England's noble men—in heart, soul, and deed.

As a pioneer in the revolution of methods of education he stands without a peer, and the effect of his "secret society" upon mankind in Europe was ever a puzzle to the multitude until it was discovered that the secret society to which much of his correspondence seemed to refer, was the Rosicrucian Order. Then it was found that some of his literary co-workers were his official emissaries or deputies of the Rosicrucian Order, making periodical journeys to foreign jurisdictions.

It was Bacon, who, as Imperator of the Rosicrucian Order, wrote the now internationally famous book called the *Fama Fraternitatis,* and to which the fictitious name of Christian Rosenkreutz was signed —meaning Rosy Cross. Through the discovery of the secret Code in this manuscript, and the several acknowledged writings on secret codes, it was further discovered that Bacon wrote the famous plays attributed to the one who produced them, Shakespeare. An examination of the pages of the original plays shows not only the name and titles of Bacon concealed in the strangely arranged lines of text, but the Rosicrucian and Bacon symbols are found as water-marks in the paper. The writing and production of plays at that time was considered a low, mean, and sordid occupation, and while the "Shakespeare Plays" were of a very high type and quite different from all previous plays, the very nature of their intimate revelations would forbid the author from admitting his connection with them under penalty of having them destroyed. It was a most fortunate circumstance for civilization that Bacon conceived his wonderful plan of writing and issuing the plays under the name of the principal actor, yet preserving within their text the name of the real author.

It was Bacon who first planned the Rosicrucian invasion of America. He published a book called the New Atlantis (often referred to as "The House of Solomon") in which the whole scheme is given in fascinating symbolism. Many years later, in 1693, a specially selected army of Rosicrucians, with their families, gathered from all parts of Europe at one port, and set sail for America in their own chartered boat. They arrived at what is now Philadelphia in the early part of 1694, and established many of the first educational institutions in the United States. Their record, well preserved in the archives of this country, testifies to the magnificent influence of the Rosicrucians in the foundation of this great Republic.

Bacon's transition occurred April 9, 1626, in the very height of his Rosicrucian work and while he was making some important scientific tests.

The full-page illustration of Bacon, shown elsewhere, accompanied by many of the symbols used in reference to him, was made by our Imperator, Dr. H. Spencer Lewis, in 1919, as a frontispiece to a book he was compiling on *Bacon's Mystic Symbolism*. It has been reproduced a number of times and is drawn from the best known portrait of Bacon, with other decorations and features known so well to Rosicrucians. It is unlike any page to be found in any of Bacon's books in entire composition, but duplicating parts of many. Thus our members have an excellent souvenir of the eminent Rosicrucian Imperator of the seventeenth century.

DR. H. SPENCER LEWIS, F. R. C.

Imperator for North America, A. M. O. R. C.

The following brief biography is compiled from facts gathered from our various official publications and from official records.

Harve Spencer Lewis was born in Frenchtown, New Jersey, on November 25, 1883, at 12:38 noon (corrected, astrological time). His parents were engaged in educational work at the time and he was given a good schooling, and later brought to New York with his two brothers. He is of Welch extraction, descending from the family of Lewis whose great forbear was Sir Robert Lewis and whose other descendants included Merriweather Lewis of the famous Lewis and Clark expedition, and many others prominent in early American history.

Educated in New York City schools he united with the Methodist Church and was one of the early members of the well-known Methodist "Metropolitan Temple," of which Dr. S. Parks Cadman was the first clergyman and marvelous promoter of great good.

Devoting himself to scientific studies he also entered the art world as a profession, and in many parts of America today are paintings in oil, pastel, and water-color, as well as hundreds of pen drawings from his prolific pen. Many of these have become nationally known. Before his twenty-first year he was in charge of special art features of the New York Herald.

At about this same time he was elected President of the New York Institute for Psychical Research, and among the many able associates in his work were Ella Wheeler Wilcox and "Fra" Hubbard, founder of the Roycrofters. Both of these later assisted in the establishment of the Rosicrucian Order in America and were on the first American Council of the Order when Dr. Lewis was elected Supreme Grand Master of America.

After many years of continuous scientific and psychic research, even in the fields of wireless (radio) when this science was little known, he made his first contact with the work of the Rosicrucians through obtaining copies of the secret manuscripts of the first American Rosicrucians, who established their headquarters near Philadelphia in 1694. A member of the English Branch which sponsored the first movement in America, Mrs. Colonel May Banks Stacey,* descendant of Oliver Cromwell and the D'Arcy's of France, placed in his hands such papers as had been officially transmitted to her by the last of the first American Rosicrucians, with the Jewel and Key of authority received by her from the Grand Master of the Order in India, while an officer of the work in that country.

---

*See Portrait on Page 12.

For several years correspondence was maintained with different representatives of the foreign Jurisdictions until proper investigation could be made establishing the worthiness of Dr. Lewis to carry out the warrants then in his possession. Finally in 1909 he was directed to make his appearance before certain high officials in France. He visited Toulouse, the ancient center of the Rosicrucian international conclave, and returned from that country in possession of further authority. This, and the papers possessed by Sro. Stacey, were presented to a Committee of over a hundred American citizens and the foundation for the decreed revival of the work in America was laid, with Sro. Stacey as *Grand Matre* of the Order, and Dr. Lewis as *Supreme Grand Master.*

Since then many high honors have been conferred upon him by foreign and American societies, academies, scientific institutions and learned bodies.

His wife, Martha Morfier Lewis, a descendant of the famous French General, Morphier, was the first lady in America to cross the Threshold of the Order in the new regime, and his four children have been raised in the work; his son, Ralph M. Lewis, being the Supreme Secretary of the Order for North America.

NUMEROLOGY AND THE REAL SYSTEM

Thousands of our members inquire of us each year in regard to the various systems of Numerology, or NAME NUMBERS, now on the market in book form, and being supplemented with new and contradictory systems each month. Many of these believe that because our studies cover so many subjects we should include *Numerology*.

The more serious letters tell us that these persons have changed their names or are about to go to some considerable expense in order to change their names in accordance with the advice of some number system; others say that after having changed names for a number of years, and having experienced much confusion thereby, they find no radical change in their personal affairs. All want some helpful advice from us.

We believe that a presentation of the facts about these systems will save much trouble, time, and expense. Therefore, read carefully the following logical statements:

It is claimed that the continued *pronunciation* of certain names by ourselves, or by others in our presence, will affect our careers, our health, our psychic development, etc. It is also claimed that each letter of the alphabet has a certain number, or vibration rate, and that these vibrations affect us.

It is a mystical fact that the continued, or occasional, and proper pronunciation of certain vowel sounds, such as "Oom" or "Aum," will produce certain psychic effects, but it is stretching the point to say that because a boy bears the name *Harry*, the sound of that name, used by him or others, will cause good or bad conditions in his life.

Let us look at the matter critically. Granted that sounds of the letters, when pronounced by us or others, affect us, it becomes apparent at once that it is not due to the vibrations of the letters or their *numbers*, but to the *vowel* sounds. In other words, the sounds are important, but the letters composing the sounds are not; for the letters are *not* the true guide to the sounds.

Let us illustrate: If a person born on a certain date should now have a name that "vibrates to 12" but should have one that vibrates to 13, how will you determine the proper name?. By the numbers given to each letter? That will not do, for how can you assign the name Harry, and give 4 to the letter *a* in the name Harvey? They do not have the same vowel sound; how then can the number be alike? How will you sound the two letters Vi in Violet and Vincent? The two sounds are quite different, yet, so far as the two letters are concerned, they would have the same numbers in the Numerology systems.

All of the systems on the market today give one number to each letter of the alphabet. Let us say that the letter *o* is given the number 6 in the system we are examining. It will have to be measured by that number in all cases, whether the *o* appears in the name John or Oliver, Oscar, Otis, Orville, Dora, Doris, Louis, or Howe. And yet there are a number of distinctly different sounds to the one *o* in these names.

So we maintain that a number system based upon the assignment of numbers to the letters of the alphabet is not true and correct. If the vowel sounds have any effect, then the sounds, and not the letters should be numbered. There is no such system popularly distributed, and only the Rosicrucians have carefully tabulated the real numerical value of vowel sounds. But such knowledge is not published and sold for the pastime of changing names, with the consequent confusion and expense.

And what would you do with the foreign names? You may figure out the vibration numbers of the name *Madeliene* as you use it in America, but let a Frenchman pronounce it for you and you will note that the vibrations are different from those resulting from pronouncing the word in English.

We advise, on excellent grounds, that you do not change your name, but make it serve you, and at the same time bring honor and esteem to it. If there is nothing more serious afflicting your rise and progress in life than the numerical value of the letters of your Christian, or given name, then thank God that you have an unusually free and clean Path to great success and happiness.

Whatever may be your birthday, whatever may be the configuration of the aspects between the planets in your horoscope, whatever may be your hereditary traits, your Karmic debts, your given name, your phrenological bumps, you still have within you the creative, corrective power of God's consciousness, to which all these other things are slaves and over which YOUR OWN WILL has dominance. Use your Divine Heritage, direct it, give it greater expression, and make all the material handicaps stepping stones to success and power.

The Rosy Cross

Mechanically and Symbolically Formed

PART TEN

The Great White Lodge

ATTAINING PSYCHIC ILLUMINATION

and

The Rosicrucian Code of Life

A SPECIAL MANUSCRIPT PREPARED FOR THIS MANUAL BY THE IMPERATOR

ATTAINING PSYCHIC ILLUMINATION

▽ ▽ ▽

"WHEN THE STUDENT IS READY"

The question may be asked: "What is the ultimate goal of Rosicrucian study and preparation?" It is an old question that has been answered thousands of times in each country by the attainment that has come into the lives of the most devoted students.

It is well that the Neophyte and the Adept alike should be reminded again of the real purpose of the work we are engaged in and the reward that may be theirs when found ready and worthy.

There is a very old and well-founded injunction that "when the student is ready the Master will appear!" This has been very greatly misunderstood and is used by thousands for refusing to unite with any school or organization, preferring to "wait until the personal teacher manifests."

The injunction distinctly says: "When the student is ready, the Master will appear!" What is meant by being *ready?* Surely it is not merely a matter of time! It must mean precisely what thousands have found it to mean: When the student is ready *through preparation and worthiness.*

This leaves the matter very clearly in the hands of each student. He may prepare slowly through selected reading, through long hours of meditation covering many hours, or through the occasional attendance at lectures and discourses. If time is of no consequence, then a student may wait until the close of this incarnation or even another, for the appearance of that Master who is to be *his personal teacher.*

Here again we may ask: What Master, what teacher? Surely not an earthly Master, for such do not require the preparation and development necessary for Cosmic illumination. The sincere student who truly prepares himself and becomes worthy of the personal instruction from a Master soon develops beyond the point where any earthly Master would satisfy. Only a Cosmic Master would meet the requirements of one who is ready.

HOW TO PREPARE

How, then, shall the student prepare most efficiently and with the utmost economy of time? This, too, is an age-old question, asked in the mystery schools of Egypt, as it is asked in the arcane schools of our Order today.

There is but one answer: By taking the preliminary and graded steps in the earthly schools of the Masters and attaining the degrees of readiness through *directed preparation.* Hence the establishment of the arcane schools in all lands; hence the Great Work allotted to them by the Masters.

Where are the Great Masters and how are they contacted? Here we find more difficulty in answering, not because our knowledge is meager, but because language is inadequate to express the sublime facts. There are some conditions of Cosmic life which even the language of the Shakespeare gems could not describe. We may comprehend, we may apprehend, and there may come to us, through words, some faint conception of the beauty, magnificence, and divinity of the Cosmic scheme, but never a complete realization until we have made the personal contact and found Cosmic Illumination.

Know, then, that there is a wonderful union or assembly of Master Minds, Master Personalities, which constitute the *Holy Assembly* of the Cosmic. One of these masterful characters, Kut-Hu-Mi, the Illustrious, is shown in a portrait in another part of the Manual. He was one of the two Masters referred to by the ancient mystics and made somewhat known to advanced Theosophists by the late Mme. Helen P. Blavatsky, who was one of the personal students of the Master.

THE GREAT MASTERS

The Master K-H-M is *Deputy Grand Master* of the Great White Lodge of the Great White Brotherhood. He was at one time known on earth as Thutmose III of Egypt, and at one time resided at Lake Moeris (Morias). He was referred to in the Zend-Avesta as the *Illuminator* and was also known in Egypt as the Kroomata (Kai-Ra-Au-Meta) from which comes our Rosicrucian word used in our rituals and salutations: CROMAAT. (It is interesting to note that if we take the initials of the title of our Order: *The Ancient and Mystical Order Rosae Crucis,* and reverse them, we have CROMAAT.)

The Master K-H-M (often called "K-H") passed through a number of reincarnations and was an important character on this earth many times, and has lived for over a hundred and forty years in each incarnation. At the present time he abides on the earth plane again and is at a secret monastery and temple near Kichingargha, called variously Kichinjirgha, Kichi-jirg-jargha, or Parcha-jarg-hatba by the Tibetans and Sikinese.

THE GREAT WHITE LODGE

There are a number of others, twelve in all, who compose the *Holy Assembly* of the Great White Lodge; some are on the Cosmic Plane, carrying on their great work while awaiting their next incarnation, and some are on this earth plane directing the physical work while developing for the Cosmic Plane period.

Under their care a certain group of high Initiates are prepared in each incarnation for still higher work in a next incarnation, and some of these are assigned the duty, the service, *and the real labor,* of maintaining the positions of Imperators, Magi, and Hierophants in the several branches of the Great White Brotherhood organizations, of which the Rosicrucian Order is the highest. These Imperators, Magi, and Hierophants in various lands compose the *Great White Lodge* under the personal direction of the twelve Masters referred to above.

The Great White *Brotherhood,* on the other hand, is the school, or *Fraternity,* of the Great White Lodge, and into this *invisible* Brotherhood of *visible* members every true student on the Path prepares for admission.

COSMIC INITIATION

Hence, the real preparation of which we were speaking is for the purpose of ultimately being admitted, by Cosmic Initiation, into the Great White Brotherhood, that herein the Master will appear to the student who is ready, take him under personal instruction, and lead him (or her) on to higher development, where, some day, Mastership in the Great White Brotherhood is certain, and assignment to service as Imperator, Magi, or Hierophant in some phase of the work on earth will then bring affiliation with the Great White Lodge.

How is such instruction given by the personal Master? It is, truly, personal, and is given through the *media* of the Cosmic. In other words, it becomes what is generally referred to as *Cosmic Illumination,* or *Cosmic Consciousness,* for at certain hours, days, or weeks of one's life one becomes *conscious* of some new and astounding knowledge, often with, and sometimes without, being aware of the presence or contact of the personal teacher.

In other words, the student, who attains membership in the Great White Brotherhood, after due preparation and real worthiness, first discovers this by becoming conscious of having passed through a series of events constituting a true *Initiation.* Often these occur during the night, or while on periods of rest and meditation in the mountains or valleys, away from active worldly affairs. This consciousness is accompanied by an influx of Divine Apprehension and Spiritual Awakening, affecting even the physical body to such an extent as to bring about a real re-birth of the body with rejuvenation, increased vigor, restored functioning in organs and parts that were tired, depleted, or subnormal.

COSMIC CONSCIOUSNESS

This is followed by a sudden increase in the functioning of a sense which is mistakenly called *intuition* at the time, for it seems to be like unto the intuitive faculty that was being highly developed during the earlier stages of preparation leading up to the original Initiation into the Great White Brotherhood. It is not intuition, however, but

Cosmic Consciousness of events now occurring and decreed to occur in the near future. It is *knowledge*, and not a prophetic impression. Then follows guiding instructions and definite knowledge of laws and principles, facts, and actualities, in accordance with the needs and desires of the member. From then on the member attends the earthly Lodge as a worker to help others who are on the Path, and to assist in the Great Work; but he receives no instruction through an earthly Master by means of books, lectures, papers, or diagrams.

This is why we urge those who have gone fairly high in the development of their psychic bodies, and have attained certain knowledge and powers in our Order, to maintain a close contact with the Order, with its Masters, and its Imperator, for through such contact these members may find at any time, unannounced and unexpected, the *Initiation* that will take them into the Great White Brotherhood. The last three grades of study and preparation in the Rosicrucian Order are designed especially to prepare the members, in the most minute and varied details, for the *ultimate goal.*

What, then, do we suggest to our members to aid them in attaining this ultimate goal?

That, above all else, they be loyal and devoted to the ideals of Rosicrucianism, and *maintain every physical contact* with the physical organization known as AMORC in North America and by similar names in other lands.

BENEFITS OF OUR LESSONS

The mere intellectual study and comprehension of the specialized lectures and lessons issued to student members is not sufficient. Of and by itself, such study is but a third of the work of preparation leading to *readiness* and *worthiness.* The lessons are designed to accomplish two things:

- (a) Train the brain and augment the knowledge of the mind in regard to fundamental laws and principles leading up to a comprehension of the higher laws;
- (b) Give and suggest certain experiments and tests which will consciously and unconsciously develop certain psychic centers in the member that will quicken his psychic powers and abilities for more complete Mastership and control of natural forces.

Many members look upon the lectures and lessons as if they were intended to cover only the *first* of the above purposes. To them the lessons in all the grades are like unto discourses in philosophy or metaphysics, often seeming to be simple and inconsequential. It is difficult, indeed, to make them appreciate the fact that unless the various exercises and tests are performed each week, or even each day, for a few minutes, there will be very little psychic development accompanying the comprehension of the lessons, and, of course, no real progress made.

On the other hand, another most difficult point to make plain to many members and students is that *not all* of the psychic development and awakening of psychic centers will be manifest or objectively conscious to the student. To think that it should be is to believe that all of the functioning of the psychic body should make itself continuously or periodically known to the objective mind. This will appear unreasonable when one stops to consider that not one-thousandth of the functioning of the parts of the objective, physical body is realized by the objective mind. Is one conscious of the functioning of the kidneys, the spleen, the pancreas, the brain, the air chambers of the lungs, or of the solar plexus, or the plexus around the aortic arch of the heart, or a thousand other places?

Very often the most devoted student and the most regular applicant of the tests and experiments feels that he is making little progress because he senses no particular development from within. He is apt to become discouraged, knowing that he is familiar with each law and principle he has studied, with no apparent manifestation of *unusual abilities*. But if he is persistent, as well as patient, there comes a time when, having need of the laws in a truly practical way, and not merely in a test, he finds a sudden impulse to power, a sudden quickening of a faculty—and there is a marvelous demonstration! Or he may go back over some experiment that puzzled him for weeks and find, now, a manifestation that was impossible before.

Such students are always urged to continue their studies and diligently test each principle, try each experiment, and apply each law in the way described in the weekly lesson. They should give each lesson a full week's trial, and then if no success has been attained—or not such success as was expected—go on with the next lesson as though success had been attained. Try the new lesson diligently, and then the next lesson, and so on. After several months have passed, if the student goes back and reviews some of the experiments which were not successful, he will find that he has some slight or large degree of success. Such reviewing does not interfere with the study and practice of the new lesson and does not delay, but assists, the progress.

PSYCHIC DEVELOPMENT

The lessons are all arranged so that the exercises lap over one another in affecting certain psychic centers. Three different exercises in three successive weekly lessons may appear to be unrelated, yet each of them may pertain to the same end in view; and by going on to the second or third one, when the others did not show any success, it will aid in continuing the development started by the first.

For it must be kept in mind that the exercises and experiments DO start certain degrees of development each time they are tried, whether a successful issue to the experiment is manifest or not. Once a serious application of a law is made, an awakening of some center results, and four or five applications in one week for the same purpose will start a process of development that may not be realized by the outer-self, but will continue for weeks and months.

Therefore, to repeat, the mere study of the lessons, as one would read a book of law to memorize the principles, is *not* sufficient for psychic development. And—psychic development requires TIME in each human being, more or less according to the stage of development when the study is started. We come into each incarnation at a point in psychic development where we left off in the process at the time of transition in the previous incarnation. While the soul and psychic self are on the Psychic Plane awaiting reincarnation, certain work is being accomplished and certain knowledge attained; but that phase of psychic development which is capable of manifestation while in the human body must be developed on the earth plane; and this ceases, to some degree, while on the Cosmic Plane. Therefore, not all of us are born alike in Psychic Development; some will have certain experiences early in the lesson work, and some will have them a little later. But when those who have had to wait begin to manifest, the process is rapid and wonderfully satisfactory. (Right here, to anticipate any questions which may be sent to us by members, let us say that it is impossible for the Officers of the Order to tell any member *when* she or he may expect to have certain manifestations, or to what degree a member is developed psychically before being able to make any manifestation of his development. After development has started to manifest and the member can apply the development, it is a simple matter for the member, and others equally developed, to sense the development and its degree.)

PROGRESS AND DELAYS

The most rapid development is made by the student who is least concerned, during the first few grades of study, about his or her psychic status. Careful study of the lecture for an hour on the night of the weekly lesson, and a few minutes' meditation on it each day, at a convenient time, plus an occasional test of any exercise, will do more for the new student (or the old student who is starting over) than anything else.

Previous studies and beliefs are the greatest source of trouble. Members who have studied Theosophy, New Thought, Christian Science, Yogi Philosophy, or Practical Psychology for one year, two years, or five years—as is often the case—believe that they should see some special good coming from the Rosicrucian teachings after ten weeks of study. They attempt to compare the knowledge gained through our teachings in ten weeks with what they have learned in five years from other systems—always deciding that they are receiving very little from us in comparison to what they *know*. In truth, they should compare what we give them with what they *believe*. It is necessary to take all these *beliefs* out of their minds before we can have them start on our work, unhampered by previous doctrines, theories, and speculative dogmas.

Attainment of some success in psychic matters through the teachings in other systems does not indicate any special preparedness for the Rosicrucian work. Very often we hear the remark made: "Before I took up your Rosicrucian teachings and exercises I had visions that were prophetic, could at times see other persons at a distance, and make them sense me, and could even heal by laying my hands on others; but now all of these things have stopped, and I find I have gone backward in my development. What is wrong?" Without being unkind in our intentions we say to these persons: "Yes, and you may be able to play several pieces of music quite well on the piano without knowing anything of music, and after taking up the study of music for a while you will find you cannot play the old pieces at all. But would this indicate that you had gone backward in your talent?"

CONTROLLING PSYCHIC MANIFESTATIONS

Many persons do have unusual experiences of a psychic nature before they ever take up any course of *practical*, psychic development. This is because they attained some degree of development in a previous incarnation and those faculties are striving to manifest, and DO MANIFEST AT TIMES, but without *control* and *direction* by the person. What must be done is to learn how to control and direct the faculties and develop them to a more perfect state of functioning. To do this, the spasmodic action of these faculties must cease for a time; and nature stops them until the time comes to use them UNDER CONTROL after the laws and principles have been learned.

So our members are guided and directed in their individual development. And, in addition to the study and practice of the lessons, the one who is truly on the Path will give the utmost of devotion to the Order, to assist it and its other members, that the Masters may be helped by the very ones who will later on seek help and guidance from the Masters.

SPECIAL HELP IN DEVELOPMENT

Always ready to render some service to the Order, through the Order, or *because* of the Order, is a form of devotion that pays each member the greatest dividends in development; for by such service he obligates the Order and the Cosmic to him, and from the Cosmic he can expect compensation. That is why the Keynote of the Rosicrucian Order is SERVICE. All through the graded work in the Temples of our Order the student is impressed with the fact that SERVICE is the duty he owes to it and all mankind.

Few new members realize, of course, the many ramifications of the Rosicrucian Order, and in its public literature it says very little of this phase of its Great Work. But it is a fact that not only has AMORC in North America, for instance, three or four very definite associate organizations under its direction, but it has twelve definite avenues of service and labor in behalf of its members, and about the same number in behalf of mankind generally. All of these activities—often carried on to a high degree without being known except to a few hundred of America's foremost newspaper editors, scientists, judges, lawyers, physicians, and educators—require trained experts to do the work in secret, funds to meet emergencies, secretaries to keep records, and space for the preservation of the work in our national organization.

Perhaps one of the greatest services rendered to our members is through the personal correspondence to and from Headquarters. Do our members ever think of the nature of that correspondence and the cost—the tremendous cost—to maintain such a service department? Take, for instance, the students of a law course issued by a correspondence school of law or by a college in personal instruction. The students of such a course must confine their written or oral questions to points of study in their LAW lessons, and cannot expect answers and detailed help on other subjects. Or take students of an engineering course; they must confine their questions and appeals for help to matters strictly limited to the subject of the phase of engineering they are studying at the time.

But take the students of our work! They are not studying any one definite course of instruction, nor are they striving to attain mastership in just one direction. And we, as directors of their studies, friends of their interests, Brothers of the whole membership, and officers of a very broad and inclusive system of humanitarian activity, must be prepared to assist in thousands of ways. The interests of our members are our interests; their personal problems are our problems; their success and failures are ours also. The father of a family may be the only one in that family who is a member of our Order, but the problems of that family and each member in it become of vital interest to us as to him. Were he a student of a law or engineering course, the school from which he receives his instruction could not be expected to show any interest in the members of his family. Not so with us! Likewise his business affairs, his health, his social affairs—all these are of importance to him in his progress through life and MUST, therefore, be of interest to us.

Here is where the correspondence department, the welfare department, and the specialized directors of certain branches of our work render the great SERVICE which has made the Rosicrucian Order famous as a practical institution of real benefit to its members.

LOSING PSYCHIC CONTACT

When a member, for any reason, voluntarily closes his contact with the Order, or suspends his affiliation for a short period, through a mistaken idea that he has gone far enough in the work for the time being, he automatically closes the door to the most important part of the Order's benefits. He may suspend his studies for a time because of traveling, but such circumstances make the average member realize the need for *close contact* with the Order, and they never permit their membership in the Order to lapse for one hour.

It may be true with some organizations that "once a member, always a member." That may be so in the sense that once initiated and in possession of the secret passwords, grips, and signs, these things cannot be taken away by the lapsing of membership. But in the Rosicrucian Order, *membership* means CONTACT, *active affiliation.*

We have said that the simple study of the lessons, without proper practice of the exercises and tests, does not constitute proper studentship. We may add that the mere payment of the dues, or the possession of a membersip card, does not constitute good membership, either. "Honorary Membership" is conferred upon the high members of other jurisdictions of our Order, but it is not conferred upon those who are not active, affiliated members of some branch of our work. There would be no *honor,* indeed, in such a compliment. The greatest honor the Rosicrucian Order can bestow upon any man or woman is *active* membership in its rank and file of working members.

Therefore, to make progress toward the ultimate goal, each member should be jealous of his contact, his devotion, his active participation, with the others of the Order. No member ever really knows the loss he will sustain in a sudden emergency in his own affairs, or those of his family, by severing the contact, the affiliation, for a day, a week, or a month.

DIVINE ILLUMINATION

The Great Goal of the Great White Brotherhood is ever before the vision of all sincere Rosicrucians. The sublime joy of Cosmic Consciousness, Divine Illumination, can be known only through experience; and those who have made the contact have written in hundreds of books in the past ages such alluring descriptions as were calculated to tempt the seeker on the Path to be patient and persistent in his journey toward that Goal.

You will realize, of course, that the Great White Brotherhood and the Great White Lodge have no visible organization. They never come together in one united session; their members are never assembled in any one meeting; they have no Temple known by their names; and they have no earthly rituals, physical organization laws, or material form as a Brotherhood or Lodge. That is why it is often said, in mystical writings, that the "real Rosicrucian Brotherhood is an *invisible organization.*" The Rosicrucian ORDER is truly visible, but the Great Brotherhood back of it is not *visible* as a body.

THE WORK OF THE GREAT MASTERS

As we have said, Mme. Helen P. Blavatsky was the first to popularly introduce one of the Masters of the Great White Brotherhood to mystic students. She had the permission of her Master to do this, and it was well, for it helped to remove some of the misconception prevalent at that time. We have read in her private correspondence with her trusted initiates, and in some of her rare manuscripts, how her Master would change and correct statements she had written, even though HE was many hundreds of miles distant; and how HE would intercept some of her letters in transit and change words written therein to conform to HIS better knowledge. She gave many interesting descriptions of manifestations of her Master and the Associate Master. But what she explained and revealed were but the *simple* manifestations which were safe to give to the public. We, who have contacted her Master and others, and who are working under their direction, know what marvelous things are done by and through them daily, although we are often directed in strange ways and unknown methods to carry out their plans, *the end of which we know not until they are completed.*

Therefore, our members will realize that statements they see in print, or hear, to the effect that a "branch" of the Great White Lodge is *located in some city* and is issuing *secret books of instruction,* etc., are not only untrue, but impossible. And when we read or hear that some prominent character, connected with some psychical society or association, is conducting a line of work that brings disgrace, sorrow, or scandal to its members, claims that he was "initiated" into the Great White Lodge, we know at once that it is not so; for no such person could ever attain such initiation. In one prominent case the claim is made that the character "fell from grace into sin and error *after* having been initiated in the Great White Lodge." That explanation may save the face of the leaders of the movement, who sponsored and endorsed the statement of his high initiation for their own good purposes, but it is an impossible claim; FOR THE MASTERS OF THE GREAT WHITE LODGE ALWAYS KNOW WHAT YOU WILL DO IN THE FUTURE AS WELL AS WHAT YOU HAVE DONE IN THE PAST, and they would not initiate anyone who *would be capable of* "falling from grace." If the great Masters did not have such knowledge they would not be infallible in their judgment, and if they were not infallible in Cosmic knowledge they would not be the GREAT MASTERS.

INDICATIONS OF PROGRESS

How will a student know that he is truly progressing toward the Goal? By many indications that will come to him as he maintains his active interest in the Order. First of all he will receive, from time to time, slight indications that the Master of his Lodge, then the higher officers, and finally the Imperator of his country, are showing some personal interest in his progress.

Such indications may be in the form of a call for a personal interview at the Lodge or offices of the Order, or by a personal note commenting on some experiment, or a letter verifying some psychic experiment. There may be no reference to the Goal, none to what is in the mind of each (the student and the Master), or anything else that another could understand as being a reference to a personal interest.

THE INNER URGE

Then, there will be a consciousness of a desire to assist the Order or one of its Lodges; this will be the result of a growing desire to become a part of the Order, more closely allied with its activities. The desire for more *Light*, more lessons, more knowledge, is not the only indication of progress toward the Goal, for even the beginners on the Path are most anxious in this regard. Members often voluntarily plan to review the old lessons, and the Masters of the Lodges know that this is a very serious indication; it spells magic to the heart of every officer who is anxious to see his members make real progress.

There also comes to such members the continued urge to SERVE; they want to go out and become disciples—lecture, promulgate the great principles, spread Light where there is darkness. They seek for opportunities to assist their Lodge with real physical labor—in accordance with their trade, their profession, their art. Artists seek to decorate, and paint, and beautify their Lodge Temple with symbolical pictures and ornaments; carpenters, electricians, and mechanics offer to build, repair, and improve the material structures; physicians and scientists ask for means of assisting, and so on. It is a notable fact that all of the Egyptian and other Oriental temples of our Order in North America, as in Europe, have been built and decorated by the voluntary services, as far as possible, of the members. All a work of Love! And what wonderful rewards have come to "The Builders" in most cases!

Also, those who cannot serve contribute in some way, perhaps financially, or by gifts that will help in research, in mechanical processes. They are anxious to make some sacrifice, contribute some part of their blessings, and thereby become a part of the ORDER other than a student member.

Naturally there is no thought of reward, special advancement, or sureness of progress because of their offers. No officer of the Order can assure that; none will accept any help or gift on that basis; and the one who is truly on the Path, making real progress, knows that his "gift" is inspired by the inner impulse to want to be a more intimate worker in the Order, and by that sign or token he proves his worthiness to advance.

SPECIAL OPPORTUNITIES TO PROGRESS

As soon as the higher officers of the Order learn of the progress of those who are headed in the right way for the Goal, they diplomatically offer them further opportunities for study, for service, and for personal test. We have said that there are a number of special avenues of work connected with the Order and that there are several allied organizations under the direction of AMORC. Into these the progressing members are directed from time to time without anything being said as to *why*. Some members are suddenly called upon to do certain things. They may refuse, they may hesitate, they may *impulsively* and enthusiastically accept. And thereby hangs the fate of their progress; whether it shall be rapid or regular. Not that any officer of the Order can deter or accelerate a member's psychic development, but the Cosmic is ever mindful of the intents and motives that actuate all mystic students who seek its blessings. The more *impulsively* and whole-heartedly one responds to an inner impulse or urge, the more definitely it is registered in the Cosmic records.

Various ways are used by the Order to assist its progressive members of the higher degrees to attain greater mastership of the laws and principles. In the early Grades a close and sincere application to the studies and the practices is all that is required or necessary. But after advancement through the first five or six grades there comes a time in the journey of each member when he may safely rest a while in his progress and dwell at the "Houses" of special preparation. These Houses will be pointed out to him diplomatically, and he may not even suspect that he is pursuing some study or branch of work that is not shared by others. Petitioning on the part of the member for such special opportunities when he is not ready will mean nothing to the Officers, who are guided by no ulterior motive and can profit nothing personally by the delay or advancement of any member. Nor does the Order exact any financial or material compensation through its special interests in any member, for there are no special fees or dues to be paid by those who are given opportunities to advance their own interests.

All of this may be difficult of comprehension for our members, for it is difficult to explain, as we explained in our opening paragraphs. Nevertheless, the discerning student of our Order will read between the lines and find encouragement.

THE LENGTH OF TIME FOR MASTERSHIP

Always arises the question of TIME. New members, who have been studying with various schools and systems for years, and frankly state in their application blanks that they have been seekers for five, ten, or fifteen years, wish to know HOW SOON they may expect to manifest occult or mystic powers. When they read that it requires a year to complete the preliminary work (which enables them from the very start to apply many important laws) they feel that it is a long time. Not until a member reaches the higher Grades in his second or third year does he begin to realize that time is of little consequence, SINCE EVEN A WHOLE LIFETIME WOULD NOT BE SUFFICIENT TO LEARN ALL THAT THERE IS TO LEARN, and with much already accomplished, great things are possible.

What are five years or three years compared with the twenty-five, thirty, and forty years you have lived WITHOUT SPECIAL KNOWLEDGE, and the twenty, thirty, fifty, or sixty years, or more you will live WITH THE NEW KNOWLEDGE? Why, then, be impatient? Looking at it broadly, the five or six years required to bring the average member to the very threshold of Mastership, as compared to one's whole cycle of incarnations, is like a pencil dot on a line a mile in length. But how we can magnify that dot and lose sight of the line!

THE ATTAINMENT OF DESIRES

The full attainment of our desires is almost impossible at best. That which we desire today, and will go far to attain, becomes small in importance after we have it, and discover through it what else we may attain—and our desires are at once increased and made more difficult of attainment. Members just admitted into the Order often frankly state that it has been their desire for many years MERELY TO CONTACT THE ORDER and now they feel they have attained their greatest desire. Ah, how that sense of attainment is forgotten in the first weeks of study!

Each lesson, each lecture, each experiment and test of the early Grades arouses new and stronger desires. In their anxiety to get into the next grade, and the next, the great desires of the heart before admission into the Order are forgotten. With each lesson the definite benefits therefrom simply accelerate the desire to progress.

Each member will find, however, that not a single lesson, from the first one of the First Grade, is without some special benefit that empowers, strengthens, augments his abilites, his faculties, and his special psychic functionings. This, provided, as we have said, the member *practices* the exercises as well as *reads* the lectures and lessons, and does not become impatient because such development of certain faculties is not made manifest *at once*.

EVOLVING INSTRUCTION

The work of the Rosicrucians is not an arbitrary plan or scheme developed by some individual or discovered by some leader of a cult. It is an evolved plan, worked out by the Master minds of many ages and still being evolved. It is designed to give the utmost help and advantage to every sincere student on the Path and every devoted member of the Order. Nothing is left out of the teachings that will help. No modern thought revealed by any Master mind that is practical is ignored, but immediately added to our teachings, so that our members will have all that is worth while. To believe that some mystic of India, or Persia, or some other land, possesses secret knowledge known only to his cult, which he has offered to students for *years* at a commercial price, that is not to be found in the Rosicrucian teachings, is to believe that the Order is unmindful of its obligations to its members, unacquainted with all sources of real wisdom, and inconsiderate of its own best interests. If any *real knowledge* of truly practical help to sincere students of occultism and mysticism is known to any group of students anywhere, it soon becomes a part of the Rosicrucian teachings, IF IT IS NOT ALREADY A PART OF IT. It is this fact that makes the Order the eminent repository of great wisdom. That is why members are urged not to spend money and time in private lessons from foreign or domestic teachers of personal systems, or in buying new books as they are issued rapidly by firms and individuals solely for the purpose of presenting in a new and puzzling form some of the ancient wisdom, or personal systems of *discovered* knowledge —and often at high prices.

Therefore, be devoted in your work, be loyal to your promises and the Great Oath of the Order, be sincere in your studies and practices, and you will find yourself, sooner or later, at the very Portal of the Great White Brotherhood, and *ready* for the Master who is to appear when you ARE ready. The Order of AMORC is happy to serve you, and through SERVICE, on the part of both the Order and its Membership, is the ultimate Goal attained.

▽ ▽ ▽

THE ROSICRUCIAN CODE OF LIFE

The following rules are taken from old and modern manuscripts wherein certain regulations are set forth for the guidance of Rosicrucians, who are devoting their entire lives to an idealization of the Order's principles.

Perhaps only in the Rosicrucian monasteries of India, or those in Tibet, could one live strictly in accordance with all the ancient regulations; but those selected for publication here can be adopted by a great many of our members in the Occident. We know from practical experience that most of these can be adhered to by any man or woman without interference with the necessary duties and obligations of present-day living; and we know, also, that most of our Officers and advanced members are living the Rosicrucian life in accordance with the rules suggested here, much to their own great advancement, the joy of their associates in family and business, and the betterment of mankind generally.

It will profit you greatly to *try* to adopt as many of these rules as possible.

1. Upon arising in the morning start the day with a prayer of thankfulness to God for the return of consciousness, because of the opportunities it affords to continue the Great Work and Mis-

sion of your life. Face the geographical East, inhale fresh air with seven deep breaths, exhale them slowly with mind concentrated upon the vitality going to each part of the body to awaken the psychic centers. Then bathe, and drink a glass of cold water before eating.

2. Upon retiring, and after conducting all psychic experiments scheduled for the night, or attending to any special psychic or Rosicrucian work contained in your weekly lesson or program, give thanks to God for the day and its fruits; ask the Cosmic Hosts to accept your psychic services while you sleep, to use your consciousness as they desire, and, if it please God and the Masters to have you live another day on earth, So Mote It Be! Then, with thoughts of love for all living beings, and a sense of Peace and Harmony with all the universe, close your eyes and fall asleep, visualizing your inner-self in the consciousness of God.

3. Before each meal wash the hands clean and hold them, palms downward over the plate of food for a fraction of a minute, then mentally pray that the benediction of God be granted to the food you eat that it may be magnetized with the spiritual radiations from your hands and thus greatly supply the needs of the body. Then, before eating the first morsel, say, mentally: "May all who need food share with me what I enjoy, and may God show me how I may share with others what they have not."

4. Before accepting any blessing from the material world (whether purchased by money, labor, or exchange, or whether received as a gift), say, mentally: "By the privilege of God I receive this and pray that it may help me to better fulfill my mission in life." This applies to even such things as clothing, personal requisites, periods of pleasure at the theatre, church, musicals, etc., or even to such small things as books, helpful reading matter, etc., and of course includes the receipt of money as salary, commission, gifts, or otherwise.

5. Whenever any special blessing is received, such as long desired things from the material world of any nature, or a small or large luxury, or an unexpected piece of goodness, do not use or apply it to your own personal use in any way until you have retired to the silence somewhere for a few minutes to meditate and ask this question: "Have I truly deserved this blessing and is there any way in which I can share the benefit of it—directly or indirectly—with others or for the benefit of man?" Then wait for an answer from the Cosmic. If you receive no word that it is undeserved or should be shared, or passed on to another, then say: "I thank God, the Cosmic, and the Masters for this blessing; may I use it to the Glory of my Soul."

6. If any special honor—military, governmental, political, social, or otherwise—is being conferred upon you, always act with the utmost humility, proclaim your unworthiness (for who is truly worthy of all things?) and with a mental resolution that it must not make you proud or selfish, accept the blessing with a prayer of thankfulness and assert that, in the name of those whom you can serve better with such blessing, you receive it.

7. If, in giving testimony, in court or elsewhere, you are asked to take an oath, or to swear or promise upon some sacred book or emblem, bear in mind that to *you* there is no symbol or emblem more holy or sacred than the Rosy Cross. (In most courts of the world individual selection of such sacred symbol for such purpose is permissible.) Then say that as a Rosicrucian you prefer to make your statement "before the Sign of the Cross," and make the Sign (as directed elsewhere in this Manual). After making the sign, make your statement, and remember that if an untruth is knowingly stated at such time it will create a Karmic condition that can never be set aside except by the fullest compensation, according to the Law of Compensation.

8. Never permit yourself to enter discussions of other persons' religious beliefs, except to point out the soundness, goodness, or possible benefits of certain doctrines and thereby show them the good that exists in all religions. Hold not your religious thoughts as superior. Speak well of them if need be, point out how they serve *you*, but do not create in the mind of others the thought that they are in sin or error because of their beliefs. That religion is best for each which enables one to understand God and God's mysterious ways.

9. Be tolerant on all subjects and bear in mind that destructive criticism creates naught but sorrow. Unless you can constructively comment on matters, refrain from speaking.

10. Attempt no direct reforms in the lives of others. Discover in yourself what needs correction and improve yourself, that by the Light of your Life you may point the way to others.

11. Flaunt not your attainments, nor boast of your Rosicrucian knowledge. You may be a Rosicrucian as a member of the Brotherhood, but as a Rosicrucian in knowledge and power, the greatest and highest among us is but a child of the studies and unworthy of Rosicrucian recognition. Proclaim yourself, not as a Master, but as a Rosicrucian student—ever a student—eternally.

12. Seek to share what you can spare, daily, even if in small ways and meager amounts. Go out of your way to find where that which you can give or do will be a blessing to someone or many, and while performing this duty shun all personal glory and let it be known that you are simply "about the Masters' work."

13. Accept no personal thanks for any blessings you bestow, any gift you give, or any help you render. When "thanks" are expressed it is customary to say: "Please thank me not, for it is I who am grateful. I seek, and must seek, to serve and labor for the Masters; you have afforded me an opportunity. But, now the obligation to pass it on rests with you; may you, too, find an opportunity to serve someone else."

14. Accept no gifts of a material nature for any good you do unless you agree with yourself in the moment of accepting, and so state to the giver, that you will divide the blessing with someone where it will continue to carry on its mission of relief and help.

This is essentially necessary when the material gift is of a nature—like money, food, clothing, etc.—that can be divided and is a common necessity on the part of many.

15. Bear in mind that through your Rosicrucian Order you always have an open portal to help many, and that by sharing with them any blessings you pass on to others, who are Brothers and Sisters of the Order in need, the blessings which come to you, perhaps as a trustee of the Cosmic.

16. As you give so shall you receive! As each opportunity to give is seized upon with utmost impulsiveness, so will future blessings, sought or required, be granted to you by the Cosmic. The greater the impulsiveness—with little thought as to personal sacrifice—the greater will be the compensation credited in the Cosmic.

17. Let not a day pass by without speaking to someone of the work of the Masters through the portal of the Rosy Cross Order. Each day makes someone more familiar with its Great Work, not always by soliciting, not always by preachments, but by simple statements of facts, simple demonstrations, and the kind words of recommendation.

18. Respect all women; honor thy father and mother; be sympathetic to the sinful, helpful to the afflicted, and serving to the Masters. He is greatest among you who is the greatest servant unto all. Hence the Master of a Lodge, the Supreme Master, and the Imperator, are greatest, because they may be the greatest servants.

19. Provide now, while consciousness can assist you, to take care of those who may be dependent after your transition; and if you have no one who will require a share of your earthly possessions after your transition—or you have sufficient to more than do for them—be certain that you grant, in proper and legal manner, a disposition of some of your worldly blessings to the superior body of your Rosicrucian Order—the Supreme Grand Lodge—that it may be helped in the work it is doing for others.

20. Go to the assistance of any living being, regardless of race, creed, or color, when you can render direct or indirect aid in any emergency; if you cannot give aid in person, but can call or solicit aid, this, too, is imperative; in quiet and peace perform your work, render your service, and retire with as little recognition as possible.

21. Maintain one place in your home that is sacred to you and your Order. In it find Peace and time for meditation daily. Profane it not with pleasures of the flesh, but sanctify it with your higher thoughts.

22. Give your support, moral or physical, to some church in your community, that it may have your help in carrying on the great work in its Light.

23. Assume no political office without properly and duly notifying all who may sponsor or support your attainment of your definite views and principles toward humanity at large, that they may not

expect or depend upon your submission to principles of a lesser degree.

24. Judge not, unless you are so placed that those to be judged come legally and formally before you as an accredited servant of the multitude; then in sympathy understand, in mercy comprehend, in leniency estimate, and with love be fair. For the Law of Compensation will make adequate demands, and the God of all is alone a truly competent Judge of all facts.

25. Repeat no slander, tell no tales, and support no reports that injure or condemn unless accompanied by more than the same degree of constructive criticism and comment, and *only after you have completely investigated and learned all the facts.*

26. Seek the good in all beings and give public praise to what you find. Look not upon the changing character of the outer-self, but discover the real self within. Learn to know all beings and love them.

27. Gamble not with the lot of another who in ignorance may lose and suffer what you gain.

28. Avoid all extremes in thought and act; be moderate in all desires, and subdue your passions in all directions.

29. Attempt no radical or sudden changes in the natural scheme of things; remember the Rosicrucian injunction: Not by revolution, but through evolution, are all things accomplished in permanency.

30. Hold sacred and above all criticism the ideals of the Rosicrucians; permit no slander to affect the good name of your Order; live that life which will prove the goodness of your principles; and be ready to defend the emblem of the Rosy Cross with the might of your life and the light of your being.

Members may procure a very handsome, printed card in several colors containing the Rosicrucian creed which differs from the above code in brevity and nature. It may be procured from the Rosicrucian Supply Bureau, San Jose, California, at very small cost.

▽ ▽ ▽

INTERESTING FACTS FOR OUR MEMBERS TO EXPLAIN TO INQUIRERS ABOUT AMORC

The following facts are based upon an examination of 1,000 application blanks taken at random from our files. They are typical, therefore, of the entire membership.

GENERALITIES

Males, 64%; females, 36%; average age of all members, forty-four; average age of males, forty-three; average of females is forty-five, in regard to marriage, 62% are married. These figures show that the average member is a serious person with certain responsibilities and problems, and not an esthetic dreamer.

SOCIAL AND POLITICAL

All living within the United States must pledge allegiance to the American Flag. Of these we find that 81% were born in America and only 19% were born in foreign lands, and are naturalized. This is a high standard of Americanism in a national organization. We also find that 42% of our members have college, academic, or honorary degrees, 47% of the females have such degrees. This is another high percentage for a national organization.

PREVIOUS OCCULT STUDIES

The records show that 98% of our members have studied along similar lines for over four years before uniting with us; 68% have studied for over ten years before joining with us, and 52% have been students of these subjects for over twenty years. They came into AMORC because they had not found the Light they sought.

OCCUPATIONS

Eleven per cent are physicians of various schools; 9% are practicing lawyers and judges; 12% are teachers and professors in schools and colleges; 42% are in the trades and arts requiring a skilled education; 14% call themselves "just housewives;" 12% are retired from business or are students of specialized courses.

▽ ▽ ▽

Part Eleven
ROSICRUCIAN DICTIONARY

A

Absolute—That which includes all; hence the Consciousness of God, perfect, complete, embracing every Divine Law, working in harmony, constructive, positive.

Actual—That which comes within the positive domain of the objective and is in conformity with the standards of the objective senses, having weight, breadth, length, bulk, etc. Any phenomena which the objective mind accepts as sensible to it, is actual, whether it be a delusion (mental creation of the objective mind) or not. Actualities need not be realities. (See the term *Reality*.)

Alden (Pronounced Awlden)—Sometimes spelled Ahldain; A'ldain; the name of a former Master of the Great White Brotherhood, who gave jurisdiction over the establishment of mystical centers on the North American Continent during the fifteenth century, and after whom the first Temple in this country was named in 1603. His personality still affects much of the work in this country.

Amen—A Hebrew word introduced into the Egyptian mystic rites at an early date as a term used to express the hidden and invisible God, or a truly inspired representative of God. In this latter sense the term is used in the Christian Bible just once; in Rev. iii, 14, Jesus is called "The Amen." But at a much earlier date the same word, with the same mystic vowel sounds was used to designate the name of the God of Thebes, and the term Amen-Ra came to express the name and hierarchy of a powerful God among the Egyptians. Amenhotep IV changed his name to Khuen-Aten because of the significance of the term Amen. As used in modern religious practices, the term, Amen, means *verily*. The origin of the word is found in the Sanskrit *aum* and also in *om*.

Arcane—That which is not hidden, but visible only to those who attune to it or are ready for its revelation; mystical, Divine, Cosmic.

Astrology—An ancient science based upon close observance of the coincidence of human characteristics with the date and hour of birth; time and careful analysis have proved the coincidences to be based upon fundamental laws regardless of whether the planets have any effect upon birth or upon the nature of man after birth. Only the fanatical extremist makes—or believes—the claim that we are ruled by planets; at the utmost, planetary influences can inspire and urge or tempt; the influences may indicate, but not control. All mystics should have a knowledge of the fundamentals of this old and evolving science.

Astral Plane—The Cosmic, ethereal, Divine plane. Rosicrucians recognize but two planes of existence; that which is the worldly or material plane where we live in both objective and subjective consciousness, and another plane, which is beyond the material—call that other plane the Astral, Psychic, Cosmic, or whatever best expresses your idea; it is that plane where the Soul of man functions free from the limitations of the body and where the subjective mind of man functions at times independent of the objective.

Aten—A name for the symbol of the "sole God" made understandable by Amenhotep IV after he established a monotheistic religion in Egypt. Aten was represented by the sun disc, the sun being the symbol of the life-giving radiance of the invisible God. Not as God or even as a sacred symbol is the sun disc used by modern Rosicrucians, but as an objective symbol of the creative mind and Divine Essence of God.

Atlantis—The name of the continent once occupying a considerable portion of the space occupied now by the Atlantic Ocean. Atlantis was well advanced in civilization in parts and was the ancient home of mystic culture. Mt. Pico, which still rises above the ocean among the group of Azores Islands, was a sacred mountain for mystic initiation (see ritual of Fourth Grade). The story of the lost Atlantis was first told by Plato; another story of mystic peoples using the name Atlantis is told by Sir Francis Bacon (read *The New Atlantis*). Recent investigations by France and America have proved that there is the contour of a continent at the floor of the Atlantic Ocean. (Read also *The Lost Atlantis*, by Ignatius Donnelly.)

Atom—The smallest division of any definite nature of matter; the first distinctive character that electrons form after perfect unity. Divisions of matter smaller than atoms are electrons (see *electrons*), and such smaller divisions have no characteristic nature. (Refer to *Dalton's Atomic Laws* in our grade lectures.)

Aura—That magnetic or electrified field which surrounds the animal body particularly, and which contains colors due to the vibratory rate of the energy in the field. The energy is a result of the psychic development and the vital forces of the body. The aura changes color as psychic development proceeds, reaching a brilliant violet and then pure white in the highest states. The aura is visible under many conditions and has been photographed, and will affect certain instruments balanced to receptivity. Every living cell has its aura as well as groups of cells.

B

Belief—Considered from the mystical point of view belief implies lack of knowledge; it is like unto hope without foundation. A mystic should have no beliefs, but should supplant them with knowledge or a frank admittance that he does not know. (See *Knowledge*.)

Birth—Mystically, birth occurs when the animal body takes its first Breath of Life. Then the body becomes a conscious being. Birth is the opposite phrase of the passing of the Breath (and consciousness) which is falsely called death. (See *Death*.)

Black Magic—A term used, anciently, to indicate mysterious practices or secret methods—methods and practices which today we understand and know to have been strictly scientific though little known. Today, however, the term is used in some philosophies and by some ignorant minds (and sometimes used wilfully to frighten) and is meant to convey the idea that one mind can call into play certain forces of nature to work injury upon another mind or body at a distance. It is assumed that the Cosmic space existing between two minds or persons can be utilized by one of them to transmit evil and destructive thoughts to the other. In fact, however, the Cosmic space will not transmit such destructive thoughts and the person who tries to direct them into space suffers from the attempt and from the creation of such thoughts, which remain in the consciousness. The only power there is to Black Magic for others is the *fear of it.*

Brain—The physical organ for the objective functioning of the mind. Mind can, however, make many manifestations without the use of the brain.

Breath of Life—In Rosicrucian teachings this term is used to refer to Nous. It is a combination, so to speak, of both the Vital Life Force and Cosmic Consciousness. (See *Nous* and *Vital Life Force.*)

Borderline State—This term is used to designate that mental and psychic condition where the objective consciousness and objective mental functioning of man is merging into the subjective. This state can be induced through concentration, or occurs naturally on going to sleep, or when awakening, or through suggestion it may be externally induced (but not without the cooperation or willingness of the self). A similar state exists where the objective mind or the objective functioning of the brain is made abnormal through drug, fever, injury, fright, or strain; in such cases, however, the benefits derived from a proper borderline state are lost, for there is not an intelligent and comprehensive exchange of ideas or communication between the objective and subjective faculties. Often, just prior to so-called death, the first stage of transition is a borderline state which is remarkable for its Cosmic touch.

C

Cell—Where this term is used in the Rosicrucian teachings, regardless of whether in connection with physiology, physics, chemistry, or electricity and magnetism, it means a body of spherical or other shape having a wall with negative polarity and a nucleus of positive polarity.

Concentration—A mental (and physical) state where the whole objective attention and comprehension is focused upon one definite or indefinite point, place, condition, or principle. Perfect concentration of this kind results in complete inactivity of four of the five objective faculties at one time. When concentrated upon seeing, then seeing must be the only faculty not inactive. It is impossible to completely concentrate when two or more of the faculties are active at the *same time*. Two faculties, such as seeing and hearing, may rapidly alternate in their concentration so that it may seem as though both were concentrated at one time, but this is not so. We can be conscious of only one objective impression at one time. All else is rapid alternation. (See *Borderline State*.)

Conception—In our Rosicrucian teachings we are told that our concept of anything we comprehend through the five objective faculties depends, for its accuracy and its effect on us, upon our knowledge and beliefs. Our concept of material things changes as we grow older, more experienced, and more illuminated. Not the actuality of any thing but our reality of it and our interpretation of it form our concept. By conceiving and giving our conception the power and reality of an actuality do we tend to create. In the beginning of all creation there was—and always will be—conception. (See *Reality*, also *Actuality*.)

Cosmic—The Universe as a harmonious relation of all natural and spiritual laws. As used in a Rosicrucian sense, the Divine, Infinite Intelligence of the Supreme Being permeating everything. The creative forces of God. It is an intangible, unlimited source from which radiates the immutable, constructive powers of Divinity. The Cosmic, therefore, is not a place, but a state or condition of order and regulation.

Cosmic Consciousness—That consciousness, radiating from God, which pervades all space (and hence all things), having vitality, mind, constructive power, Divine Intelligence. Into this consciousness is projected all the psychic consciousness of all Masters, and all Adepts may attune with it. It knows all, past, present, and future, for it is all. (See *Absolute*.) After preparation through study and meditation, after deserving through serving, after attuning through practice and with nobility of desire, there comes to all Adepts an influx of illumination and inspiration which maintains a continued connection with Cosmic Consciousness. This is called *illumination* by the Mystics. This is one of the gifts desired by all Adepts.

Cosmic Mind—Referring more specifically to the mind or intelligence that forms a part of the Cosmic Consciousness. It is also called the Divine Mind. (Compare with *universal mind*).

Conscience—The term in our ritual and teachings to indicate the "still, small voice" of the Master Within; the Cosmic Mind with its inspiration and urge; the Mind of the Psychic Self, knowing all truth, all law, all principle, ever constructive in desire, dependable, "ever present when the tempter tempts."

Cremation—Mystically this is a process of reducing the material elements of the body to the primary elements through fire, as though an alchemical process were being used with crucible and fire. It carries out the ancient law that the body shall return to the dust of the earth from whence it came. Cremation simply hastens the natural process in a most sanitary way. The custom of burying the dead in the ground to decay was always considered a barbarous and unclean practice by the ancient mystics, and cremation is not a modern method and will in time become universal among civilized people. The Rosicrucian burial service and ritual call for cremation of the body and the scattering of most of the ashes upon running water in brooks or rivers or in the opened soil within seven days after transition. (See *Death* and *Funeral Service*.)

Cromaat—The word *Maat* is an Egyptian word meaning truth. When combined with *Cro*, it means *as in truth*. It is a salutation quite frequently used in the rituals of the organization, both in the Temple Lodges and in the National Lodge rituals. Peculiar to note, if you reverse the letters of the word, *Cromaat*, they constitute the abbreviation of the words: *The Ancient and Mystical Order Rosae Crucis*.

Cycle—A period of time, evolution, process, method, or manifestation. Mystically every progressive action is in cycles, definite and important. The cycle of human life is divided into periods of seven years, each of which is a cycle in the growth and development of the mind and body in the being; even the prenatal period is divided into cycles. The evolution of the universe, the evolution of man from a primitive being into the present can be divided into cycles. The twenty-four hours constituting a day is divisible into planetary cycles. The consciousness of man is at present in the early part of the Aquarian Cycle. Cycles form an easily understandable and significant method of measuring time and progress.

D

Death—The mystic not only looks upon death as inevitable, but as a necessary element in the cycle of life. Death and birth are synonymous in this sense, for so-called death is birth into another plane, while birth is likewise a transition. The transition of soul into a body is considered just as strange and fraught with unknown possibilities by the mystic as the transition of soul from a body. Both constitute the Great Experience. Both are a form of Initiation affording an opportunity for greater advancement. Therefore, both are looked forward to by the soul without grief or fear. On the other hand there is no death, whether we consider the transition from a material or spiritual view-point. Matter is indestructible; that is a fundamental law of matter; it can only change its form or nature of manifestation, and matter is in constant change—another fundamental law. The soul is immortal and cannot be destroyed, lessened, increased, or otherwise modified, except in growth of experience. After transition the material part of man, the body, does not cease to live, but is in fact still vibrant with spirit energy, even to the most minute cell. Hence neither body nor soul ever dies, and there is no death. (See *Birth* and *Cremation*.)

Deduction—A process of reasoning. The objective mind can reason by all processes, inductively, deductively, syllogistically, etc. The subjective mind, on the other hand, tends to reason deductively all the time. Starting with a true and understandable premise or basic fact, reasoning by deduction therefrom, one will come to a logical conclusion, if the deductive reasoning has been logical in accordance with law. It is the excellent reasoning ability of the subjective mind that brings about the correct conclusions through deductive reasoning. Bringing about a Borderline State of Mind will enable one to take advantage of the subjective reasoning.

Disease—A local or general disturbance of the harmonious constructive process of the living, creative cells. Regardless of the cause, the condition is, fundamentally, the same. The disturbing, breaking-down process among the diseased cells is being strongly or weakly fought by the healthy, normal cells, according to the general constitutional state of the body. Through the creative, constructive powers of the healthy cells, nature attempts to end the destruction and renew the disease cells and restore health. The battle calls for concentration of energy and robs the general system of its normal status, while the disease is also disqualifying many cells, organs, tissues, and parts of the body for normal, constructive work; hence fevers, weakness, mental and physical disturbances, and pains, The logical procedure is to help nature, mostly by not interfering and by ending the cause of the disturbance when it is known. Proper breathing, proper eating, proper exercise, sleep, and thinking are the first essentials in helping nature and removing the cause of interference. Giving to the blood, the nerves, and the general system that which was lacking (and which caused the disturbance) or is now lacking in helping to restore normalcy, is the next essential. Hence the various schools of therapeutics may assist and contribute to the restoration of health, but solely through assisting nature. While so-called death or transition is inevitable, disease is not necessary. The physical body can reach a state of age and exhaustion where the breaking-down process of cells and parts of the body is more rapid than the reconstruction, and as a principle of economy the Soul will cast off or vacate the body and await another and more useful one; but such breaking-down and gradual weakening of the whole system need not be accompanied by any specific disease and can be free from any pain or suffering.

Dreams—Dreams always occur just as one is passing from the complete sleep state to a waking condition; this transition is a state where the subjective condition is gradually merging into the objective. (See *Borderline State*.) Such a state is very short in duration, usually, and in the brief period of two or three seconds one may "dream" a long story or experience. This is because the experience is simply realized by the mind as one realizes a picture after a glance of two seconds, but must use hundreds of words many minutes in explaining or describing. After one awakens one cannot be sure just when the dream was experienced, except in such cases where the awakening interrupts the dream. The causes of dreams are many. The most common cause is that the first objective thought or idea that passes from the objective to the subjective mind, at the beginning of the Borderline

State, starts a train of deductive reasoning on the part of the subjective mind; or some long-forgotten picture or idea lingering in the memory storehouse of the subjective mind is sensed by the objective mind at the beginning of the Borderline State, and the objective mind, not keenly and logically awake in its reasoning functioning, distorts or adds to and creates a story based on the first idea. Other causes are: External suggestions from cold air blowing over the face or partly uncovered body; slight noises not properly interpreted by the waking mind, a movement of the body as consciousness starts its return; a mental impression received by the subjective mind from some other person who is concentrating upon the one who is at that time dreaming, thereby consciously or unconsciously sending an impression. Of course, such a Borderline State may occur at any time during sleep.

E

Ego—The Subjective Self as distinguished from the Objective Self. This term is not used often in Rosicrucian teachings for the term Psychic Self or Psychic Mind expresses more correctly what is meant.

Electron—The first form into which spirit essence concentrates preparatory to material manifestation. The essence when stressed under certain conditions gathers into very minute magnetic cells which we call electrons. They are both positive and negative. Electrons do not manifest any definite chemical or material nature until they unite in certain combinations to form atoms. (See *Atoms* and *Molecules.*) Single electrons are invisible, but streams of them may be seen and measured.

Electricity—Current electricity is a vibratory force in action; static electricity is a potential vibratory power inactive and under stress ready to manifest itself under certain conditions. These terms and definitions are not as one finds them explained in scientific works but will make plain the terms as we use them. Electricity is a vibratory energy; natural electricity is the result of the radiations of the sun (therefore, one of the manifestations of spirit essence and Nous); all other electricity is artificially made through chemical and mechanical action.

Element—One of the many different natures expressed through combinations of electrons into atoms. There are 144 elements composing all material creation. Of these, 81 are definitely known to science in perfect form; others are known through analysis of the vacant places in the periodic table of elements. Some can be sensed in a psychic manner only so far as their nature and purposes are concerned.

Elementals—Sometimes called Salamanders and other terms used by early philosophers and by some modern schools of strange thought. In this sense an elemental is supposed to be—"nature-spirit presiding over the elements of fire, air, etc." A superstitious belief exists that these elementals or beings can cause good or evil, or that they can fill a room and cause disturbances or manifestations, or influence our thinking, hearing, and seeing. It is needless to say that there are no elementals in this sense.

Emanations—The radiations or projections from all material and psychic forms. The emanations are extensions of the vibrations within the form—the vibrations of the spirit essence composing the form. It is through the emanations reaching us from all things that we sense, either subjectively or objectively, the existence of all things.

Evolution—The progressive growth and perfecting of all that is manifest or in the conception of the Cosmic Mind. Even so-called devolution or disintegration is a part of evolution, is one of its phases. Evolution implies onward and forward. It is the fundamental law of nature and every element in nature is tending toward perfection and becoming higher in its rates of vibrations and more evolved in its manifestations.

F

Faith—We find the term faith often defined as "active" belief, or a belief which amounts to a basis for action upon the accepted premises. From the mystical view-point, however, this is not exact. A distinction must be made between faith, belief, and knowledge. The mystic should have no beliefs, but knowledge; his knowledge may create faith or give him faith in certain laws and principles, but it would supplant belief. Therefore, we may say that faith is an expression of confidence, and confidence is born only from experience—knowledge. (See *Knowledge*.)

Fourth Dimension—From the Rosicrucian teachings there is nothing mysterious about the fourth dimension. Two points should be remembered: It is a *dimension* and it is the fourth. The other three dimensions are length, breadth, and thickness. Each of these is expressible by numbers—whole, fractions, or decimals. Each of these three dimensions, when expressed in numbers, helps us to have an objective realization of some attribute of the things referred to. We may write on paper these figures, 2"x4'x3". At once we know that whatever the thing may be it is four feet long, three inches wide, and two inches thick. Regardless of how irregular in form the thing may be we can mentally picture it or express its form with numerals, and from these actually draw upon paper a diagram of its form. (Note the complicated yet exact designs and diagrams of parts of machinery, architectural elements, etc., expressible with numbers.) Intelligently as do these three dimensions express a thing to our consciousness there are still essential elements missing in the expression—one or more attributes or qualities lacking. What is the *nature* of the above thing that is 2"x4'x3"? Is it wood, or iron, or stone? What is its weight, its color? Is it hard or soft? We say that all these questions can be answered by expressing the fourth dimension, and expressing it in numerals as the other three are expressed. In this case, as an example, the figures 2"x4'x3"/12,0147 would mean that the thing referred to was a piece of South American (not any other kind) mahogany, with a color equivalent to a certain line in the sun's spectrum, and having a specific gravity, a certain degree of hardness, tensil strength, etc. With the first three dimensions, and knowing the specific gravity, one could figure the exact weight of the piece of wood to within a dram, if the first three dimensions were exact. On the other hand, these figures: 6'x7'x?/12006.042 would mean that the thing referred to was a misty light blue-gray cloud of a certain density or opaqueness, but unknown thickness, covering an area of six by seven feet and formed of Cosmic energy in a very high rate of vibration, so balanced in space as to be easily controlled (moved) by mental power. (Members in the Eighth and Ninth Grades will appreciate this.) By means of the fourth dimension (and a dictionary of all the figures) one could easily express the nature and attributes of all things made manifest on the objective plane. Likewise one would be able to determine what fourth dimension would neutralize or combine with another. The fourth dimension is nothing more or less than the rate of electronic vibration. All qualities and attributes manifested by all material things result from this rate. From another point of view the fourth dimension should really be the first. It is the projection from Cosmic space, into the worldly, material plane of manifestation, of all material things. Such projection is the first phase of manifestation. The coming together of electrons into atoms, and from this into molecular formation, constitutes the first phase of creation into the material world of objectivity. The next step or phase is that of limitation, or form, caused by natural laws or by man's desires and handiwork. Hence the three dimensions of length, breadth, and thickness should follow the dimensions of *objective proportion*, which is a more correct term for the fourth dimension. Mystics will see, now, why the fourth dimension, in its true nature, has always interested the philosophers and was one of the laws carefully studied and utilized by the alchemists of old, and the advanced mystics of today use the law in many strange manifestations.

Funeral Service—The Rosicrucian funeral service is a ceremony of celebration in its spirit, at which time those assembled around the body of the Brother or Sister take part in a ritual significant of the passing through a Higher Initiation of the one who is no longer limited by the work of the Order in its material form on this plane. Purple, rather than black, is used to express the sacredness of the occasion (that is, wherever decorations or drapings are used in the Temple or home). Flowers are used to express the beauties of life. Sorrow is expressed only because of the absence of the members from such personal contact as had been enjoyed in the past. The time for the Temple Ceremony is late in the evening so that the service may end about midnight and the body remain in the Temple (before the Altar in the East) until after sunrise the next morning, when it may be taken to a vault, but preferably to a place for cremation (See *Cremation*). Those not members of the Order may be invited to the service and such friends and members of the family should be seated on special seats at the Northeast of the Temple. The rule is that the R. C. ceremony must be the last ceremony performed; if there is any other religious or fraternal organization ceremony, it must precede the R. C. service. One of the most beautiful parts in the ceremony is when, after the opening of the service, a special prayer, and some other points, the Master of the Temple permits the Guardian of the Temple where the Brother or Sister had attended, to stand beside the body and remove from the Lodge apron (which is on the body) the Rose, while speaking these words: "From our midst has departed one expression of Soul we have loved. Across the Cosmic Threshold has passed another Initiate into the Temple of God. In that Temple there are degrees of understanding, grades of advancement, cycles of progression, and then the Sublime Degree of Perfection wherein thou, oh, departed one, shall be one of the Divine Illuminati and enter again the School of Experience where we shall once more enjoy thy noble, loving companionship. In this earthly initiation, the Rose and the Cross were given unto thee in the form of this apron to wear as a symbol of your readiness to serve humanity. Thy body and personality were ensconced by the Rose and Cross. In thy Divine initiation thou shalt have no need of the Cross, for thou hast borne thy Cross well and God hath laid it aside; but the Rose in all its sweetness and perfect development shall remain with thee as a symbol of the unfolding of thy soul experience. To symbolize this, I, Guardian of the earthly Temple of thy work, do now remove from thy apron the Rose and in the hand of thy earthly body I place another Rose, fresh from Life, Fragrance, and Purity, that it, too, may return unto the dust of the earth to rise again and through resurrection become manifest in all its glory."

G

Ganglion—A mass of cells organized into one body, which body serves or functions as a center for various nerve impulses, the exchange, translation, or transmutation of such impulses, and a coordination of the influences passing into or through such body. A ganglion is, therefore, like a central station of a telephone system or a switchboard for certain electric trunk lines. The ganglia of the Sympathetic Nervous System are intensely interesting in their functioning and intended purposes. The nervous system and the physiological and psychic functioning of ganglia are explicitly and interestingly presented in the work of the Sixth Grade of the Order.

God—To Rosicrucians there is but one God, ever living, ever present, without limiting attributes or definite form of manifestation —it is the *God of our hearts,* a phrase found throughout our ritual and meditation practices. The God which we conceive, which we can be conscious of, which sooner or later manifests in that strange intimacy within us, becomes the *God of our hearts.* Rosicrucians are of many creeds and religious faiths in all parts of the world, but there is absolute unity in this one idea of God, the Supreme Intelligence, the Divine Mind. In ancient rituals we find this as part of the Rosicrucian pledge: "Man is God and Son of God, and there is no other God but Man." But this has a mystical meaning and is not to be taken literally. We repeat the famous statement of Max Muller: "There never was a false God, nor was there ever really a false religion, unless you call a child a false man." When the so-called heathen prays to or worships an idol he is not worshipping a false God, but rather a false interpretation of the one true living God, the God that he is trying to idealize, attempting to interpret—the God of his heart.

Gravitation—In the earliest lectures of the lower Grades of our work as given in America many years ago, the statement was made many times that the force of gravitation is not a pull but a *push*. The postulations of science in the last few years tend to prove that the Rosicrucian contention in this regard is correct. While in the ultimate manifestation the results are the same, in the fundamental laws involved there is considerable importance in the difference between a push and pull action, especially as regards gravitation. It is impossible to overcome the force of gravitation; at best it can be lessened in its actions; its best application is in being utilized. If it could be overcome it would not solve any of the great problems now confronting scientists, but would bring about greater problems than man could cope with.

H

Habit—In the early Grades of the Order habit is carefully analyzed and studied. There is a short, too short, definition given to the effect that habit is an unconscious law of the subjective mind. This brief explanation, following the long explanations and presentment of laws, is quite understandable to the student, but of and by itself it may give a wrong impression. A better form for the brief definition would be that habit is a law of the subjective mind, which law has become unconscious to the objective mind. Habits are usually, if not always, formed consciously by the objective self; such acts are not habits at the time, regardless of how systematically they may be performed, nor are such acts intended to become habits unless one is striving to make the acts or series of acts a subjective or unconscious practice, such as maintaining rhythm in music, the formation of letters in writing, etc. It is only when the act becomes subjectively performed that it is a habit, a law of the subjective self, unconscious to the objective self.

Health—(See *Disease*.)

Hallucination—Imaging of the mind. Such imaging may become fixed in intensity and interest and limited in regard to subject, or unlimited, and is then an hallucination. On the other hand, imaging may be rational, intense, not fixed, but under control, in which case it is creative thinking. A definite hallucination, such as that which characterizes the unsound mind, is a fixed idea born of illogical or purely deductive reasoning and which becomes the obsessing thought of the subjective mind, while the objective thinking may be caused by injury to the mind or any other cause of unsoundness. Such hallucinations are of the subjective entirely; they can be removed or modified only by dealing with and through the subjective; for the objective, being incapable of sound reasoning, cannot be utilized to assist; but once the objective is due to physiological causes, these should be remedied first, but thereafter the subjective should be reached and enlisted in the work of curing the mind. This calls for psychic processes applied by those well experienced and knowing all the laws.

Hypnotism—A subject it is well to approach carefully and in detail. There are two distinct methods of inducing a hypnotic condition—by the use of drugs or by means of mental processes. In either case a condition of sleep need not result nor is the condition of sleep an indication that the person is under control mentally or physically. Whether hypnosis is produced by drug or by any mental (or mind) process there must be certain cooperation on the part of the subject; in the case of mental induction such cooperation is not only essential but fundamental, and without it hypnosis cannot be induced. Hence the process of induction is not a contest between minds, the stronger overcoming the weaker, but a case of the stronger mind concentrating its whole attention upon the idea of passivity. Unless this is the attitude and the ability of the subject a small degree of success will be attained, no matter how competent the operator. Only certain classes of minds cannot yield to some degree of hypnosis —the infant mind, the unsound mind, and the drugged and intoxicated. A weak mind can rarely exercise sufficient concentration to assist in bringing about hypnosis by any mental process. Occasionally hypnosis is not dangerous to either the mental or physical organization of the body; continued experiments with one subject makes that subject enter states more readily as long as the same operator conducts the experiments. No one was ever placed in the state against his or her will and cooperation, for it is impossible (except in some rare cases where drugs are used, and then the state will more nearly approach a heavy or deep sleep as when choral, sulphonal, hypnal, ether, and similar drugs are used; in this state the subject is not under the mental control of the operator or physician, and the mind of the subject is not inhibited as when a mental process is used). But while all this is true and is intended to dispel the fear and false statements about hypnotism, there is seldom any need for its use (especially that which is induced by mental processes) and the practice should be limited exclusively to physicians or scientists who have made a careful study of the laws and principles, and who have naught but the highest ethical and scientific reason for inducing the state. Psychically, it is a state where the objective mind is at least four-fifths passive or dormant in functioning and the subjective mind is consequently and proportionately active or superactive. For psychic experience of the average and desirable nature the Borderline State is more efficient and calls for no assistance from any operator. (See *Borderline State.*)

K

Knowledge—The Rosicrucians ever held that one could not know of anything except through personal experience. For this reason a distinction was made between belief and knowledge. The experience, which is thus necessary, may be through objective realization or psychic reality, but there must be the personal realism. It is customary for a mystic to say that he either knows or does not know when speaking of the experiences, problems, or facts of life and nature; nothing is accepted by him on faith and he has no beliefs.

Karma—A term used by us to mean the working of the law of compensation. Rosicrucians do not contend, however, that the exactions of the law of compensation will result in any reversal of the law of evolution, as is claimed by some modern schools. That a human being may be reincarnated in the form or body of a lower animal as a punishment is inconsistent with the law of reincarnation and evolution, both of which teach us that each stage is progressive and we shall never descend in the scale of physical expression regardless of the Karmic debt to be paid. One of the fundamental principles of the law of compensation is that for each sorrow or pain we cause another, we shall suffer in like degree and manner and at a time when the lesson to be gained thereby will be the most impressive. On the other hand, this principle does not exact an eye for an eye or a life for a life, for there is no vengeance in the process, and no intention to cause suffering; the sole purpose of compensation is to teach us the lesson, to make us realize the error and to evolve the understanding thereby.

For these reasons one cannot be sure just when or how the law of compensation will exact its requirements. Of this we can be sure, however: we will not suffer through any requirements of Karma and be unconscious of the fact that it is a Karmic debt we are paying. Such suffering, without a keen realization of why it is so and what we are compensating for, would be inconsistent with the fundamental principles of Karma—that we will learn a lesson through it and advance in our understanding.

L

Life and Life Force—The mystery of all ages. Two methods of examining its nature lead to false conclusions; the chemical method would reduce all life to chemical action; the spiritual would reduce all to divine essence and ignore the material elements or actions. Rosicrucians insist that due consideration be given to all parts and all actions, realizing that in its pristine essence all life emanates from

God through Cosmic forces, but animal life-force, as it expresses and manifests on this earth plane, is not solely a spiritual essence devoid of chemical action.

M

Magnetism—Every electrified body has its aura, and when that aura is active it constitutes a magnetic field and the aura is sometimes called magnetism. Magnetism, from a purely electrical point of view, is described somewhat differently; but even so, the fundamental law involved in the foregoing definition remains. The fact that some minerals are "naturally" magnetic, as iron of a certain nature, while others can be made magnetic, indicates that magnetism is not a result of the atomic or molecular structure of matter, but rather of an electrical action that is taking place within the substance or which can be set up in the substance. In electrical science we are instructed how to induce magnetism in a metallic body by surrounding it with an electrical charge; but this further illustrates the law that magnetism results from action in the aura that surrounds all matter. This aura is fundamentally an essential part of the electron, and the molecule, therefore, has an aura which is a mixture of the auras of the electrons composing it. Some auras are passive, some are receptive or repulsive, and some are alternating in their action. Those, which are not passive, cause a manifestation which we term, in physical science, magnetism, with either an attractive or repulsive tendency or positive or negative polarity.

The cells composing the human body are surrounded by an aura and the body of man also has an aura. This aura can be made active, radiating its magnetic energy, or passive, or even repulsive or receptive. The human mind, with its control of the electrical energy in the body, is the guiding factor in the process of exciting the electrical charge that arouses the aura of the human body to its fullest power. The word mind is used here in the psychical sense.

Master—The term is used in several ways in our work, but we will not touch upon the use of the word to indicate one who is an officer of a Lodge or director of a grade of the work. Otherwise the term is used to represent one who has attained some degree of perfection in evolution or a high sense of mastership of laws and principles. In this sense we have visible and invisible Masters. Those classified as visible are Masters living in the flesh on the earth plane and seen by us with our objective, physical senses; and those living in the flesh on this plane, who are able to project their psychic bodies, thoughts, and impressions, irrespective of distance, so that such psychic bodies become visible under certain conditions, and the thoughts and impressions become sensible to our psychic or objective comprehension. Invisible Masters, on the other hand, are those who have passed from this plane to the Cosmic plane and from thence project their personality to the psychic plane and never function or express upon the earth plane until reincarnated. In order that we may sense these Masters—not see them with the objective eyesight—we must attune ourselves to the psychic plane to such a degree that, for the time being, we are psychically functioning on the psychic plane completely (that is, with our psychic bodies, while our physical bodies are dormant or inactive in all functioning except that of a purely physical nature, as when sleep in a passive state or in deep and profound meditation), and at such time contact the personality, mind, thoughts, and messages of the invisible Masters. These Masters may be "seen" at such times, but not with the objective eye; in fact, it is not seeing at all, but a Cosmic state of sensing which we interpret as seeing, after we have returned to consciousness on the objective plane, for want of a better term to describe our sensing.

Complete functioning on the psychic plane for a few minutes or hours at a time, as desired, and there contacting the personality of the invisible Masters, is a condition much desired by all mystics and is attained by careful study and preparation, many preliminary experiments, and a pureness of purpose. It is in this way that Cosmic Illumination or Cosmic Consciousness is realized.

Matter—Rosicrucians view matter from almost the same view-point as physical science. Differing from some schools of metaphysics, we know that matter is essential to expression or existence on this plane, has its place in the scheme of things, and should not be negated, ignored, humiliated, or—aggrandized. We know that matter has no consciousness or mind independent of that consciousness or mind which resides in all living forms; and we know, further, that matter does not exist independent of the spirit energy that animates it. This knowledge enables us to place matter in its right category and shows us how to make it serve us rather than rule us. The fundamental laws regarding the composition of matter are fully covered in the lectures of the First, Second, and Fourth Grades.

Mind—The mystic makes the important distinction between brain and mind. The brain is a physical organ for some of the functioning of mind, just as the lungs are organs for the functioning of breathing. Mind works through the brain to a great extent, but not exclusively through that organ. It is possible for the mind to function in many ways after the brain is removed. This has been proved with tests on lower animals. Mind is divided into two domains of functioning—subjective and objective; while it is common to speak of these two domains as two minds, it is not correct in a broad sense. The mind of man is immortal, because it is a part of the soul and personality, while on the other hand, the brain, like all the physical organs, is mortal. Mind and personality persist after transition from the physical body, and retain, as part of their attributes or equipment, the complete storehouse of memory. The psychic body utilizes the subjective functioning of the mind as its essential consciousness; hence in all psychic work and projections of the psychic body the subjective mind is keenly active. (See *Borderline State*.)

Molecule—(See *Atom* and *Electron*.)

N

Naming (Christening)—The Rosicrucians have a ceremony for the naming of children, to be performed in their Temple. No restriction is placed on the age of the child, but one or both of the parents must be members of the Order and certain promises are exacted from the parents; such as that the child will be properly educated, during its youth, in non-sectarian schools, that it will be taught to know and love obedience to God's laws, that the child will be given every opportunity to enter the Order at the proper age without interference or unnecessary urge. Such Christening may take the place of any other ceremony or may supplant it. The ceremony is, of course, non-sectarian.

Natural Law—Is that law or set of laws decreed in The Beginning by Divine Mind as the working basis of all creation and without which no manifestation can occur and exist. Such laws are universal as to scope and manner of operation. Natural law operates alike on all planes and in all kingdoms. Natural laws are extremely simple and direct, as all such fundamental laws must be. Their mission is to insure progressive gradations or cycles of evolution in spite of all the obstacles placed by man to thwart their operation. Therefore, natural law establishes such powers, functions, attributes, and phases in the various kingdoms of the universe as will unswervingly impose strict adherence to them in the search after the ideal in each plane, kingdom, class, etc. The idea, the motive, back of natural law is the preserving of life for the attaining of the ideal of expression; such preservation for such purpose recognizes no man-made ideal, no man-made law, no dictates of civilization where these are contrary to the best purposes as decreed by Divine Mind.

Natural law is always constructive, constructive even when it seems indisputably destructive. In this it follows the method symbolized by the "law of the triangle." Natural law is that basic principle which, while demanding, commanding, and insisting on strict obedience to its dictates throughout, is elastic enough in one sense to allow for much and frequent blending of the entities of any plane so long as such blending harmonizes with its purposes. Thus is it seen that there can be no such thing as super-natural law, a term which not only is a misnomer but grossly misleading. Miracles are not the result of so-called super-natural law; they are the result of obedience to the demand of natural law. Miracles as such are so only to those who do not understand what is meant by natural law.

Negative—That phase of polarity which is the compliment of the positive. It is that phase or condition which receives the positive elements and nurtures them to fruition when the result will manifest the blending of the two phases of polarity. The negative is passive, static, receptive, and nurturing in contradistinction to the positive, which is active, creative, and dynamic. The negative registers a hunger for the positive, while the positive registers an urge, an impulse toward union with the negative in order that it may, with the cooperation of the negative, cause a manifestation or creation. Neither can, of itself, produce any result, for one complements the other, supplies what the other lacks. The coming together of the negative and positive under proper conditions allows for the perfect blending of the two when a third element, the product of the two, is created, revealing in better manner the characteristics of both negative and positive.

Nerves—These may be likened to the wires in an electric circuit. They are the channels through which power is carried, both to and from the central station, the brain. Power sent out from the brain to all parts of the body, manifesting as growth and action, is sent along the *efferent nerves* while the *afferent nerves* are used in receiving such impressions and information of the world outside the brain as will cause the brain to make use of in guiding and protecting the body for its preservation.

The function of the nerves is a simple one; merely to serve as channels for the dissemination of power, whatever the nature of that power may be, just as the electrical current is sent over wires from the source of production to the point where it is to be manifested in furnishing light, heat, motive power, etc.

Nervous System—Still making use of the analogy existing between an electrical circuit and the nervous system, it can be said that this system, like unto any electrical circuit, consists of a central station, the brain, and the nerves functioning as do the wires, while the ends of the nerves are the termination at which the manifestations are produced. Just as an electrical circuit requires two wires or sets of wires in order that it may function properly, so does the living organism require two sets. This is due to the fact that the living organism is dual in nature, requiring one set for each phase, yet each set being also dual, *afferent* and *efferent*.

Therefore, the nervous system in a living organism consists of a Spinal Nervous System for the material aspect, and a Sympathetic Nervous System placed at the disposal of the immaterial, invisible aspect. It is the function of the Spinal Nervous System to provide that power of the grosser and more material nature as will care for the needs of the earthly body, while the Sympathetic Nervous System cares for the more subtle requirements of the immaterial one.

Since, according to Divine Decree, the soul makes use of a physical body for expressing its mission on this plane, provision is made for affording to each phase or expression that set of nerves which will best cater to its requirements. The soul, immaterial and invisible though it is, while functioning through a physical body, requires the use of such tools as will allow it to do its work normally and with the least interruption. So that system known as the *Sympathetic Nervous System* is allowed to the immaterial side of a living organism, the side that functions psychically, that is in constant contact with the Cosmic and allows the soul to function through a material body. Such system is naturally more sensitive, and so created that it can receive more subtle vibrations and transmit them into power than can the Spinal Nervous System, which is created solely to provide for the maintenance and preservation of an earthly body.

The Spinal Nervous System finds its central station located in the cerebrum; the Sympathetic Nervous one in the cerebellum; and over all is the brain proper as a whole. The points of intercommunication, the points where the two nervous systems unite to found a perfect, harmonious plan of cooperation and collaboration, are in the two small glands in the brain about which so little is known generally.

To recapitulate, the brain may be said to be found everywhere in the living organism, taking into consideration that the two nervous systems, each with its afferent and efferent nerves and nerve centers or substations, according to the analogy of the electrical circuit, may be said to be a brain that is elongated and made use of by mind, the earthly, material, objective mind making use of the Spinal Nervous System and the immaterial, subjective mind making use of the Sympathetic Nervous System in order that the soul may function normally on the earth plane through a physical body and so fulfill the demands of the evolutionary plan.

Nous—is that energy, power, and force emanating from the Source of all Life, possessing positive and negative polarity, manifesting it in vibrations of various rates of speeds which, under certain conditions and obeying the dictates of natural law, establish the world of form, be that form visible or invisible.

Nous possesses within itself all potentialities; that is, all manifestations of any kind are within it, uncreated, awaiting the right moment, the precise time, the exact locality for manifesting as entities. Nous is the essence out of which all creation comes. While it is the substance, the Divine Substance, out of which things are made, yet it is amenable to natural law.

Nous is vibratory in character, dual in nature, triune in manifestation. It operates through a system of harmonies by means of a Cosmic Keyboard of sixty octaves of twelve groups or periods, each period consisting of five octaves of twelve notes each. An interesting and significant point in this regard is that each period is related to a sign of the Zodiac, the first octave beginning with the Sign of Aries.

Each note represents a definite number of vibrations of Nous, beginning with one vibration per second for the first key, and ending with trillions of vibrations per second for the last key.

Octaves constitute not only groups of twelve notes but groups of manifestations. Thus, the first ten octaves produce the sensation of feeling and hearing—manifestations of action which may be felt and even seen, and those of Sound. The next octaves give different manifestations, and so on throughout the sixty octaves of the Cosmic Keyboard.

Nous, in more understandable language, may be said to be a combination of Vital Life Force and Cosmic Consciousness moving from the Source toward earth in an undulating manner, in an infinity of waves, traveling at different rates of speed, each rate characteristic of a special phase of manifestation. Within these waves, traveling with the same speed as the waves themselves, are to be found those particles of Nous essence, which, grouped together according to specific number combinations, make cognizable all manner of creation. It is due to the vibratory rate of each Nous wave that the created masses themselves are able to send forth the vibrations by which they are known and recognized.

Nucleus—This term is used to denote the focal point, the center of action, the source of aggregational manifestation. This point is the heart of any creation possessing, latent within itself, all the potentialities of development commonly used in connection with a cell. But what applies to it in a cell applies equally as well in larger masses of matter. The nucleus is endowed with a polarity complementary to that of the rest of the mass of which it is the nucleus.

On the earth plane the nucleus of a cell is positive in polarity while the retaining wall and the space between the two are negative. It is due to the dynamic, creative quality of the positive polarity that search is made by the nucleus for its complementary negative in order that the business of life may be started. In this manner is the law of attraction observed (as well as it was established in the beginning of time) and it is according to its dictates that there is formed between the nucleus and periphery the field of operation in which the stressed condition existing between the two polarities may be eased in creating. This field is known as the magnetic field and is in actuality the meeting or mating place of the two polarities.

On the immaterial plane the elements are in reverse order; that is, the nucleus will have the negative polarity and the outer wall and environs will have the positive polarity, but the *modus operandi* will be the same for cells, whether single or collective, on both planes.

The nucleus possesses, within itself, all the elements lying in a dormant state awaiting the proper conditions for awakening that are necessary for the growth, assimilation, and reproduction of the cell. It has crystallized within itself all the characteristics of former unions in previous generations and in each successive manifestation blends in the additional characteristics of the present union, thereby establishing the conditions and qualities of heredity. This union of the nucleus with the complementary polarity in the field of manifestation, each with its inherent and acquired traits and with their inevitable blending, is what makes evolution possible.

O

Objective Mind—is the Mundane Mind, the mind that operates in a material world, through a physical body, and in a selfish manner for the main purpose of preserving the physical vehicle or tool of the soul as it manifests on the earth plane. The objective mind must necessarily be selfish in purpose, but that selfishness should be constructive in purpose and principle. As it commonly is, the objective mind is destructively selfish. By constructively selfish is meant that selfishness which tends to preserve the body, and all its powers and functions, at its best in order that the soul within the body be not hampered in its mission here on earth. Being constructively selfish means that an individual seeks to better himself in every direction in order that he may serve and make the world a better place to live in. Such selfishness has divine sanction. To attain its purpose and end it was given an objective mind that could and would cope with the purely worldly or carnal conditions and problems. But to be destructively selfish means that the objective mind, in such case, is seeking benefits to be used not in service for others but for the one and only self primarily.

The purpose and function of the objective mind, as has been said before, is essentially a worldly one. Its scope is looking well-nourished, in normal condition, and ready at an instant's notice to obey the demands of the soul as they manifest through the subjective mind. The objective mind, like the physical body is subservient to the subjective. Its province is to tell the subjective of existing mundane conditions in order that the subjective may be guided as to how it is to express Divine Cosmic ideals in a material world. The province of the objective mind is over the five physical senses and their functions, over the voluntary acts, over recollection, inductive reasoning, and finally complete reasoning, all of which will easily demonstrate how important is the objective mind functioning through a physical body and brain in the Divine Scheme of Things.

Omnipotent—having illimitable power. A term used in referring to the powers of God and the Cosmic. But such power, illimitable as it is, is amendable to Cosmic or universal law as established in The Beginning. While it may seem that omnipotence is, therefore, lessened, it is, on the contrary, increased or strengthened, for by adhering to its own laws nothing is impossible. Adherence to these laws insures that system and harmony, that plan of number, that peace that establishes omnipotence. So it may appropriately be said that God is omnipotent because in His Wisdom He established those laws and principles, not only for His Creation, but for Himself, adherence to which gives omnipotence.

Ontology—according to Rosicrucians, is the TRUE science of ALL being. And in perfect accord with this definition and the standard which it involves are the teachings of Rosicrucianism. Those laws and principles alone can help humanity solve every problem that is universal in character and application. Such must, perforce, be based on divine truths and ideals, not with the idea or purpose of making goody-goodies out of humanity but of making it NORMAL. Such laws and principles, because they are simple and direct, are easily demonstrable to the entire satisfaction of anyone willing to take the time to prove them. They are operative in the daily life of every creature. When observed they bring happiness, success, and ecstasy. When they are ignored, intentionally, or through ignorance, they allow unhappiness, failure, and despair to manifest, not for the purpose of punishing in a retaliative spirit, but solely for the purpose of teaching through fixed laws and principles and fulfilling their decrees.

It may seem strange to the unthinking reader that the study of the law of vibration, with its seemingly endless ramifications, should give us the knowledge whereby we learn to solve economical, social, ethical, and religious problems, yet it does do precisely that. For universal laws are operative in like manner and degree through all the planes of creation, in all conditions.

It may seem stranger yet that by studying the universal and natural laws, as they manifest and apply in the purely material world, mankind should know how they operate and manifest on the immaterial, spiritual world, yet each study does just that. By studying all about the SEEN world by recognizing the laws that apply to them, by learning how to make use of those laws and putting them into operation, if altruism is the motive actuating the purpose, the UNSEEN world becomes not only intelligible but as intimately known, contacted, and associated with as the SEEN. By learning how to use natural, universal laws in transmuting material, physical conditions and things can mankind learn to transmute unfavorable conditions of whatever kind. Ontology teaches what are the universal and natural laws. It teaches how to use them in transmuting destructive conditions into constructive ones. It teaches, further, that what is mastered in regard to purely material things can be used, if the purpose is in accordance with Divine Ethics, for spiritualizing the purely mundane and raise such to the higher plane of manifestation. Ontology teaches, moreover, not only mastery of physical and Cosmic forces, but teaches that more difficult subject, the mastery of the self, giving each individual the right blending of the humble, the noble, the magnetic traits that characterize MASTERSHIP wherever it may be found. It gives these through KNOWLEDGE.

P

Perception—is that faculty of the objective mind which obtains knowledge through the five objective senses and faculties. It is the process of getting that infinity of facts of a material or mundane nature which goes to make up the sum total of our objective knowledge after such facts have been classified by another process of mental functioning.

Personality—to the Rosicrucian, in contradistinction to individuality, is that distinctive manifestation of character, with its peculiar and innate qualities, which reveals or establishes the identity of any entity. Personality pertains to the Inner Man, the Soul, the Psychic, or Divine Being who resides within the physical body and expresses the character which the soul has evolved through the cycles of time from the hour of the creation as a soul. The personality reveals all that has been garnered up through numberless experiences and absorbed as part of its very essence of expression. It demonstrates all the qualities which have been adopted by the soul as its own peculiar characteristics or earmarks, so to speak. And so there are all kinds of personalities according to each soul's evolution. It is due to the personality of the soul that certain acts or deeds are performed which we recognize as being those performed by any particular personality. Personality reveals the true psychic identity of each individual of the human race.

Individuality, on the other hand, refers to the transient and mortal objective side of man. While it is true that individuality signifies that which may not and cannot be separated, this term applies not to the soul, which is not separable from its Creator, but to the objective individual, who possesses a body composed of units which cannot and may not be divided or separated one from another without destroying the objective manifestation. The individuality is essentially worldly and material because its purpose in life is to function on the mundane plane. The personality is essentially unworldly and immaterial because its purpose is to function on the immaterial plane. The two, personality and individuality, or the psychic and mundane, the immaterial and material working in unison reveal an entity recognized both through its individuality and personality as it expresses itself in daily life. (*See Reincarnation.*)

Pineal and *Pituitary* glands, in their physiological purpose, have to do with the regulating of various functions of the body like the circulation of the blood, the growth of the bones and tissues, and the development of the sex and emotional functions. They act in this sense as governors essentially. In the psychic sense, they are transformers, stepping down for objective sensing those exceedingly rapid vibrations which come from the spiritual or psychic planes or stepping up the slower vibrations of a material nature that they may be sensed on the immaterial plane. By a series of exercises these glands may be brought up to that standard of functioning decreed by the Creator and which has not been generally in evidence for many ages. It is one phase of the work of mysticism to afford the sincere, earnest seeker after Light, Knowledge, and Power the privilege and means of bringing up to normal these most essentially important glands in the human body. Such a one will have, among other faculties, the powers of seer and prophet. Any standard work on physiology or anatomy will give the description of these glands, together with their function and place in the physiological economy. This may be found under the heading of ENDOCRINE Glands. But the description of these same glands, together with their place and function in the psychic economy of man, is NOT to be found in any book nor is the knowledge given to the idle seeker for the mere asking. These glands have to do so greatly with the spiritual side of life that they must be developed slowly so that their pristine normalcy be regained.

Plastic—refers to that which is endowed with all manner of possibilities but which lacks form or definite and characteristic expression. That is plastic which allows of being moulded or shaped according to the ideas of the moulder.

Polarity—is the predominance of one or the other phase of electrical or magnetic force possessed by any manifestation of creation, and which gives it its distinguished character of positive or negative. This is contrary to the commonly accepted understanding of the term polarity, which is defined as that which has two poles. In actuality it is more than the quality of having two poles. It is the quality of having in addition more of one phase or the other of that which is found at the poles. This applies to all forms and kinds of creation, for each has its individual and characteristic polarity by which it is distinguished from the other manifestations of its own class and of other classes. Here may be found a key to the explanation of personality, its power of attraction and repulsion when thinking of polarity as applied to mankind.

Potential—refers to that state or condition of anything which is not in an active state. It is a static condition and not a kinetic one. It is dormant, awaiting that touch which will change it from its inactive condition to an active or dynamic one. Any potential condition has crystalized within itself all the qualities and essentials needed in the kinetic or active state of manifestation. The potential state lacks nothing which it would not have in the active state. Its inactivity is all that characterizes this condition. This is in contradistinction to that condition which lacks that which is essential to its active state.

Prayer—a petition, a supplication or entreaty, addressed usually to the Creator, for the granting of some special request. In many cases, the Divine Laws and Principles involved in the granting of prayer are completely ignored or overlooked by the petitioner. Yet neither negligence, nor ignorance, nor wilfulness will abrogate them nor diminish by an iota their efficacy or reduce their operation. God, in His Wisdom, decreed and established certain laws of universal operation in order that there might be system and order in the world. Such laws are applicable to all and infrangible—therefore, any prayer which does not meet the requirements of such laws will not be answered, for, could or would God answer all prayer, irrespective of its motive and purpose, chaos would result.

The mystic well knows that should he petition for any purpose he must base his prayer on that which concords with Divine Ideals. Therefore, he asks, first, not that his prayer be granted, that his plea, out of a world full of pleas, be singled for fulfillment, but that he be given Light and understanding of the Laws involved in the granting of the prayer and of the consequences to accrue from its fulfillment. Next, the mystic assures himself that his prayer is altruistic. It is not necessary that it be wholly altruistic but it must be over fifty per cent so, as in the case of asking benefits and blessings for ourselves. It is right to ask for these when we desire them in order that we become better fitted to serve others.

Having asked for understanding of Divine Decrees and Laws, having asked that it be shown us if it is right that our petition should be expressed, having assured ourselves that our prayer is, in the final analysis, altruistic in nature and purpose, we proceed to give expression to the prayer with a feeling of confidence. This feeling of confidence is not an impossible one, for as our prayer is formed in harmony with the Divine Scheme, meets the requirements of the Laws, and is based on altruism, we find that there is nothing to prevent us from having the feeling that we will obtain the object of our petition since we are doing all that is possible in fulfilling the requisites imposed. And so, having achieved our feeling of confidence, and knowing that our prayer will be fulfilled, we express our thanks for the fulfillment, for spiritually it is ALREADY granted under these circumstances.

From the foregoing it may now be apparent why prayer is so often unanswered. God, in His mercy, refuses to answer our entreaties knowing how great the penalties for us would be could He and would He abrogate His own laws to grant our prayers, however agonizing the need from our human point of view. But that prayer is answered which meets the requirements and standard of the Creator, because it is a prayer, which the granting of, will add to the general betterment, not only of the individual, but of the greatest number. One other wonderful feature to be noted, as a result of basing prayer according to the Divine Principles, is that the manner, ways and means of fulfilling the prayer are indicated to us and we proceed to demonstrate that God helps those who help themselves.

Projection—is not only the act of releasing at will, on the psychic plane, of the psychic body of man with all its consciousness, mind, powers, and functions, but it is also the psychic body freed from the limitations of time and space and other hampering and confining conditions. Projections are made for the purpose of contacting such as we wish to aid or by whom we wish to be assisted and inspired.

Projections are endowed with all the distinguishing traits, characteristics, and mannerisms that distinguished the *personality* of any entity. Projections carry with them these earmarks: Traits developed through the incarnations making the projections recognizable anywhere at any time through these very characteristics, because the soul and psychic body are immortal.

Projections are endowed with five psychic senses and faculties, allowing for their sensing and expressing psychically in the same manner as the five objective senses and faculties allow the physical and objective individuality to become conscious of conditions and circumstances. Projections are guided and directed by the soul and impregnated by the soul's ideals and hopes. Naturally, in communing with other psychic bodies and subjective minds, a projection will act in full accord with the ethical code characteristics of its soul.

So strong are the powers of the soul, and so forceful its ways of making itself felt, that to those who can see and hear and feel psychically the soul is recognized by its projection as easily and completely as is one physical body or manifestation recognized by another physical one. This is most commonly done during sleep. But it can be done at will by those trained to do so, trained to release the psychic body, manifesting at any specific place at any definite time for a very particular purpose. Sensing the psychic body in a projection and recognizing it as the personality of any entity is also a matter of training. Both these privileges and powers are part of the birthright of man.

Psychic Plane—is that plane or condition in the Divine Economy which has been provided by Divine Mind as the meeting place and field of action for the psychic bodies of the dwellers of the Cosmic (where dwell only those freed from functioning in physical bodies) and earth planes, wherein they may meet to their mutual benefit. It is here that our loved ones, who have cast off their earthly bodies, may be contacted. It is here that our thoughts, hopes, plans and requests are projected along with our personalities. It is here that in response we receive the inspiration, guidance, direction, and illumination we are in search of when appealing to those whom we feel are better fitted and ready to give. It is here that we, too, carry on our psychic work as our share in the uplift of mankind. And this plane may be reached at any time provided the purpose is pure and noble.

Psychology—from the common point of view is the science of mind, or the science which treats of the analysis of the laws of connection and condition of mental phenomena. From the Rosicrucian point of view it is more than this: It is the science which treats of the soul, its attributes, mind, and consciousness and its purpose, place, and function, as well as its influence in our lives as regards habits, their formation, their adoption, rejection, or transmutation, the action and interaction of the two phases of mind, the objective and subjective, and many other forms of psychic and mental existence.

R

Reality—The Rosicrucians make a very definite distinction between realities and actualities. As stated under the term ACTUALITY, the actualities of life are those things which conform to the laws of sensibility of the objective mind. On the other hand, realities are real things to the subjective or psychic consciousness, regardless of the lack of actuality. We may easily select, from our own experiences, many instances of realization of realities which had no actuality in the purely objective world, and there are thousands of actualities in this strange world which to date have brought no realization, or created no reality, in our consciousness. The important point with true mystics, is, however, that we are affected, as living organisms, by both actualities, and realities. So far as our consciousness is concerned, it is our reality that affects us—our realization of things—whether actual or not. Therefore, mystically, we live in the world of realities, or realization, and anything or any stimuli, impulse, urge, or inspiration which causes a realization in our consciousness is affecting us. It may not affect all, it may affect only one of us, but, to the one affected, a reality of the consciousness is as actual as a material thing of the objective world. (*See Actual.*)

Reincarnation—The Rosicrucian doctrine of reincarnation is unique in some respects, yet it represents the one religious or ethical doctrine more universally held in the world today than any other, because it is non-sectarian, just, understandable, and revealing. In brief, it is that the soul of man, a Divine Essence, has as an attribute a memory and consciousness which constitutes the personality of the individual ego. This personality is immortal, as the Soul Essence is immortal. The Soul Essence is unseparated from the universal Cosmic or Divine Essence, only a part of which resides in each being during an earthly incarnation. The personality is, however, distinct and unique with each being. This personality manifests in the human body during its earthly life as the ego or character of the person, and at transition moves on and into the Cosmic Plane along with the Soul Essence. There it remains until the right time for another incarnation with the Soul Essence in another physical body, for more and different earthly experiences, which are added to the Personality memory and remain intact there as the accumulating knowledge and wisdom of the inner-self. The Personality remains conscious of itself on the Cosmic Plane, as it was conscious of itself on the earth plane, and can carry on the Psychic manifestations of itself more easily from the Cosmic Plane than it could from the earth plane. Each personality may incarnate many times, the limit being unknown. Rosicrucians know that the Personality never retrogrades or enters the bodies of lower animals, and only occasionally enters a body of a different sex.

Religion—The knowledge of God and God's ways lead to a real religious devotion on the part of Rosicrucians, and the Mystic is always a true student of essential theology. But, aside from uniting with sectarian churches in order to assist in the great work they are doing, the Rosicrucian is broad and tolerant in his religion and finds God in everything and for everyone of His creatures.

S

Shekinah (pronounced usually in the occident as sheh-ky'-na)—It is from an old Egyptian word, though for centuries believed to be a Hebrew word because it is found, in the Hebrew religion, to mean the same symbol. In the Rosicrucian Temples it is a triangular altar, thirty-six inches high and thirty-six inches wide on each of its three sides. The sides are covered with black satin, the top with blood-red satin, with a gold cord binding the red to the black at the edge. On each of the three sides there is a gold cross attached to the black satin, formed of gold braid or ribbon (four inches wide). Such crosses are about eighteen inches high and twelve inches wide; in the centre of each is a red velvet rose. On the Shekinah, which may have a glass top to protect the red satin, three candle sticks are placed, one at each corner of the triangle. A vessel of incense may burn in the centre of the triangle. The Shekinah is usually placed for all convocations with its points as follows: (1) toward the West; (2) toward the South, the Chaplain's station; (3) toward the North, the station of the High Priestess. A small footstool is also placed before point 1. It may be covered with red and black satin. The Shekinah represents the presence of the Concentrated Power of the Holy Assembly of the Cosmic in the centre of the Temple. The Sanctum of each Temple is that area between the Shekinah and the East platform of the Temple.

Solar Plexus—One of the most important groups of a number of small plexuses forming the largest plexus in the human body, located in the centre of the abdomen. Its objective or physical functioning is very important, but far more important is its psychic or sympathetic functioning. It was believed by the ancients that this plexus was the centre of the Soul in man, as the sun is the centre of the solar world; hence its name. Many systems of so-called mystical instruction pretend to tell how to use the Solar Plexus for attaining certain results, but it requires many years of careful development of this plexus to make it a real value in true mystical work.

Soul—We wrongly speak of the Soul in man, or man's Soul, as though each human being—or each conscious organism—had within its body on this earth plane a separate and distinct something which we call Soul; and, therefore, in one hundred beings there would be one hundred Souls. This is wrong, indeed. There is but one Soul in the universe; the Soul of God, the Living, Vital Consciousness of God. Within each living being there is an unseparated segment of that universal Soul, and this is the Soul of man. It never ceases to be a part of the universal Soul, any more than the electricity in a series of electric lamps on one circuit is a separate amount of electricity, unconnected with the current flowing in all the lamps. The Soul in man is the God in man, and makes all mankind a part of God—Brothers and Sisters under the Fatherhood of God. (See *Personality*.)

Spirit—Rosicrucians were the first mystics to make a distinct difference between Spirit and Soul. Spirit is a universal essence pervading all nature, even unconscious matter, and manifesting in many ways, such as cohesions, adhesions, etc. It is a divine, universal, essence-like Soul, but of a lower rate. Spirit essence makes its first material manifestation in the formation of electrons, which enter into the composition of atoms. Soul, as an essence, can manifest only psychically, because of its very high rate of vibrations.

Spiritualism—A religious doctrine attempting to use some of the psychic manifestations of Soul, some of Spirit, and some of Personality, to sustain a theoretical scheme of the Soul's activities here on earth, or in the Cosmic, after the change called transition. Spiritualism as a system or a "science" is taboo with Rosicrucians, for they know that the spiritualistic explanation of much phenomena is wrong, that most so-called mediums are unaware of the facts, know little or nothing of the laws and principles which they are attempting to demonstrate, and often bring serious situations and sorrows into the lives of those who are being guided by them. Furthermore, Rosicrucians KNOW that departed "souls" do not return to earth in a material form, and that departed "spirits" do not make materialized demonstrations as entities, and that communications received from the Cosmic, or through the psychic bodies of living persons, are not always what they seem to be to the spiritualists.

Subjective Mind—The mind in man may not be dual—it may be but one mind, manifesting in two distinct domains at times, or in two phases, but since the manifestations group themselves into two distinct classes, called objective and subjective, it has become common in psychology, and especially mysticism, to speak of the mind as being dual—subjective and objective. For the functionings of these sections of one mind, the student must refer to the many lectures of our studies, where all the details are carefully given.

T

Therapeutics—Generally used to mean any system of healing or method for the alleviation of pain and physical suffering. The ancients, however, used the word in a mystical sense and a branch of the Rosicrucians in Egypt was known as the Therapeuti. This was a branch of the ancient Order, which at that time used various names in different lands so as to conceal the mystical part of its work. The same organization was known as the Essenes in the Holy Land, and researches in the past century have revealed the fact that the Therapeuti, Essenes and other similar organizations were a part of the Egyptian mystery schools, or arcane schools, in which the Rosicrucian organization had its birth.

Transition—This term is generally used to indicate the condition called death in modern times, but since there is no death in natural law, any more than there is in the spiritual or so-called supernatural, the term is not only erroneous, but absolutely contradictory. The great change that takes place at the time when death is supposed to occur is, after all, a mere transition and transposition of the various component parts which, being united, constitute a living human being or a living entity of conscious matter. This transition consists of separation of the dual parts of man (soul and body) and also changes the constructive processes of the physical body which have been holding together, to some degree, the material elements composing it, permitting a new condition to exist whereby these elements begin to separate and return to their primary form of living matter. Therefore, it is truly a transition with no indication of death to any part of the former physical and spiritual expression.

Transmutation—This is not merely an alchemical term but a mystical term, and transmutation may be mental, as well as physical, and can be spiritual in a broad sense. Transmutation means the changing of the vibratory nature of a material element or the vibratory expression of a spiritual manifestation so that the manifestation or expression is different after the change. The ancient Rosicrucians claimed that it was possible to transmute the baser material into the more refined and they demonstrated this in their day, as we do in our day, in a material or chemical world, by the transmutation of gross metals into gold or platinum, both of which represent a higher and more refined expression, but they also claim, as we demonstrate today, that the highest demonstration of transmutation and the more ideal, profitable, and noble demonstration is that which occupies our greatest attention in the world today as Rosicrucians: This is to transmute the baser elements of our physical natures into the highest ideal expressions and to transmute our desires and thoughts into living spiritual ideals. Thus all of us are striving to become true alchemists and demonstrate the real art of transmutation.

U

Universe—This word is significant to a mystic because it indicates the Cosmogony of one cell, and if the word is worthy of being used at all it should be used to indicate that all that exists is a universe or within one great cell, the Macrocosm, a replica of the smallest cell, the Microcosm. The ancients taught that there was but one earth, one cellular world, one sun, the sun that is visible to us, and that it is the centre of the universe. This would indicate that the universe is a limited cell of enormous size, and the idea that space is limited and in the form of a cell is not more difficult of comprehension than the idea of limitless space, and the mystics of the Orient today point to the fact that nothing that has been discovered through astronomy, or any of the sciences, disputes this contention. Mystically, the idea of one universe as a cell, with God and all of His human expressions within it, gives the foundation for the general idea of one God and Father of one Brotherhood of mankind.

Universal Mind—This term is often used to indicate the Cosmic mind or the mind which is the consciousness of God and which pervades all space in the universe. It is not only the mind of God but the consciousness and mind of all living men, of all living beings on the earth plane so united as to be a consensus of mind and thought in which every inspiration, idea, and impression of universal importance is registered and may be contacted through proper attunement with this Universal Mind.

V

Vestal Virgin—This is another term that has often been used in the place of the word Colombe (see explanation regarding Colombes in the forepart of the Manual regarding Officers of Lodges). It was believed for many years that the Vestal Virgins were an institution of Roman origin, but research has shown that in the arcane schools of Egypt, and in the earlier Rosicrucian Temples, there were one or more Vestal Virgins, who not only kept the important symbolical and holy fire in the Vestal Stand ever burning, but served in the ritualistic work and in the mystical exercises as a symbol of fire, light, life, and love, as well as the dove of consciousness. Hence the word Colombe, which means dove, and which symbol has always had an important place in the mystical and religious ceremonies of ancient and modern times.

Vital Life Force—This term is fully explained in the lectures and teachings of the various Grades and refers exclusively to that form of energy which vitalizes the human body at the moment of birth and which leaves the human body at the moment of transition. It has naught to do with spirit energy, which prevades all space and which does remain in the human body and is active after transition, and which also exists in all living matter, whether conscious or not. The vital life force is from the same source as all energy, but is of a distinct and different rate from that which constitutes spirit energy and soul energy.

SOME INTERESTING QUESTIONS OFFICIALLY ANSWERED

To save much correspondence and at the same time arm our members and readers with official answers to questions often asked, we publish the following list, taken from our records as typical of those asked hundreds of times each week in the correspondence:

Q. What does A. M. O. R. C. mean?

A. It is the abbreviation of the term: Ancient and Mystical Order Rosae Crucis (Ancient and Mystical Order of the Rosy Cross).

Q. Has the Order any other name?

A. Yes, the complete Latin name as used in some foreign jurisdictions. See introduction to the Constitution in the forepart of this Manual. The Order is often briefly referred to as the Rosicrucian Brotherhood.

Q. Has the A. M. O. R. C. any relation to other American Rosicrucian societies?

A. No. The A. M. O. R. C. has no connection with any society, fraternity, or movement using the name Rosicrucian unless it uses the title A. M. O. R. C. or its equivalent in Latin or some other language. The A. M. O. R. C. is an ORDER and always uses the word ORDER and not society or fraternity.

Q. How can there be a number of Rosicrucian Societies without being related?

A. Because the word *Rosicrucian* has become a general term to mean *arcane, mystical, metaphysical, etc.* There is no law prohibiting its use, unfortunately, except in the Cosmic, by those who seek to attract attention through its use. The term ROSICRUCIAN ORDER, however, is protected and is never used except by the real organization.

One will find in the city directory of New York a very large number of organizations, movements, groups, and commercial propositions using the word *Columbia*. There is the Columbia Academy, the Columbia School, the Columbia Society, the Columbia Laundry, and the Columbia Meat Market. But there is only one Columbia UNIVERSITY. No other educational movement or institute would think of using the term *Columbia University*, though they might use Columbia School or College, for various reasons, much to the confusion of casual readers.

Q. Has the A. M. O. R. C. any relation of the past or present to the Roman Catholic Church or the Jesuits?

A. Absolutely no. There was a time in the ancient periods of the Order when some Jesuits were greatly interested in the teachings and some even joined the Order; but today no Jesuit or official representative of the Roman Catholic Church is in any way connected with the Rosicrucian Order in this country or foreign lands.

Q. What relation has the A. M. O. R. C. with other metaphysical or mystical societies including Theosophy?

A. No relation at all, although the Order does look with brotherly kindness on every movement promoting good will and arcane knowledge. The A. M. O. R. C. in every land is connected with no other movement or society or Order than its own. It is absolutely independent.

Q. What attitude do you take in regard to the Rosicrucian Fellowship and the work of the late Max Heindel?

A. We say over and over that Mr. Heindel was a keen student of the Theosophical teachings under a private teacher, and after years of careful thought wrote and published a few books which contain his interpretation of a philosophy essentially Christian and Theosophical. We have said that these books are inspiring and profitable. The work of his movement is devoted to the sale of these books and the formation of groups to promote the study of his books, but does not consist of TEMPLES, LODGES, and COLLEGES like the Rosicrucian Order, and the teachings are NOT those of the Rosicrucian Order of international affiliation. The ORDER never has and never will issue and sell to the public the real teachings and instructions in book form, and they cannot be found in book form in any country. We have naught but the kindest feelings for the Fellowship, but it is not a part of the International Rosicrucian Order, and the German Rosicrucian Order in which Mr. Heindel says he was initiated has officially denied that he was ever an initiate or student.

Q. In what way is the A. M. O. R. C. distinctive from other mystical or scientific, occult schools?

A. In the first place the A. M. O. R. C. is NOT primarily a school or publishing house, nor is it simply a brotherhood. It is an international fraternity with its schools or secret teachings as an adjunct to help the members master such laws and principles in life as will enable them to help themselves and help others. The object, therefore, is the practical demonstration of humanitarian principles and mutual cooperation in the evolution of the races of man. It is not a theoretical or speculative school, but a practical organization. Its teachings are given to members only, in carefully graded sequence, covering various periods of development from one year to ten years.

Q. Is it not commercial since it charges dues?

A. It charges dues like any other society or order, and these dues are not for instruction, but to cover the operating expenses of an enormous SCHEME which embraces many features of co-operation and practical demonstration of real help. Only twenty-five per cent of its national and international activities is in the form of educational work; the remainder of the activities have to do with solving the personal problems of its members, healing, directing important moves in the lives and progress of its members, scientific and medical research, archaeological discoveries, promotion of national welfare plans, contributions to better citizenship, the correction of evil systems affecting the happiness of many, and similar lines of activities. The regular monthly dues of the members DO NOT and CANNOT meet all of the operating expenses of such an institution as A. M. O. R. C. in any land; and the large deficits in its monthly and yearly budgets have to be met with private donations on the part of the supreme officers, including the Imperator, and those high-grade members who, as of old, would sacrifice all they possess to maintain the integrity and good work of the Order. The Order is incorporated as a non-commercial, non-profit body, and all who are acquainted with the Order for more than a year learn of the truth of these statements. It is this fact of non-commercialism that has made the Rosicrucian Order what it is today.

Q. Has the A. M. O. R. C. in America ever experienced any legal difficulty or unkind criticism or exposure?

A. No. The Order has carried on its work publicly for many years and has never had other than very high and kind praises in newspapers, magazines, books, and pamphlets. It has never had any so-called *exposure* or uncomplimentary attack. It has naught to do with politics, attacks on religion or Church, deals with no impolite or immoral subjects, has no under-cover practices and is not likely, therefore, to be entangled in any unpleasant notoriety. It has had more newspaper publicity of a kindly nature in the past ten years than any other metaphysical secret school in the world.

Q. Do the Rosicrucians have any "coming world master" as do other mystical schools?

A. No. The Rosicrucians know better than this. They know that the next great Master to come to each being will be the *Master Within,* and not some foreign person of one tongue, affiliated with one school and limiting his redemption to those who are within a certain fold. And the Rosicrucians have never solicited funds for the support or propaganda of such Masters.

Q. What are the religious convictions of Rosicrucians?

A. Since the Rosicrucian Order is a universal movement, with Brothers and Sisters living in all lands and of every creed and tongue, its religious principles *must* be non-sectarian. Universally, all Rosicrucians are convinced of the existence of God, and the Divine Ruler, Architect, Mind and Father of all men, regardless of creed or doctrine. In Christian countries Rosicrucians acknowledge the Divine Selection of the Master Jesus as a special Messenger and Representative of the God-head. In non-Christian countries a very similar attitude is held by the Rosicrucians, except that the Son-ship of Jesus is considered as having been attained through worthiness and preparation as an Avatar of God. In America you will find Rosicrucians in every denomination, often as Ministers, Clergymen, Rabbis, etc.

There is nothing in the Rosicrucian teachings which will affect your religious beliefs except to strengthen them.

Members of the Rosicrucian Order may procure a copy of the booklet entitled, "Rosicrucian Catechism," which sets forth definite answers relative to the nature, purposes and activities of the organization, which the members may use for his own information and also to furnish information to inquirers. This may be procured by writing to the Rosicrucian Supply Bureau and enclosing a three cent postage stamp.

ARE ALL SEEKERS WORTHY?

This is the big question which every organization such as AMORC must solve. Most organizations attempt to find an answer to the questions through investigation *before* admitting the applicant. AMORC makes its preliminary investigation through the usual channels, then investigates along its own psychic lines. After this a certain number of inquiries are rejected. The others are admitted into the three preliminary TEST grades, which cover nine months of close examination and preparation. After that those found *worthy* are admitted into the regular work for one year or fifteen months, during which more tests are applied while preparing the seeker for further advancement. Then, those finally adjudged worthy are admitted into various branches of the work not generally known to those who are uninitiated.

Our statistics show that out of ever thousand persons who answer our public notices—

Only 402 are admitted into the preliminary test grades;
Only 329 are admitted into the higher work;
Only 260 pass the second tests;
Only 248 are permitted to continue;
Only 239 reach the Seventh Grade;
Only 224 reach the Ninth Grade;
Only 199 reach the Twelfth Grade;
Only 101 reach beyond the general work of the Order.

Every possible encouragement is given to the worthy and sincere, and it is our ambition to make every one who enters the first grades truly prepared to continue. We regret each loss and seek ever to change these figures so that more will reach the top. But, certain standards must be maintained and we cannot alter the Cosmic, Psychic, and Mundane rules that apply to all things.

Volume I.

ROSICRUCIAN QUESTIONS AND ANSWERS WITH COMPLETE HISTORY OF THE ORDER

This volume contains the first complete, authentic history of the Rosicrucian Order from ancient times to the present day. The history is divided into two sections, dealing with the traditional facts and the established historical facts, and is replete with interesting stories of romance, mystery, and fascinating incidents.

This book is a valuable one since it is a constant reference and guide book. Questions that arise in your mind regarding many mystical and occult subjects are answered in this volume.

For many centuries the strange, mysterious records of the Rosicrucians were closed against any eyes but the high initiates. Even editors of great encyclopedias were unable to secure the weird, fascinating facts of the Rosicrucian activities in all parts of the world. Now the whole story is outlined and it reads like a story from the land of the "Arabian Nights."

The book also outlines answers to hundreds of questions dealing with the history, work, teachings, benefits, and purposes of the Rosicrucian fraternity. It is printed on fine paper, bound in silk cloth, and stamped in gold. Price, postage prepaid, $2.00.

Volume II.

ROSICRUCIAN PRINCIPLES FOR THE HOME AND BUSINESS

This volume contains such principles of practical Rosicrucian teachings as are applicable to the solution of the every-day problems of life in business and in the affairs of the home. It deals exhaustively with the prevention of ill health, the curing of many of the common ailments, and the attainment of peace and happiness as well as the building up of the affairs of life that deal with financial conditions. The book is filled with hundreds of practical points dealing especially with the problems of the average business man or person in business employ. It points out the wrong and right way for the use of metaphysical and mystical principles in attracting business, increasing one's income, promoting business propositions, starting and bringing into realization new plans and ideas, and the attainment of the higher ambitions in life.

"Rosicrucian Principles for the Home and Business" is not theoretical but strictly practical, and is in its fourth edition, having had a wide circulation and universal endorsement not only among members of the organization, who have voluntarily stated that they have greatly improved their lives through the application of its suggestions, but among thousands of persons outside of the organization. It has also been endorsed by business organizations and business authorities.

The book is of standard size, well printed, bound in silk cloth, and stamped in gold. Price, postage prepaid, $2.00.

VOLUME III.

MYSTICAL LIFE OF JESUS

This is the book that thousands have been waiting for—the real Jesus revealed at last! It has been in preparation for a number of years and required a visit to Palestine and Egypt to secure a verification of the strange facts contained in the ancient Rosicrucian and Essene Records.

It is a full account of the birth, youth, early manhood, and later periods of Jesus' life, containing the story of His activities in the times not mentioned in the Gospel accounts. The facts relating to the immaculate conception, the birth, crucifixion, resurrection, and ascension will astound and inspire you. The book contains many mystic symbols, fully explained, original photographs, and a new portrait of Jesus.

There are over three hundred pages with seventeen large chapters, beautifully printed, bound in purple silk and stamped in gold.

Here is a book that will inspire, instruct, and guide every student of mysticism and religion. It is one of the most talked-about books ever written on the subject. Read it and be prepared for the discussions of it that you will hear among men and women of learning.

Sent by mail, postpaid, for $2.25.

VOLUME V.

"UNTO THEE I GRANT . . . "

This is one of the rarest, Oriental, mystery books known. It is translated by special permission of the Grand Lama and Disciples of the Sacred College in the Grand Temple in Tibet.

Here is a book that was written two thousand years ago, and was hidden in manuscript form from the eyes of the world and given only to the initiates of the temples in Tibet to study privately.

Out of the mystery of the past comes this antique book containing the rarest writings and teachings known to man with the exception of the Bible. Hundreds of books have been written about the teachings and practices of the *Masters of the Far East* and the Adepts of Tibet, but none of them has ever contained the secret teachings found in this book. This book is divided into many parts, each part containing a large number of sections or divisions and chapters.

The book deals with man's passions, loves, desires, weaknesses, sins, strengths, fortitudes, ambitions, and hopes. All are treated in detail with illuminating implicity. The book is beautifully printed and bound in stiff cover, and contains also the strange mystic story of the expedition into Tibet to secure this marvelous manuscript.

Price, per copy, postage prepaid, only $1.25.

Volume VI.

A THOUSAND YEARS OF YESTERDAYS

Here is a book that will tell you about the real facts of *reincarnation*. It is a story of the Soul, and explains in detail how the Soul enters the body and how it leaves, where it goes to and when it comes back to earth again, and why.

The story is not just a piece of fiction, but a *revelation of the mystic laws* and principles known to the Masters of the Far East and Orient for many centuries, and never put into book form as a story before this book was printed. That is why the book has been translated into so many foreign languages and endorsed by the mystics and adepts of India, Persia, Egypt, and Tibet.

Fascinating—Alluring—Instructive

Each who has read the book says that he was unable to leave it without finishing it at one sitting. The story reveals the mystic principles taught by the Rosicrucians in regard to reincarnation as well as the spiritual laws of the soul and the incarnation of the soul.

It is well printed, neatly bound, and worthy of a place in anyone's library.

Price, per copy, postage prepaid, only 85 cents.

Volume VII.

SELF MASTERY AND FATE WITH THE CYCLES OF LIFE

This book is entirely different from any ever issued in America dealing with the secret periods in the life of each man and woman wherein the Cosmic forces affect our daily affairs.

The book reveals how we may take advantage of certain periods to bring success, happiness, health and prosperity into our lives, and it likewise points out those periods which are not favorable for many of the things we try to accomplish. It does not deal with astrology or any system of fortune telling, but presents a system long used by the Master Mystics in Oriental lands and which is strictly scientific and demonstrable. One reading of the book with its charts and tables will enable the reader to see the course of his life at a glance. It helps everyone to eliminate "chance" and "luck," to cast aside "fate" and replace these with Self Mastery.

Here is a book you will use weekly to guide your affairs throughout the years. There is no magic in its system, but it opens a vista of the cycle of the life of each being in a remarkable manner.

Well printed, bound in silk cloth, and stamped in gold to match other volumes of the Rosicrucian Library. Price, postage paid, $2.00.

Volume IX.
MYSTICS AT PRAYER

The first complete compilation of the famous prayers of the renowned mystics and adepts of all ages. By MANY CIHLAR, F. R. C., *Austrian Philosopher and Mystic.*

The book, "Mystics at Prayer," explains in simple language the reason of prayer, how to pray, and the Cosmic laws involved. You come to learn the real efficacy of prayer and its full beauty dawns upon you. Whatever your religious beliefs, this book makes your prayers the application not of words, but of helpful. divine principles. You will learn the infinite power of prayer. Prayer is man's rightful heritage. It is the direct means of man's communion with the infinite force of divinity.

"Mystics at Prayer" is well bound, embossed in gold, printed on art paper in two colors, with deckled edge and tipped pages, sent anywhere, postpaid, $1.00.

Volume XI.
MANSIONS OF THE SOUL
The Cosmic Conception

The Doctrines of Reincarnation Fully Explained

Here is the most complete presentation of the doctrines of birth and rebirth of the soul ever compiled by one who has spent the greater part of his life studying and analyzing all that the ancient teachings and philosophies have said on this subject, and all that modern science has discovered as a verification of these doctrines.

The book deals with the nature of the human Soul, its source and origin, and its purposes in earthly incarnations. It reveals the fact that all of the ancient religions, including the Jewish and Christian, accepted the doctrines of reincarnation as fundamental, scientific laws. Quotations from the Holy Bible and other sacred writings show that the doctrines of reincarnation are not contrary to the teachings expounded by Jesus the Christ and His Disciples, and an explanation is given as to why these doctrines have been partially stifled in the

Christian religion in the Western world. The periods of birth and rebirth of the human soul are explained, and the strange references in the Bible and other sacred literature to the Mansions of the Soul in the heavens are explained. The nature of character, personality, individuality, and ego are also revealed, and hundreds of questions regarding the mysterious principles of reincarnation are answered in detail and in a convincing manner.

Well printed, bound in silk cloth, and stamped in gold. Contains over 300 pages. Price, postage paid, $2.20

Volume XII.

LEMURIA—THE LOST CONTINENT OF THE PACIFIC

Beneath the rolling, restless seas lie the mysteries of forgotten civilizations. Swept by the tides, half buried in the sands, worn away by terrific pressure are the remnants of a culture little known to our age of today. Where the mighty Pacific now rolls in a majestic sweep of thousands of miles, there was once a vast continent. This land was known as Lemuria, and its people as Lemurians.

We pride ourselves upon the inventions, conveniences, and development of today. We call them modern, but these ancients and long-forgotten people excelled us. Things we speak of as future possibilities, they knew as everyday realities. Science has gradually pieced together the evidences of this lost race, and in this book you will find the most astounding, enthralling chapters you have ever read. How these people came to be swept from the face of the earth, except for survivors who have living descendants today, is explained. Illustrations and explanations of their mystic symbols, maps of the continent, and many ancient truths and laws are contained in this unusual book.

If you are a lover of mystery, of the unknown, the weird—read this book—remember, however, this book is not fiction, but based on facts, the result of extensive research. Does civilization reach a certain height, and then retrograde? Is the culture and progress of mankind in cycles, reaching certain peaks, and then returns to start over again? These questions and many more are answered in this intriguing volume. Read of the living descendants of these people, whose expansive nation now lies at the bottom of the Pacific. In the minds of these descendants is the knowledge of the principles which in by-gone centuries made their forbears builders of an astounding civilization.

The book, "Lemuria, the Lost Continent of the Pacific," is beautifully bound, well printed, and contains many, many illustrations. It is priced economically at $2.20, postpaid.

VOLUME XIII.

THE TECHNIQUE OF THE MASTER

The Way of Cosmic Preparation

A guide to inner unfoldment! The newest and simplest explanation for attaining the state of Cosmic Consciousness. To those who have felt the throb of a vital power within, and whose inner vision has at times glimpsed infinite peace and happiness, this book is offered. It converts the intangible whispers of self into forceful actions that bring real joys and accomplishments in life. It is a masterful work on psychic unfoldment.

It is well bound in cloth, with deckled and tinted edged paper. Secure this treasure for yourself. Economically priced, postage paid, at $1.85.